Dragon Removal Service

E.C. Stever

Published by Looka Books

Print Edition first published March 2019 by Looka Books.

Print ISBN: 978-1-949026-06-1
Ebook ISBN: 978-1-949026-05-4

However, the fairies are real.

For more works by this author, visit:

ecstever.com

DEDICATION

To my wife, Deanna. For the pressure, and the space.
And for laughing at the right times.

CONTENTS

ACKNOWLEDGMENTS

I would never have been able to write this without help from the universe, and more specifically: My two daughters, for crying when I told them what would happen to the fairies; My two Kathys, for commenting on the early chapters and laughing about potatoes; The students of Sundance Elementary, for inspiring me to keep writing this; The Bearlodge Writers Group, for cracking my shell; Rivo T. (best bass guitarist in Estonia) and Eneli (taker of wine, eater of apples), for hosting us in Estonia and showing us the sights and tastes and smells. We owe you so much!

And finally I would like to acknowledge the Stever family in whole (no matter what time zone or latitude), for joining me on this houseboat we call *life*.

AUTHOR'S NOTE

This is not a good story for people who like dragons, because the dragons are already dead.

The Sorcerer is dead too (mostly) and the heroes are off celebrating. So in addition to the dead dragon issue, this is also not a good story for people who like heroes and sword battles and evil sorcerers getting their just desserts.

And, in fact, there are just not many desserts in this story either, because one of the characters is allergic (which is why he eats dessert five times a day).

Instead, this is a story for girls and boys who like things tidy and neat. This is a story for those who, secretly, *don't like magic.*

Because magic is rather silly, if you stop to think about it. Because, after the magical war is over, and the Sorcerer is defeated, and the dragon is dead . . . somebody has to clean it all up. *Right?* All the other magical creatures are still around, farting with their armpits to get your attention, or pinching you and flinging fairy poo at your head. Somebody has to take care of those little *squirts*, don't they?

So this is the story of the dead dragon, and the left-over magic, and the lonely eleven-year-old girl (who wasn't really an orphan, and certainly wasn't eleven). This is the story of that girl, Gulchima, the one who thought she could get rid of the magical pests, once and for all.

And this is the story of what happens, *next.*

"Five years I was gone, and I didn't age a day. You want to know what happened, right? How I came to run the Outfit? Why I'm still eleven and everyone else is five years older? Well, it's the same reason everything else is wrecked around here: Magic. Stupid, useless, left-over magic. It ruined my life."

-The Collected Lies of Gulchima Brixby
(94/100: **The One True Thing She's Told Us**)

CHAPTER 1: GULCHIMA AND THE EGGS

THE SECOND EGG-WAGON jittered halfway across the bridge before the *lunkers* got to it. That was an improvement. The first wagon hadn't even made it that far.

Gulchima watched from the far side of the wooden bridge, as the second egg-wagon sped toward her. Her client, the Egg-Meister, stood next to her. He was a fussy little man, with his precise mustache, and a puff of black hair spun up on top of his head. He spoke half his words through his nose. "That wagon's almost made it over the bridge. I think we won't need your help after all, little girl. Those magical creatures are too weak."

On the opposite side of the bridge, a long caravan of egg-wagons waited to cross. The Egg-Meister waved to the next wagon driver, urging her on. But the driver refused to cross the bridge. Her oxen mooed anxiously.

"Maybe," Gulchima said. She glanced at the heap of slime

and wood floating in the river, all that remained from the first egg-wagon. Or maybe, the next crash would be spectacular.

Gulchima made some calculations, taking into account the additional speed of the second wagon, the twelve-foot drop between the flat clapper bridge and the river. She stepped three paces to her right. "I wouldn't stand there," she told the Egg-Meister.

He patted his poof of hair and ignored her.

The egg-wagon rattled past the bridge's final stone piling. In the morning sunlight, Gulchima saw a flash of fur, hands reaching up from under the bridge, sharp nails digging into the wagon's axle. She saw the *lunkers*—their hands anyway—plucking springs and hinges and pieces of necessary metal from the passing wagon. They were magic. Stupid, useless, left-over magic. Magic had already ruined her life. Now it was ruining breakfast.

The second egg-wagon accelerated as it left the bridge and clattered onto the packed gravel road. But the lunkers had gotten to it. The right wheel flew off, rolling back down to the river. The wagon, over-laden with eggs, skidded then tipped. The oxen screamed, eyes bulging, twisting in their yokes.

The driver jumped free—he'd seen the first crash, so he was ready. Half the egg cartons launched out of the back, smashing into a stand of Tamme oak behind Gulchima. Eggs splattered across their trunks like a gooey wave. Two dozen eggs flew into the air, paused at their highpoint, and then pelted the Egg-Meister, dousing his tunic in a hail of yellow and brown.

Gulchima walked back over to him, picked a shard of brown eggshell off the ground and examined it.

"So here's your problem," Gulchima said to the Egg-Meister. "Your eggs break too easily."

The Egg-Meister spat, flapped his arms, and then stalked back across the bridge, where dozens of wagons waited to cross. "Loose planks," he explained to the waiting drivers. "Not magic. This route is magic-free, as promised. They will fix the planks and then we can cross."

The wagon drivers passed the message down the line.

The Egg-Meister seemed angry. It was hard for Gulchima to tell. Adults were always getting angry after Gulchima explained things to them. She wondered, was it because she was eleven-years-old, or because she was always right?

Probably a combination.

A movement from the bridge caught her eye. Gulchima watched as the lunkers fiddled with the laces on the Egg-Meister's boots, tangling them into a knot.

His boots were tied together!

The Egg-Meister screamed as he started to fall, which was unfortunate.

Because when he toppled face first into the steaming pile of ox poop, his mouth was wide open.

Wide open.

Everybody knew that an ox pooped when it got scared. And this one had been *terrified.* The poop coated the Egg-Meister's face like a mask.

Gulchima shook her head. "What a mess."

It wasn't just the ox poop. Left-over magic caused such a *mess* these days. But whose problem was it? Who cleaned up after the war was over? Not the heroes. They were focused on the impressive, parade-worthy goals, like stealing the magic amulet, or killing forty guards to rescue some friend of minor importance. Heroes didn't worry about things like logistics, or clean water, or keeping the *trangles* out of your garden after some tottering old magician turned the wall into a clay monster. So who cleaned up? Not the heroes, certainly. And not the villains either, if there were such a thing.

Uncle Rattbone clomped over to her. He was a big man, strong, with bold bawdy tattoos on his arms that Gulchima wasn't allowed to look at. He tied bones in his beard like wind chimes.

"Hey Gulch, you sure we can fix this bridge?" Uncle Rattbone looked around. "With all the *loose planks* and all."

"Of course," Gulchima said automatically. "I'm head of the Outfit, and the Outfit can fix anything. Even magic."

They both watched as the Egg-Meister scrambled over to the river to wash the ox poop from his mouth. A furry hand darted out of the water, and popped several of the clasps off his tunic. When the Egg-Meister leaned forward to reach for them, a second furry hand yanked on his manicured mustache, ripping half of it out.

He screamed again, but stopped after the lunkers shoved a live crawfish into his mouth. It pinched his tongue with both claws.

"Mostly, anything," Gulchima corrected.

Uncle Rattbone laughed, then covered it with a coughing fit that fooled no one. The Egg-Meister was their client after all. It was unprofessional to laugh at the people who paid you. At least in front of them.

"I'm not doubting you. You're the boss, applesauce," Uncle Rattbone said. He put his meaty hand on her shoulder. "It's just, I've never dealt with these lunkers before. I fought more of the tooth-and-claw variety of magic in the war."

She glanced at his hand. Gulchima always felt small standing next to Uncle Rattbone. Not physically smaller—but of course she was smaller—but smaller in importance. He was so vibrant, colorful, easy to talk to. Gulchima was pale, and straight-backed, and had just enough freckles that you wouldn't notice. Her hair was dark, her mouth perfect but a few sizes too small. She was eleven-years-old, born sixteen-years-ago, and magic had ruined her life.

Gulchima smiled up at him. "I haven't fought a lunker either, but let me tell you what I have fought: A badger. They can't be worse than that. They can't."

Gulchima saw one of the lunkers pull the wagon wheel under the water. They were poor swimmers, and hung to the underside of the bridge like furry barnacles. Their fingers were as long as her hand.

"Well we better get to fixing then," Uncle Rattbone said. The steady warmth of his hand slid off her shoulder. "What's the plan?"

The plan? If they got this job done today, the money would pay their local debts, plus feed the entire Outfit—both houseboats. It was easy. Just a few creatures underneath the bridge. So what if they were magic? She'd fought a badger once. She'd stared down a bearded bear. Sharp teeth were sharp teeth, it didn't matter how they got that way.

She just had to trap them and get paid, and she could feed everyone. Pay off the local debts too, so their houseboats wouldn't be chained up anymore. Maybe then, the adults in the Outfit would start listening to Gulchima, instead of acting like her sister was still in charge. It was her company now. Officially.

"We need to find out what the lunkers look like, how many of them there are," Gulchima said. "I'll go see what happens."

Gulchima looped one of her bootlaces, so that it made a lasso. Then she started to walk across the bridge.

Uncle Rattbone said nothing. They'd talked about this. If she really was the leader of the Outfit—both houseboats—

then he had to treat her that way. At least in public.

Gulchima walked up and down the bridge.

Nothing happened.

She kept her eyes on the boards, and stomped twice. Still nothing.

She tap-danced. Again, nothing.

Had the lunkers gone? Would it be that easy?

Uncle Rattbone called to her. "Maybe they got what they-"

Her left boot twitched, then tugged, knocking Gulchima off her feet. The loop in her bootlace had caught one furry hand. The hand skittered across her boot, frantic. Gulchima took out her loop of ironstem rope, then wrapped it around the lunker's wrist, snaring it.

But it was strong. The creature's hand popped free of her bootlace, then tugged on the slack ironstem rope and disappeared off the side of the bridge.

It dragged her towards the water.

Gulchima skidded to the edge of the bridge, her legs splayed out in front of her. Splinters dug into her calf and thigh where her rabbit-skin leggings had drawn up. She wedged her boots against the running-board at the edge of the bridge, but the lunker pulled harder.

Gulchima levered against the running-board, and was pulled back up to her feet. She teetered, almost falling off the bridge. She could smell the sedges and muck plants at the river's edge. Worse, she could smell the lunkers. Like rotting cotton dipped in oil. Like fish covered in packing grease.

What would those things do to her? Drown her? Strangle her? Pull out her hair?

Horrible as they were, she didn't mind the creatures she could see, so much. *But the creatures in the dark? The ones you didn't see, until it was too late . . . .*

She shuddered.

Gulchima yanked backwards, slammed her backside against the bridge as she fell to a sitting position. The rope pulled her forward again, and she almost lost her grip. No! She needed this job. She needed to catch these lunkers.

Gulchima pulled back savagely, her lower back popping with the effort. But it wasn't enough. Gulchima scraped forward. A large sliver of wood stabbed into her thigh, drawing blood.

She wouldn't let go, not now. But if she didn't, the lunkers would pull her into the dark cold water. Gulchima might go back into the dark again, and she couldn't do that. Not after five years of it. Not after what she had seen—

Gulchima felt Uncle Rattbone's strong hands on her shoulders, felt him pull her back to the center of the bridge. She did not loosen her grip on the ironstem rope. The lunker had gone limp, but it might be faking.

"Did it scare you?" Uncle Rattbone asked. His breath rattled in his chest. The small bones in his beard trembled. "Because I think I was scared enough for the both of us, to be honest."

"No, it just *surprised* me," Gulchima lied. She breathed in deeply, regained her composure. "I thought they would be bigger."

"That's magic that is. Always a surprise."

"Oh, magic." Gulchima raised her eyebrows. "And all I have is technology, foresight, and hundreds of years of human ingenuity."

She started to pull on the rope, hand over hand, drawing the lunker up to the surface of the bridge.

Gulchima paused and then grinned up at Uncle Rattbone.

"I wonder if it *hates* fire."

CHAPTER 2: HUBWARD LIKES CANDY

HUBWARD LOVED SWEETS. He told himself this each morning as he laid out a row of chocolate raisins like pills from a herbalist, and dutifully choked down each.

He professed his love each afternoon as he forced pudding after pudding into his rumbling, protesting guts. Minutes later, as he sat grimacing on a squat-toilet, Hubward wondered when he would next get the opportunity to enjoy the obvious and entirely normal pleasure of eating sweets. They were not at all disgusting. They were a delight.

It was clear that Hubward was a normal ten-year-old boy, and normal boys like him loved sweet things. They couldn't stop chomping those oozing cherry chocolates, the limp licorice, the sappy, glue-like lollipops. And young boys with sweet-tooths (or was it sweet-teeth?) were certainly not known to do magic. Boys with sweet-teeths were safe. Unless you were a chocolate egg.

On his last day in town a flabby, fluffy, and definitely non-magical Hubward trudged to the sweet shop. He was pale and sweating by the time he reached it. Hubward forced himself to push open the shop's door and smile, despite the sickly sweet stench of candy.

"Back again," Hubward said, tremulously. He retched as the stink of chocolate covered pretzels wafted out the open shop door. Hubward turned, as if to vomit, but swallowed it instead. *They've just ruined pretzels*, he thought. *Forever.*

"I'll just . . . stay outside today. Like always."

Hubward threw two copper thalers into the shop. He closed his eyes, held open his bag, and whimpered an order. It was the same thing he'd ordered every afternoon for the last three months.

"Whatever you have is fine. Just hurry up. I love sweets, so very much, that I . . ." He started to choke and cough. The vile reek of butterscotch, made his eyes water.

"I must eat them. Immediately."

One of Gulchima's favorite lies:

"Everybody in the Outfit wants to know what happened. I mean, I was missing for five years, but I didn't age a day. I must have gone on a magical adventure, right? Was I pumped through a portal? Did I stumble through a prophecy, slip on some soap and accidentally defeat evil? I usually lie and tell them nothing happened, that I just woke up and five years had passed. But the true-truth is: I did go on an adventure. I was kidnapped.

Yep, the king of the fairies fell in love with me, and stole me away, which was pretty awkward because I was a hundred times his weight. But anyway he made me his queen and we played lutes and I drank dew out of acorns (which is not a good choice if you're really thirsty).

To be honest it's all a bit fuzzy, but as it turned out, the fairy king was evil, or maybe it was his twin brother, or whatever. I can't remember exactly what happened, but I definitely saved the kingdom. Or something like that. They called me round-ears."

-The Collected Lies of Gulchima Brixby
(23/100: **An Obvious Lie**)

What Really Happened?

CHAPTER 3: GULCHIMA AND THE LUNKER

AS IT TURNED OUT, the lunker did hate fire. That was *nice.*

Gulchima had tied it up. The lunker didn't look like anything else she'd ever seen, really. Not at all like a badger.

The creature had hidden its face, and appeared to be a harmless mottled brown-and-white puff of fur. Except it had overlong arms, and thin, agile fingers, each one as long as her hand. It had no mouth that she could see, but a pair of large black eyes told her where its head was.

Gulchima poked it with a stick. *Squish.*

"So we know that much at least," Gulchima said. *Squish. Squish.*

The lunker squirmed away from her.

In addition to fire, it seemed a lunker didn't like being poked in the eye with a stick.

Squish.

Interesting.

Uncle Rattbone stared down at it. "Must have been three or four pulling on that rope," he said. "It doesn't seem that strong."

"Maybe the sunlight weakens it somehow," Gulchima said.

"Oh that's almost never true, about the sunlight hurting magical things," Uncle Rattbone said. "Back in the war we had a saying, 'Sunlight will hurt it, when you put a new hole through its head.'" He sniffed. "Of course, that one was hard to test."

"Should we try the torches again?" Gulchima asked. She held one up near the lunker, and with a flap of a finger, it blew the torch out.

"They just run away to the other side of the bridge," Uncle Rattbone said. "And if we put a person at either end, the lunkers just run to the middle, or splash out our torches. I think we're beat Gulch, I really do."

"Then we'll just burn the whole bridge down," Gulchima said.

Besides, she didn't want to go under the bridge anyway. It was dark. She wasn't exactly afraid of the dark. Not as long as she had a torch. And a sharp knife. And a few candles, just in case. Gulchima wasn't afraid. It was just that she'd strongly prefer never to go there. Ever.

Five years, alone in the dark was enough for one lifetime.

Uncle Rattbone pulled at a bone in his beard. "Probably not going to hold up in a contract dispute . . . ."

His words trailed off. On the opposite side of the bridge stood two young soldiers, one woman, one man, both dressed in ragged uniforms. They nodded as a third soldier, a tall female warrior dressed in overlapping scale armor, gestured at the bridge.

"Debt-collectors," Uncle Rattbone said. "Professionals."

"So? We'll just bribe them again," Gulchima said, distractedly.

"Not Brunhild, that big one with scale armor. I knew her from the war," Uncle Rattbone said. "She's the toughest debt-collector in all of Baltica. She won't take a bribe."

Gulchima wished the soldiers were ugly or gross in some

way, but they weren't. They just looked like people doing a job, maybe one they didn't enjoy.

Brunhild herself was outwardly beautiful in that proud way of warriors. Rippling muscles, careless blond-hair, calm eyes that seemed to know what you were going to do. But a permanent scowl ruined her face. Her armor, made of overlapping scales, was dull and stained. It wasn't for show.

"I see you Rattbone! You Lordly Beast!" Brunhild shrieked. She started to laugh, but it curdled into a cackle. No one joined in. The Egg-Meister sidled a few paces to his left, away from her. The two young soldiers covered their ears.

"She's a little crazy," Uncle Rattbone said. He waved at Brunhild, now doubled over in laughter to the extent her armor would allow. "Maybe more than a little."

"What happened to her?" Gulchima asked. "Something in the war?"

"Crazy grows slow, usually," Uncle Rattbone said. "But she finally lost it when . . . Well, it seems I put a sword through her chest."

"She's undead? But her skin isn't blue." As far as Gulchima knew, magic had rules. Undead equals blue skin.

"Brunhild? Undead?" Uncle Rattbone exclaimed. "Naw, to be undead, you'd have to be killed first. But the stabbing stirred her up a bit. After our wedding, she—"

"Wait! You married her?"

"Well we thought we were going to die, you see," Uncle Rattbone said. "We were surrounded. Besides I owed her that much. I mean, I did stab her through the chest." Uncle Rattbone leaned in and whispered, "I think it's time we get away, while we have a river between us. If Brunhild owns all our debts, she could—"

"She can't do anything right now, we're under contract,"

Gulchima said.

But he was right. They still had a chance of running away. Baltica was a big country. Maybe the next town—but no, Gulchima hadn't told him about the next town.

Uncle Rattbone didn't know about the letter she'd received. The Outfit had a big construction contract waiting for them at the town of Bayadev. But they had to get there soon. That meant finding enough money to pay off their local debts, so they could unchain their houseboats.

It was simple. She'd catch these lunkers, then use the thalers she earned to pay off the Outfit's local debts. They'd be free to travel to Bayadev, where they'd make enough to pay off Brunhild. Once under contract, they were safe. And Gulchima was technically the leader of the Outfit wasn't she? She was eleven-years-old, she could handle the finances.

Gulchima stared hard at the lunker. There was a way, she knew it. She just had to figure it out. What would her mom do, if she was here?

"The Egg-Meister and his wagons are getting restless." Uncle Rattbone looked up at the sky, held up one hand between the sun and the horizon. "You've got four fingers to figure it out. Or it's eels again for dinner. Even if you can't do it, we'll find another way to pay the debts. If you're worried—"

"I'm not," Gulchima said.

She bit her lower lip and tried not to look at the three soldiers talking to the Egg-Meister. They had exchanged paperwork. Something was up.

"No, this is the plan," Gulchima said. "If it was easy, somebody else would have done it by now."

What *was* her plan really? What was her plan for after they defeated the lunkers? Once they got to Bayadev, they'd make such a huge profit that Gulchima could pay off her parents' debts and get them out of prison too. Then her parents could run the Outfit again, and Gulchima could go back to being eleven (technically sixteen) and annoying her younger (technically older) sister and her (previously non-existent) brother. It was simple, but not easy.

All that stood in Gulchima's way was stupid magic, from a stupid war that was over. As usual.

"So what we know is that the lunkers are not too strong, and they hate fire, and they don't swim too good," Gulchima said. "Oh and if you poke them in the eye like this—*Squish*—they don't like it."

Brunhild barked something to the two young soldiers and they started to march across the bridge. They slowed as a flurry of hands swiped at them, then retreated back across the bridge.

"Little Mouse, I've bought your debt from the Egg-Meister," Brunhild taunted. "And your other debts too. Now you owe me all of it. If this bridge is not repaired, you'll default. It'll be three years of service in the King's army, Rattbone. You and all your workers. The girl can dig ditches!"

"Got some work here, Brunhild," Uncle Rattbone said, with false cheerfulness.

"I am a Lordly Beast! Remember Rattbone?" Brunhild screamed. "You'll pay your debt to me. 'To dream of iron, is to dream of fire'!"

Uncle Rattbone cleared his throat, then spoke loudly. "I'm going to head over to that smashed wagon, see if I can make a deal for eggs. Seems like a man that'd be looking to make a quick sale." He waved at Brunhild, then whispered to Gulchima. "It's time for us to go. Now! Forget the contract."

"Wait!" The plan formed in Gulchima's mind. She'd need more help, but it could—no, it would—work. "I'm going to need you to get my sister, all the carpenters, and five or six roof thatchers in skin-boats. Do not tell Uncle Roog. And bring lots of torches and tar."

"I said we're not burning down this bridge," Uncle Rattbone said. "You're as crazy as your father sometimes."

"If I'm in charge of the Outfit, then I'm in charge, period," Gulchima said. The lines between Uncle Rattbone's eyes deepened, and she softened her tone. "But you're right Uncle Rattbone, burning down the bridge isn't going to work."

This wasn't exactly true. But you could only tell adults so much. Once they got upset, it took a few days for them to calm down.

She looked at the soldiers. They were arguing with the Egg-Meister. That would give her time.

The true-truth was that burning the bridge was only part of Gulchima's plan. They'd still burn it, of course. But they were going to build a bridge too.

They had almost four hours. How hard could it be?

CHAPTER 4:
HUBWARD MEETS THE BULLY

HUBWARD'S FACE WAS FULL AND WOBBLY, and his gentle gait caused his belly to sway in front of him. This showed the world—he hoped—how un-dangerous he really was. Hubward loved being un-dangerous. Besides the bullies, no one bothered him. And he could get on with his job of saving the world.

He scurried down the alley behind the candy shop, meek as mouse droppings. His hands were covered with chocolate, and Hubward carefully smeared some of it over his face. If an adult passed by, he'd give them a vague grin, pretend not to notice how messy he was.

Hubward fussed with the rolled up parchment beneath his arm. Maybe it would happen today. Maybe this week. He was close, he could tell, and it was only a matter—

"Hey frog-face, back for more?"

Hubward looked up, irritated by the interruption. But then he remembered where he was. Who he was. Actually, the interruption was right on schedule.

Hubward adopted a neutral expression. His default state was dull. Who was it this time? Crusher? Thumper? Oh my, it was Ani. Oddly, he was alone.

A large boy stepped out from behind the corner. All towns had large bullies like this, but Ani was something special. He loved his job. He was an artist. He didn't just hit you, he grabbed your skin and twisted. He didn't just insult you, he found the one flaw you couldn't admit to yourself. Then he made you sing about it.

A boy like Ani wouldn't rob and beat you, not for serious, not really. He smiled the whole time, like it was just a joke between pals. A game. Hubward had known people like that in the war. They'd died horribly.

In his ten years of life, Hubward had endured many insults about his cheeks, which were naturally chubby and round. Chipmunk was obvious. Frog-face, bee sting, hamster, were all pretty common insults too. Hubward's favorite had been two towns ago, when a bully called him "pudding pouch". He liked the sound of it.

"Frog-face" wasn't exactly Ani's best work, but he seemed preoccupied today. He should have started pummeling Hubward already.

Hubward wondered again, why he was alone. Ani had a crew of other boys to hold arms, and say things like "Yeah Ani," or "Can I hurt him *real* bad this time?" But the crew was absent today.

"Wh-what do you want Ani?" Hubward stammered. He'd been practicing his stammer. It lended a certain realism to the encounter. As if he really were afraid.

"Give me your thalers. All of them."

All of them? That was new.

"Here take it," Hubward held out his small cloth money pouch. "I have two thalers left over—"

"Two?" Ani asked. He grabbed Hubward by his tunic. "Not *two*. I want all your thalers. Now."

Ani shoved him against the stone wall. Hubward's head snapped back, and he saw stars.

A little rough for the first blow, Hubward thought. He started to feel the first pangs of fear, like a cold fire running up and down his arms. Not now, he thought. Not today. He was just about to find—

Hubward shook his head, trying to clear it. "I can't do that. I need them. For the delicious candy which I so love to eat." Hubward smiled weakly. "Yum?"

Ani tugged at a rolled up parchment from beneath Hubward's arm. "What's this, a treasure map?"

"You don't touch that!" Hubward yelled. The meekness evaporated from his voice, and he realized he'd just clenched his fist. No, he can't do that right now. He relaxed his spine, curved in his shoulders. He had to be the victim. He was stuck.

Ani held out the parchment, then read in a halting voice, "*My New Play: Scene 2.* Dialog-Butler, Bald: 'As you know, Madam Pills is allergic to lemons'. Dialog-Young Maid, Pretty Like Mom: 'Which is why when I served her the lemonade, I took out the peels' *dot dot dot*, wait for laughs." Ani's brow furrowed. "'Wait for laughs?' What's this supposed to be?"

"Um, I was going for *funny*?"

Ani grinned. "Well *as you know,* nobody talks like that. And nobody is coming to rescue you." He rapped his fist on Hubward's forehead. "Dot dot dot."

Hubward's eyes teared up. He hoped Ani would think he was crying.

"You're taking it too far," Hubward said. "Give me back my—"

Ani handed the parchment back, then slammed his fist into Hubward's stomach. He frowned. "What are you wearing?"

"Clothes. Normal boy's clothes." Hubward started to tear up again. Water leaked from his eyes like rain off a roof. Ani had gone too far. He'd backed Hubward into a corner. Stolen his manuscript. Hubward didn't want to lose his temper. Not now. He was tremendously close to saving the world. At the last town he'd failed because of that enchanted pig oinking its alarm, but before that was just bad luck. Well, that and the problem with the misapplied lightning. Usually it came down to pumpkins. But to fail now, because of a stupid bully? Because Hubward couldn't hold his temper?

Ani grinned, the fine sheen of oil on his nose glistened in the afternoon sunlight. "You've been holding out on me. I see you buy candy every day. Where's the rest of the money?"

"I love candy," Hubward said. "Yummy." The sweat poured out of him. His shirt was damp, the chocolate ring around his mouth had faded.

Ani looked puzzled. "No. You're hiding something." His hands padded along Hubward's stomach. "You're hiding the money in here aren't you? You have a money pouch beneath your—"

Ani stepped back. His face whitened. "It's fake. Your stomach is . . . oh *sweet sorcerer*, I didn't know. I didn't—"

Hubward smiled, but now it was a wolfish grin. The anxiety faded. Sweat dripped from his body, forming a puddle on the ground beneath him. To an outside observer, it would appear Hubward had wet his pants. But of course, Ani was the boy in trouble.

Hubward's cheeks deflated. They looked hollow. "Couldn't just leave me alone, could you?"

Hubward ate the candy because he was allergic. He hated the stuff, how it made him swell, how it kept him running to the toilet. But the candy kept him thin.

Ani shook his head, took a step back.

"You got greedy," Hubward said. "That's why your crew isn't here. You wanted all the money for yourself."

"I was just trying to rob you, honest," Ani said.

Hubward removed his false belly and let it drop to the ground. It was just a sackcloth filled with flour and water. Magical camouflage would have been detected. He twisted his neck, cracking it. It felt wonderful not to have that weight on his shoulders.

Above them, a dark mass flitted across the sun, painting shadows on Ani's face. Hubward's target was gone. The creature had sensed his magic, and gotten spooked. Again. He'd been so close, had almost caught it. He could have been done with all this saving the world nonsense, and gotten back to what mattered.

But Hubward knew where to go next: *Bayadev.* There was nowhere else the creature could go. He'd track it there, and finish the job.

"You're so skinny." Ani cringed away. "I didn't know. I saw you eat candy. I saw—"

"Not just skinny," Hubward said. "Scrawny." He ran his finger across the bold protuberance of his rib cage. "Dangerously thin."

Ani started to weep. "If I'd known you were such a weakling, I would never have tried to fight you."

"I know. I tried to warn you," Hubward said.

"I can go . . . ."

"No, you can't," Hubward said. "You've insulted me. That means we have a relationship." He tapped a thin finger on Ani's forehead. "You backed me into a corner. You hit me. That causes panic. You know what happens when you back someone into a corner, when you scare them too much. Do you know what happens, Ani? Do you?"

"They get desperate?" Ani's lower lip trembled.

"They get desperate," Hubward agreed. "And when

someone as dangerously scrawny as me gets desperate and scared, what happens? What happens when you push weak, starving people too far?"

"They . . . please, just let me go. I won't tell anyone."

"Can't do it. I've blown my cover and what I was tracking has flown off. It knows I can do magic now. Magic senses magic. And somebody has to pay the price. So what happens, Ani? Tell me and I'll let you live."

"They do . . . magic," Ani blubbered. "And the more desperate they are, the stronger the . . . the stronger the . . . ."

"The stronger the magic," Hubward finished.

Hubward reached down and grabbed Ani's shadow, pulling it upward, stretching it out into seven separate shadows, revealing them like paper dolls.

The magical shadows closed in around the big boy.

"Please, don't," Ani mumbled.

Hubward smiled, cleaned the nougat from between his teeth. He wouldn't hurt Ani too bad. But bullies always cried at the end.

"What's the matter?" Hubward taunted. "Are you afraid of your own shadow?"

"The true-truth? Okay, I admit the fairy story was a lie. The truth is that five years passed for everyone else, but not me. When I came back, my bratty younger sister was now my bratty older sister, and the war was over. Where did I go? Hard to say where I was really, because of all the apostrophes. Every place I went to had these apostrophes in its name. It's hard to pr'nounce ap'str'phes, have you noticed? You never quite c'n say them. So where did I go? It's hard to say."

-The Collected Lies of Gulchima Brixby
(40/100: **Another Lie!**)

CHAPTER 5: GULCHIMA STARTS A FIRE

"IF YOU DON'T WANT TO WORK, then who needs ya!" Uncle Rattbone roared. He picked up the carpenter and threw her over the side of the bridge.

The sun had fallen below the treeline, and a cold spring wind blew across the water. The carpenter, a steady worker named 'Anya from the Black Sea', had landed well outside the reach of the floating lunkers. She paddled efficiently, her braided liripipe swishing in the water behind her.

"You said it was honest work," the carpenter sputtered from the water below. "Nothing about magic."

Brunhild roared laughter from across the river. Sweet Sorcerer, that woman had a loud voice.

"We're getting rid of the magic," Uncle Rattbone yelled.

"Nothing dishonest about that."

The carpenter treaded water, bobbing in a thoughtful circle. "Am I fired?" she asked. She looked over at Brunhild, warily.

Gulchima thought about it. The carpenter, Anya, would be forced to join the King's army if they fired her now. That wasn't right to do. Anya had young children. They sometimes played with Gulchima's little brother, Novvy.

"She's not fired," Gulchima said, patiently. "But no eggs for her."

"Fired? Wha' for? Being afraid of magic?" Uncle Rattbone yelled. "You're not fired Anya from the Black Sea. But you're eating eels tonight, if you won't help us." He tossed a rope to the carpenter, and she pulled herself to shore.

"A two-percent reduction in debt, for that carpenter," Brunhild boomed. "The Soldier-King has need for skilled—"

"You'll get your money faster if you shut your mouth," Gulchima yelled. "She works for me."

Both young soldiers smirked, nodding their approval. Brunhild scowled.

"That's three that have outright refused," Uncle Rattbone said quietly. "The rest of them are grumbling and doing halfway-to-nothing. I'm not sure the bad-troll/worse-troll routine is working either. You sure about this Gulch?"

Was she?

Gulchima sighed. "To be honest, no. But it's the best plan I could come up with."

"That's how it goes usually," Uncle Rattbone said. He smiled. "If the plan works, everyone will say they agreed with you. If it fails, everyone will say they told you so."

Gulchima was too nervous to listen to his pep talk. She walked away from Uncle Rattbone to make one final inspection.

The thatchers had laid tar across the bridge, and swabbed it underneath too. The smell of the sticky tar burned her nose and eyes. That was step one.

The carpenters had been busy constructing a false bridge, though some had walked off the job once they realized why. The false bridge, little more than several prefabricated walls tied with rope, floated about fifty yards away. It stretched from one bank of the river to the other. Right now, the carpenters were pegging together an apex, so the false bridge at least appeared to be above the water. The apex was just two walls raised up and leaning into an A-frame, with support boards underneath.

Behind the bridge were the skin-boats, ready to tug the false bridge away. Her younger/older sister Isolde, and Uncle Roog headed that part of the operation. Moving the false bridge was step three.

And step two? Moving the lunkers? Gulchima had saved that for herself.

Gulchima breathed in deeply, then yelled, hands cupped around her mouth. Her four-year-old brother Novvy stood on the riverbank, at one edge of the false bridge, acting as a human repeater. She had to give him something to do. Uncle Roog was in one of the closer boats, and Isolde was in a boat farthest away.

"Ready for ignition," Gulchima yelled.

"Steady hold that pigeon," Novvy said.

"What about religion?" Uncle Roog asked. He really was hard of hearing. Novvy was just being a goose.

"Cheddar in position," Isolde confirmed. Hopefully she thought cheddar was just a codeword for the false bridge. Isolde didn't like the plan. Isolde didn't like anything Gulchima did. Ever. That was normal. They were sisters.

But the five year jump had altered their dynamic. Gulchima was still eleven, and her magical accident meant that, for her, no time had passed. She'd just appeared five years later, in the same spot she had been walking. The wipeberries in her basket were still fresh.

For the rest of the world, however, five years had gone by. Wars had ended. Children had been born (including her brother Novvy). Her younger sister Isolde had been eight-years-old, but was now thirteen. They were sisters. It was weird.

Isolde insisted on acting like her older sister now, and Gulchima let her. But the Outfit was Gulchima's to run. Her parents were in prison, and since Gulchima was legally sixteen, and legally the oldest, she was the boss. Isolde was angry about that too. She'd been training for the job.

Her younger brother, Novvy was now four, and had been . . . well, nothing. He hadn't existed. Gulchima was surprised by how little this bothered her about Novvy. Was it because he looked like her father? Maybe. But maybe some people were lights that made the rest of the world seem brighter. Novvy was a torch.

Isolde waited a beat, and then yelled, "This is stupid."

"Missing cupid?" asked Uncle Roog.

"I'm a new kid," said Novvy.

"Red to goop it," Gulchima confirmed. She smiled at the puzzled look of Uncle Rattbone. "That's just slang. 'Goop it' means, uh, 'to go quickly'."

"And 'Red' means 'ready'," Uncle Rattbone said. "I'm no *foozle.* I still know what's cool." He waved at one of the nearby thatchers. "Light 'em up boys. *Red to goop it*, as they say." He winked at Gulchima.

Just then, the Egg-Meister strode across the bridge. The

man had a gift for bad timing. He had removed his boots, but one of his *sockums* stuck to the tar, and he came up barefoot.

"I demand to know what is going on," he said. "When will you repair this bridge?"

"As soon as we put the fire out," Gulchima said.

"As soon as you . . . ow!" The Egg-Meister examined the new splinter in his naked foot, then looked up, wide-eyed. "What fire?"

"That one." Gulchima pointed at the river.

Uncle Rattbone floated in a skin-boat just below the bridge. A thatcher manned the oars. Uncle Rattbone ran his torch against the underside, and it whooshed into flame. At the same time, a thatcher's apprentice ran along the top of the bridge, dragging his torch, and lit that as well.

Lunkers plopped into the water, splashing at the flames. But it was too strong for them. The plan was working.

"What? Fire?" the Egg-Meister asked again.

Uncle Rattbone's skin-boat paddled backwards, then ignited a length of greased rope stretched across the width of the river. He pushed it with an oar, and the flaming rope floated across the water, towards the bobbing lunkers

"It's working Gulch!" Uncle Rattbone yelled. "They're panicking. That'll clean them out!"

The burning rope herded the floating lunkers toward the false bridge. They wouldn't leave the real bridge normally, but maybe she could trick them into latching onto the false bridge, then transport them. That was the plan.

"Fire! What—" the Egg-Meister squeaked.

Gulchima looked up and saw the Egg-Meister dancing across the burning bridge. His other sockum had tar stuck to it, and now it was ignited too.

"Stop!" Gulchima yelled, but the Egg-Meister refused to

listen to her. She was just a kid after all. What did she know?

The lunkers started to bob about, confused. On the one hand, their bridge home was burning. They could see safe planks of wood from the false bridge, and that was inviting. A few lunkers had climbed up and were roosting in the A-frame of the false bridge.

But the Egg-Meister's clomping drew them back. The idiot. She had a mind to pull out the other half of his mustache.

If the lunkers knew the real bridge was safe, they'd come back. It would all be lost. Even now, the flames sputtered. The fire was just tar burning off, not the wood of the bridge. Not yet anyway.

The lunkers started to swim back to the first bridge, a mass of soggy mottled brown lumps. The Egg-Meister had ruined her plans. Adults! Didn't they ever listen?

"We gotta get someone up on the false bridge. Make some noise on that one," Uncle Rattbone said. He picked up an oar and threw it like a spear, hitting the Egg-Meister in the middle of his back. The man fell into the water, which doused the flames.

"Surrounded by water and he couldn't figure that out?" Gulchima asked.

Uncle Rattbone shrugged.

Gulchima turned to yell out more orders, but stopped. Her little brother Novvy was already in motion.

He carried several eggs in his tunic, which he kilted up to make a basket. Novvy straddled the apex and said, "I just sure hope no one makes me break these eggs." He jumped up and down, almost fell off, but steadied himself. "Yes, that would be a turrible shame to *lost* my eggs on this *see-ka-ritt* bridge. The one them lunkers don't know about."

Novvy jumped again, then ran to one side, dumping the

eggs into a pile of leaves and needles.

"Novvy, stop!" both Gulchima and Isolde yelled. But his distraction worked. A mass of humped shapes moved through the water, toward the false bridge.

Gulchima waved for the thatchers to start extinguishing the fire on the real bridge. A line of buckets started on the top, and put out most of the flames. The tar had burned off easily. A second line of buckets worked on the underside of the bridge, which had a lot more tar applied to it.

From her position on shore, Gulchima lit another large rope with her torch, then pushed it toward the lunkers, in case any were having doubts.

None were. They clambered around the false bridge now, exploring it.

Novvy ran to the opposite end, and picked up another load of eggs. Lunker hands snatched at him, but did not find a purchase.

"Goop it!" Novvy cried. He pranced to the center of the false bridge, at the very highest point. But instead of climbing down, he started dancing and juggling the eggs.

The crowd, wagon-drivers and workers alike, erupted into cheers and chants of "Goop-it! Goop-it!"

They were cheering. Uncle Rattbone had been right. They were cheering for Novvy, for the plan, and though they didn't know it, they were cheering for Gulchima.

"Okay now!" Gulchima yelled. The skin-boats tugged the false bridge, drifting it farther and farther from the real bridge. "Take it to that far point, and leave it there."

The sudden tug was enough to jolt Novvy from his perch. His arms pin wheeled. The crowd cheered louder, thinking he was playacting. But the cheers turned to groans when Novvy slipped, and then fell backwards into the water.

Had he hit his head?

Five eggs plopped into the water where he had sunk. Gulchima waited a few breathless seconds. But nothing surfaced.

Gulchima ran through the underbrush along the river, thorns tearing at her legs, her face. She didn't care. At last she reached the edge of the false bridge.

Novvy still had not surfaced. A pack of lunkers boiled around in the water, as if searching for something. Gulchima started to cross the false bridge. The wood jostled her forward and she almost lost her footing.

Without warning, Isolde's boat slammed into the bridge, then rebounded off. She speared her arms into the water. Isolde cried out, one arm grasping something, the other slapping at a lunker. She pulled back hard, and Gulchima saw a flash of sandy brown hair, a coughing face.

Novvy! She'd saved him.

"Are you okay?" Gulchima called from shore. But Isolde waved her off, flashed her a dirty look. They'd talk about this. Later.

Isolde shoved off the bridge and launched her boat away to safety. She had Novvy, and he seemed okay. Trembling, but that was probably from the cold.

The ropes resumed their work, towing the false bridge, now laden with lunkers, to the far point. The crowd cheered again, though this time it was more subdued.

The real bridge was clear of lunkers, and already the egg-wagons were trundling across it.

She saw Uncle Rattbone and the Egg-Meister talking, exchanging paperwork. It was done. She'd done it.

There'd be no eels tonight for dinner. All the carpenters and thatchers and boatmen would say they'd helped. And she'd let them. Because who cares. She'd come up with a good plan, and it worked. Everyone would recognize that. And Novvy seemed all right. Sure Isolde had saved him, but everyone knew it was Gulchima's plan. That was obvious.

They could eat all the eggs they wanted. She'd feed them all—both houseboats—and then tell them about the next contract. There was a lot of bad magic at Bayadev. A lot that needed fixing. They'd listen now.

Brunhild stalked across the bridge. As she approached, Gulchima saw Brunhild's eyes were a dark gray tinged with purple, like bruised storm clouds. Brunhild was gibbering, laughing, slapping her own face. She headed for Gulchima.

Suddenly, Gulchima remembered: The debt, the threat.

Brunhild was coming for them. Gulchima started to run.

CHAPTER 6: HUBWARD DRINKS THE BUTTER

IT WAS HIS BIRTHDAY, so Hubward drank a mug of melted butter. Now that he was eleven, Hubward had decided on a change of approach. He couldn't be solely saving the world with sugary shenanigans every single second.

Wasn't that a mouthful? Almost as much of a mouthful, as the thick sizzling bacon, which he dipped in his mug of melted butter. Bacon in butter? Why not? It was his birthday, after all.

Ten had not been a kind age for Hubward. He wanted to forget all about ten. The confusion with the molten marshmallows and the underwear had been a momentous mistake. And so many pumpkin mishaps. Worst of all, he'd failed a third time in his quest to trap the creature. It was time to try something else.

So with a new approach, came a new outlook on diet. Adults certainly claimed a new diet would solve all of their problems. "If only I ate this, instead of that," adults always said. "Then I would be happy."

He'd try that. Eat food he liked, food he could keep down without going to the toilet every ten minutes. He wouldn't be able to do magic if he wasn't scrawny, but at Bayadev the best camouflage of all would be an utter inability to do magic. He'd be undetectable.

So Hubward sat in a birch tree, drinking his butter, and eating his bacon. The enchanted pig from two towns ago, had oinked its last warning. He'd purchased it, then brought it to a butcher. That was a nice present to himself. Very thoughtful. They said revenge was a dish best served cold. But this excluded pork products.

With all the bacon and butter, who had time for candy? Not him. So no magic for a while. Big deal. Hubward was a *Gaunt*, a magical assassin. But why did the world require all Gaunts to be the same? To look the same? He liked magic, and there was plenty left over, waiting around for him. He'd just have to pick some up along the way.

Take the pack of enchanted wolves snapping and growling a few feet below him, for instance. *They* were magic, right? With the glowing green eyes and crafty intelligence to prove it. And they were waiting for him. Well, waiting to eat him anyway.

Yes, during the War of the Ribs, magic had ruined the world (well Baltica anyway). But only because it was used incorrectly. The Sorcerer had screwed up . . . .

Hubward chewed a fatty piece of bacon, then threw the remainder below him. The wolves fought over it, with yips and growls and so on. Maybe "incorrectly" was not the right word. Magic used incorrectly, resulted in death.

What Hubward meant—he took a sip of butter—was that the magic was used *inappropriately*. But now the current king of Baltica had banned all magic. Magic was evil, the current king said.

Evil! That was like saying that since fire had once burned your hand, you should never cook anything again. Hubward sighed. *Such small minds.*

You had to cook bacon, and that meant fire. Hubward

smiled, then threw down another piece of bacon. Even the pack of magical wolves (or was it wolfs) below him would agree to that.

Yes you had to cook bacon, otherwise it was just cold pork. And so, you had to use magic, otherwise, umm . . . well . . . His point was, you had to use magic sometimes. Because if you didn't use it, somebody else would.

Hubward looked down at the wolves. He wondered about them, about how they had chased him, all of a sudden. Quite a coincidence. Anyway, he knew what to do next.

Hubward whispered to one of the seven shadows perched in the birch tree beside him. The branch bent under the weight, as the largest shadow leaned forward to listen.

After a long discussion, and much gesturing, the shadow leaned back.

"So that's how we'll do it," Hubward said. He slurped the last of his butter from the mug. "Do you understand?"

The largest shadow paused, and in a dry dusty voice, it said:

"Pumpkin?"

"Okay I admit the apostrophes story isn't true. Really, what happened was that I went to this distant land where they said magic was dangerous, but they sure seemed to use it a lot.

I mean every five minutes they would disappear in a puff of smoke. Good guys had white smoke, bad guys had red. They'd have a showdown, insult one another, and then . . . puff of smoke. How did they keep anything down? I mean was there a rule? Like you had to wait one hour after eating before you dissipate?"

-The Collected Lies of Gulchima Brixby
(13/100: **Another False Story. Insulting!**)

CHAPTER 7: GULCHIMA RIDES THE HOUSEBOAT

WHEN GULCHIMA ARRIVED BACK AT THE DOCK, one of the houseboats was already missing. The half-moon peeked over the water, and Gulchima could see the lamps from Barkers, the larger houseboat, downriver. They were moving fast.

The Biters houseboat, the one she lived on with the rest of the apprentices and junior craftsmen, was one rope away from departure. Four towboats were roped on, oars in the air, waiting to pull them to the center of the river. Someone on the houseboat waved at her frantically.

What was going on? Where was the Barkers houseboat

headed? Did Uncle Rattbone warn them about Brunhild and her soldiers? Or were they just running away, in a blind panic?

Gulchima was exhausted. She had leaves and brambles stuck to her hair, and raised red scrapes on her stomach from escaping through the needle-brush. But *tired* could wait. She had work to do.

Brunhild would have a boat too. That woman wouldn't give up easily. She wouldn't give up, period. If Brunhild caught them on the river, without a valid contract, she could put them all in debtors' prison. Or worse.

So simply drifting down the river wouldn't be enough. Gulchima had to warn Isolde and the others. Convince them to start rowing. Downriver.

More work. Won't that be popular.

Gulchima jumped onto the houseboat, just as one of the mud-boys—a mason's apprentice—loosened the last rope from the dock. What was his name? Wentick? Wartok? Tiktok? Something like that. He was about thirteen-years-old. He wasn't bad looking, but his breath could clean rust off the anchors. Underwater.

Gulchima pulled a few of the larger leaves from her hair. It still looked like a cobweb, but she felt presentable.

"Next stop, Bayadev," Tiktok called, smiling. "Took you long enough to get here, you *whiffle-waffle*."

The towboats smoothly pulled Biters out to the center of the river, then dropped the ropes. The familiar drone of *sqwatch* birds and shine-bugs lessened. It was always so quiet on the river.

And so far, there was no sign of Brunhild. At least their houseboat was underway.

"Bayadev? Who told you that?" Gulchima asked.

Tiktok shrugged, tied off the rope. "Isolde says it's the

place to be. 'Mountains of sugar, rivers of honey, uncounted quantities of near-beer'. It's our next contract. Didn't she tell you?" He smiled again, then mouthed the words to himself quietly, as if savoring them.

So they were headed to the right place too. But who else knew about the contract?

"I need you to gather a group of rowers," Gulchima said. "Then grab the oars and set up the rowbox."

Tiktok looked at her blankly. "Um, you don't need to row *downriver.* The water just pushes you."

"The debt collectors are chasing us. If they catch us—"

"Debt collectors? Isolde said we paid those off."

"Debts are like flies," Gulchima said. "You kill one and five more come to the funeral. Set up the rowbox and—"

"Isolde said we float. So we float." He took a small red onion out of his pocket and bit into it.

"I'm in charge of the Outfit," Gulchima growled.

Tiktok held up his hands. "Yeah, maybe. But when you're not around—which is most of the time—she's in charge. So *you* need to talk to *her.*"

"Okay. Where is she?"

"On the boat," Tiktok said. He took another bite of his onion. Like many boys, Tiktok thought that not answering questions made him charming.

"Very. Helpful," Gulchima said. "Do you know where Isolde is, or not?"

"It's a big boat," Tiktok answered. But his attempt at cleverness melted under Gulchima's glare. He flipped the hair out of his eyes. "Dining hall. Start there."

"That wasn't an answer," Gulchima said. "Where—"

"It's the answer I'm giving *you.*" Tiktok walked away from her to gather up the rest of the tow ropes.

"So yeah, just grab some oars and some friends," Gulchima called after him. "Make sure you get the rowbox set up. Okay? Yes?"

Tiktok waved his hand behind him, but did not respond.

"And brush your teeth!" Gulchima yelled.

* * *

Biters *was* a big boat. Not as big as the Barkers boat, but nearly so. The houseboat was about two-hundred-forty feet long, and maybe sixty feet wide. It wasn't too deep, no river boat could be without scraping the bottom of the river. But they'd built it up, level after level, and now parts of the houseboat were five stories high. It'd be a disaster in the Western Sea. Which was why they kept it to the rivers.

Gulchima needed to find Isolde and starting at the dining hall made sense. She jogged across the plaza to the dining hall, the lone building near the front of the ship. The smell of fried fish and boiled potatoes greeted her at the door.

The dining hall was a two story affair with a full kitchen and three rows of Tamme oak tables on the first floor. Dinner was finished, and though there were mountains of eggshells to commemorate Gulchima's success, the gaggle of grimy workers still sitting at the tables seemed not to notice her. Isolde wasn't there.

Gulchima picked up a boiled egg and cracked it against the small bowl carved into the table. She peeled the egg with a fingernail, then bit into it.

It needed salt. But at least it wasn't boiled eel.

"'Strength for working'," Gulchima said to a young cooker-girl, who was sweeping garbage into the drain on the floor.

"'Strength is needed'," the girl replied in a bored tone, without looking up. She snapped the drain cover closed, then sped back to the kitchen.

Okay. Not the rousing welcome Gulchima had envisioned. Obviously Isolde wasn't here, and not at the front bow of the houseboat either. Maybe she was with Novvy.

Gulchima walked out of the dining hall, and crossed the plaza, darting around the potted fruit trees and the derrick. A few of the younger children were playing *Blind-Mouse* and Tormo, a tubby eastern boy with a pockmarked forehead, crashed into her. He pulled up his blindfold.

"Sorry Gulch!" Tormo squealed with laughter. The children were Novvy's age and younger, but Novvy wasn't with them. Was he hurt?

"Have you seen Isolde or Novvy?" Gulchima asked.

"Haven't seen anything 'cause of this blindfold," Tormo said. He grinned and the rest of the children laughed out loud.

This time Gulchima laughed along with them. It was hard to be cross with someone missing both front teeth. She kept walking.

"Don't forget, Festival of Rough Peter is coming up!" Tormo said. "That means chocolate!"

"I won't forget, I'm running it this year." *That and everything else.*

Where next? She could check the *Trilogy*, the three-story living area. But that was a maze of sleeping bodies, cubbyholes, and storage bins. She'd wake up half the boat. The main building was no better. All five levels clanged and thumped as the masons and carpenters geared up for the contract. Gulchima heard the ring of sharpening adzes, the muffled thuds of supplies being sifted. She'd have to talk to Isolde about that too.

Gulchima climbed up the rope ladder to the walk-walk, a porch that wrapped around the main building. She sidled past a line of bee boxes, then ran straight into Uncle Roog.

Hello Bad. Let me introduce you to Worse.

Uncle Roog poked his mass of white hair out from behind the nearest bee box. He scowled at the bees, then scowled at Gulchima.

"Novvy is hurt, you hedgeborn pumpkin-eater," Uncle Roog barked. "And you can't not tell me about replacing us with undead laborers at the next job." He pointed a sticky finger at Gulchima. "Because I already know!"

Uncle Roog said things like this when he was grumpy or stressed out. So, basically when he was awake. He was no one's uncle. He'd earned his title because like many uncles, he showed up to events, uninvited, and then criticized whatever you were doing. But like an unpleasant spring snowstorm, you assumed he was necessary for some part of the world to keep working.

"Uncle Roog, I don't have time for your cloudy disposition," Gulchima said. "Where's Isolde?"

"Speak up, mumblecrust! Novvy's with the herbalist, not that you care," Uncle Roog said. He looked away. "Haven't you done enough, without bothering him now?"

"Haven't I done enough? Yes, I have. I saved the Outfit today, with an awesome plan. Now just get—"

"Stop mumbling! You caused this. If you hadn't, Novvy wouldn't be hurt. Look, I'm not your uncle," Uncle Roog said. "But if I were, I'd tell you what I think."

Gulchima crossed her arms. "Oh? What's that?"

"You're a *cumberworld.* Your head got screwed on backwards by that magic." Uncle Roog wagged his finger in her face. "That's what I *would* say. And you know what else? You can't replace me with the undead. All that groaning and slobbering about. They can't dig a straight ditch, let alone repair a wall. It's an art form, repairing mortar."

"What? That's not the plan," Gulchima said. She took a deep breath and looked over Roog's shoulder. Below the porch, at the back of the boat, stood Isolde. She was struggling to move both steering oars at the same time. The idiot.

Gulchima's attention snapped back to Uncle Roog.

Uncle Roog grinned. "Yeah, sure that's not the plan. Not anymore."

Gulchima turned, and walked in the opposite direction. She was shaking with anger, and didn't want to say what she thought. But then she spun around, and did it anyway.

"No Roog, the actual plan is to replace you with a real dead person. Not undead. Just dead. Or maybe a sack of ox poop. Because either of those things would get just as much work done as you. And without so much complaining."

Uncle Roog looked confused. He held up a honey encrusted finger.

Gulchima slid down the rope ladder that led to the stern.

"And stop stealing our honey!"

* * *

Isolde stood in the shadow of the curved swan neck, the oversized carving which decorated their stern in the Romaic fashion. A thin tube ran from the stern to the front of the ship and another to the spy atop the houseboat. Both were rattling a warning.

"Two steering oars, two people," Gulchima said to Isolde. "Or are you trying to crash the boat?"

She grabbed one of the steering oars and yanked it into position. It was heavy, and moved like molasses. Gulchima could see there were some weeds stuck to it. But together, she and Isolde moved the steering oars into position. The houseboat drifted away from the rocky bank, back to the middle of the river.

Isolde looked at her, startled, then gave her one of those broad fortifying smiles that melted boys' hearts. Gulchima was immune, but not ignorant. Her thirteen-year-old sister was borderline beautiful, with curly black hair, and light eyes the color of honey. Nobody would compare Gulchima's eyes to anything interesting, unless they knew a lot about soil. Hers were a brown silty-loam.

"Oh, you didn't get my message?" Isolde asked. She flapped her eyelashes like a poisonous butterfly. "We're leaving. What took you so long?"

"Must have been busy saving the Outfit and running away from . . . ."

In the distance, Gulchima saw Brunhild's longboat, loaded with soldiers, their oars slicing through the water like knives through pork fat. The carving on the prow wasn't a dragon's head. It was Brunhild's own face, carved large and laughing. She was gaining on them.

Brunhild stood at the prow, resting her arms on the carving of her own face. She spoke calmly, yet somehow her words boomed across the water. "The chase builds my hunger, lemon-drop." Brunhild laid her head on the carving. "It grows vaster than empires. Vaster than stars and seas."

" . . . from her," Gulchima finished.

"She looks like a nightmare my bad dreams once had," Isolde said. The steering oar tore from her hand, and the boat started to drift. "Sweet Sorcerer, these weeds!"

"Almost forgot!" Gulchima reached into her pocket and pulled out thirty-seven kroons. She tossed the seven lumpy coins into the water.

"You're wasting money," Isolde said.

"Can't journey without luck," Gulchima said, with a shrug. "Dad always did it."

"Well you're not Dad," Isolde said. "Moreover, after three journeys, that's a full thaler. You could buy a loaf of bread with a thaler."

"Moreover, if you act poor, then that's how the world will treat you," Gulchima said. That was another of Dad's sayings.

"So what about this letter? A new contract? Bayadev?" Isolde asked. "Were you going to tell anyone?"

"Oh you didn't get *my* message?" Gulchima parroted back to her. She flapped her eyelashes, mocking her sister. This time the oar slapped out of her hands, and smacked into the boat's side. Below her the weeds had thickened. Worse—since they were weeds and technically shouldn't be able to do this—the weeds started climbing up the boat.

"Do plants normally climb?" Isolde asked.

Gulchima looked down. "I don't know. Do they normally have a face?"

Weed covered hands gripped the top rail. Gulchima stepped back, suddenly afraid. Was there a word for worser than worse? If so, this was it.

But then, the singing started. Gulchima felt stuck in place, calm, at peace. The music was beautiful. So were the singers.

There were no weeds once they climbed aboard. That was silly. Twelve of the most beautiful women Gulchima had ever seen now stood on the deck. Their song was amazing, uplifting, inspirational. They were guardians of the river, they sang. They would help her fight Brunhild. Gulchima's gift of money to the river had sealed the deal.

"So that's what was slowing us down," Isolde said. "But . . . I don't mind somehow."

From the porch above, they heard Uncle Roog stomping

around. He threw a bag of potatoes at their feet.

"I'm not your uncle, and it's none of my business," Uncle Roog called down to them. "But those river-hags clambering up the side of the boat got my attention." He clanked down his load of potatoes and iron.

Uncle Roog stuffed a dirty brown potato into the wide bore of a pitted iron tube, then picked up a candle.

"They're helping us!" Isolde and Gulchima yelled simultaneously. "Don't shoot them with your—"

Uncle Roog grinned evilly as he held up his pitted iron hand-cannon. "Cover your ears, girls."

He lit the fuse, then pointed the hand-cannon at the closest beautiful singer.

"It's about to get loud."

CHAPTER 8: HUBWARD GETS OUT OF THE TREE

THE THREE REMAINING WOLVES growled at Hubward. That was silly. Why give away their position like that?

He strode over to them. The wolves backed to the edge of the sinkhole. Now which one was the meanest? Not the biggest one. Its tail was down between its legs.

Hubward belched. "Can any of you talk?" he asked the wolves.

They said nothing. How boring. Magically enhanced intelligence, and they still couldn't talk. What was the point?

The three wolves were cornered. Their brethren's yips and howls of pain echoed from the bear den just below them. The bearded bears in the sinkhole weren't magic. They didn't have to be. They were bears. And they were grumpy. The wolves falling into their den had woken them up.

A rock whizzed near the trio of wolves, but did not hit them.

"No, not like that," Hubward yelled at the thinnest of his seven shadows. "I told you, they can't see you. Or smell you. Stop sneaking and hurry up."

A leaf fluttered to the ground.

Hubward turned to another shadow, lugging a small boulder. "Yes I know you're hungry. There's pumpkins ahead." He rattled his parchment. "I have a map right here. Okay?

Pumpkins, yum."

The wolves cowered, trying to appear small. Their growls were angry, confused. They couldn't see what exactly was hurting them. Hard to bite a hand you can't see.

A beetle landed on a blade of grass.

"Well I suppose that might work," Hubward said to the roundest of the shadows. "But that's a tricky bit of logic. Wolves eat rabbits, and rabbits eat pumpkins. So you could eat wolves and thereby—Just be patient, all right? Pumpkins are coming. I promise."

The wind swirled, pelting him with sand.

"I double promise then," Hubward said. He sighed.

The wolves crouched down, ready for a final attack. Hubward reminded himself to be careful. He couldn't do any magic right now. He'd been drinking butter.

The meanest wolf—which was always the middle-sized one because it had to fight wolves of both sizes—leapt at him. It slammed into a tree branch it couldn't see, then fell back dazed.

"Okay, now go ahead and drop the rock on that one," Hubward said. "Don't kill it, just injure it a bit."

The boulder appeared, and bowled into the wolf, knocking it back down.

"We'll need some more whining, before it falls into the sinkhole," Hubward said. "Those bears can't be that hungry anymore." He held his fingers up to the horizon, measured the height of the sun. Three hours left. This was taking a long time.

A mouse nibbled a berry.

"I said I'll get the pumpkins! Geeze!" Hubward yelled. "Just hurry up would you? I have a job interview in Bayadev in three hours."

"The one thing I learned about being immortal? Take care of your teeth."

-The Collected Lies of Gulchima Brixby
(0/100: **Impossible, Illogical, and FALSE**)

CHAPTER 9: GULCHIMA HAS STRONG FEELINGS ABOUT POTATOES

BUH-BOOM!

Uncle Roog's first shot missed entirely. The potato sailed over the side of the houseboat before plopping into the water.

"Roog! We don't use magic in this Outfit," Isolde yelled.

"It's not magic, it's potatoes!" Uncle Roog replied. He speedily reloaded the cannon. "And a spoonful of fire medicine." He poured several handfuls of the explosive powder into a compartment on the cannon.

Gulchima was glad he hadn't interrupted the women's song. It was a beautiful lullaby from her childhood, one half remembered. Gulchima's hand loosened on the steering oar. Let Isolde steer. She could do it with just one oar. And it had been so long since she'd heard that song. Gulchima wanted to listen.

One of the twelve beautiful singers climbed up to Uncle Roog, a patient smile on her face. She gestured for him to put down his weapon.

"Oh what a pretty maiden," Uncle Roog said, sarcastically. "Want to sing me a lullaby do you? Well guess what?"

Roog pointed the potato-cannon at the singer's face. "I'm deaf in that ear!"

Buh-boom!

The potato slammed into the singer's forehead. The creature flashed a lightning-bright blue, and then flipped backwards, screaming, into the water. Its mask fell, and Gulchima saw the warts, the swampweed hair, the marsh black eyes, oily and rolling.

Those weren't swan maidens on her boat! They were river-hags!

The river-hags' spell was broken, at least for Gulchima.

Near one of the rope ties, Tiktok was kissing another river-hag, pushing away the other boys on the boat, so as not to be interrupted. Gulchima could see the slime dripping from the river-hag's lips. It was like kissing an eel.

"Roog, there!" Gulchima yelled.

Uncle Roog whirled. "Let's give them a spread of small red." He grinned as he loaded two pounds of small red potatoes.

Roog fired his cannon. The potatoes thwacked into the river-hag and the boys surrounding it. But while the small red potatoes left welts on the back of Tiktok's head, the river-hag fell as if stabbed by hot iron.

Tiktok looked at the river-hag, horrified. The beautiful young woman he had been kissing was replaced by a hideous slime beast. He wiped at his mouth frantically, but the slime had congealed, almost sealed it shut.

He screamed. Or tried to.

Boom. *Buh-Boom.* The concussion echoed off of the trees lining the river. With each blast a river-hag fell. Some of the girls from the dining hall ran over to Roog with more ammunition from the kitchen.

Behind her, Gulchima saw Brunhild's boat. It had drawn closer, but seemed to be waiting for something.

Up ahead, Gulchima saw that the river narrowed. There were two fingers of rocks on either side. Who knew how many more rocks lay just below the surface. If they hit the rocks at this speed, the houseboat would sink. This was not time for heroics. Gulchima had to steer the boat.

And her attackers knew it. The two largest river-hags moved in unison toward Gulchima.

One of the workers from the dining hall ran over and slashed at the river-hags with his short sword. The creatures didn't seem to notice. The smaller river-hag pulled the sword from the worker's hand, snapping off the nicked blade, then tossed the ruined weapon onto the deck. The river-hag's oily black eyes never left Gulchima. It shuffled closer.

"Oh there's one," Uncle Roog said. "Let's see if this russet brown, will . . . uh . . . I can't think of a rhyme."

"Just shoot it!" Gulchima yelled. The river-hags were almost to the steering oars. They smelled like swamp gas and spoiled fruit. She gagged.

"Take it down!" Isolde said. "Russet brown, will take it down."

"No, that rhyme is too obv—" But Roog had already lit the fuse. The cannon boomed, launching the potato far out of range.

Gulchima looked behind her, just as the potato slammed into Brunhild's laughing face, hitting her above the right cheekbone. It hit her real face, not the carved caricature on the prow of her ship. Brunhild toppled into the water, and her soldiers stopped rowing. The longship drifted sideways, oars lifted.

Would the soldiers save someone like Brunhild? Gulchima

wasn't so sure.

But Gulchima had other things to worry about right now. The river-hags had ganged up on her. One dug its cold claws into her forearm, and tried to push her overboard. The other larger river-hag shook the steering oar, trying to crash the houseboat. A third was fighting with Isolde, who kicked at it viciously.

"I'm on it," Uncle Roog said. "Root vegetables beat water-magic every time. It's a good thing we had all these potatoes." He pointed his hand-cannon, squinted his eyes and then . . . .

Clunk! The hand cannon exploded, spraying shards of metal across the deck. One dug into the nearest river-hag's face and the creature pulled it out distractedly. A fine meshwork of slime grew across the gash and in an instant, the wound was healed.

From the cloud of black smoke on the porch, Gulchima heard Uncle Roog yelling at one of the girls from the dining hall.

"You mumblecrust, that's a Yam! I said sweet potato." He listened as an indistinct voice replied, then said, "Yes, there's a difference!"

"The potato cannon is down," Gulchima gasped. Her river-hag was pulling at the steering oar, twisting it. Obviously river-hags had no idea how to steer a boat.

"And the rocks—" Isolde said.

"Imminent." Gulchima looked down at the bag of potatoes at her feet, and the ruined short sword. It would work. Probably. "Okay you steer backwards. These river-hags are dumb. Whatever way you pull, they'll pull the opposite. Get it?"

"No," Isolde said. Then she tried it. "Ok yes, now I get it. I'll trick them into steering the way I want to go. I pull the opposite way, and let them think they're stopping me."

But Isolde's trick was irrelevant as long as the two river-hags were messing with Gulchima's steering oar. That was step two.

Gulchima squirmed free of their grasp, then ran over to the broken short sword. The blade was fractured, but it was the handle she wanted. She leaned down and scooped up a wayward potato, then jammed it on the broken blade.

There. Instant potato-sword. Should she yell *potato-power*? If there ever was a good time to say it . . . .

"Care for a slice?" she asked the nearest river-hag. It grabbed for her, but she spun and then jabbed the homemade potato-sword into the creature's chest. It stumbled backwards, claws covering the gaping wound, then fell off of the boat. That left two river-hags.

This time, Gulchima decided she would say it. "Potato-power!" she screamed, then ran headlong at the largest river-hag. She brought her potato-sword down, but it had no effect.

The muck slime from the first stabbing covered her potato. It was useless.

She slipped and fell onto her backside, just as several fried potato chips whizzed through the air.

Gulchima looked up at the porch. Tormo and the small children from the plaza were raining potato bits onto the river-hag. Though they didn't have the force of Roog's cannon, they had numbers. The creature screamed.

A large potato chip slashed at the river-hag's forehead. A second clipped off its ear. A sling-shot tater-tot took out its left eye. The river-hag tried to pull out the tater-tot, but this time the mesh of black slime curled up and drew away from the wound.

Gulchima slid across the mucky deck and reached for the

sack of potatoes. She stood up and then swung it at the creature. It spun twice, then fell off the boat. That left one.

The last river-hag left its struggle with Isolde, and started toward Gulchima. She slipped again, and came down hard on her funny bone. Gulchima dropped the bag of potatoes.

"Gulch, here!" called Tormo. He threw down an oversized rectangularly cut potato, what the cookers called a "french-fry" for some reason. Gulchima held the french-fry up to her nose and inhaled. It smelled like oil and salt.

"Get off my boat," she said, calmly.

The river-hag held up a single claw to its face. The claw grew, until it was the length of her french-fry. "Blarrgh-rowrg-ra-roorg," it answered.

They dueled.

Neither the river-hag nor Gulchima was very good. But where the river-hag had strength, Gulchima had speed. She waited for her opening, feinting in and out. The river-hag did the same.

The deck trembled as the boat skimmed off a rock or maybe a log. Gulchima and the river-hag both stumbled, but neither attacked.

"Isolde, steer the boat! I'll take care of this one."

"Yeah, got it," Isolde said. The boat glanced off another rock, with a sickening *thunk*.

The river-hag was strong, stronger than Gulchima liked. It swung its claw around without skill, but even one blow would be enough to hurt her. And Gulchima was no sword-master.

Still she knew a bit. Uncle Rattbone had taught her to keep her feet, something the river-hag knew nothing about.

Gulchima darted in and out thinking only of her footwork, not the blade. Which was only a french-fry, she reminded herself.

Another second, another rock. This time Gulchima jumped at the river-hag. But it spun at the last second, and instead of hurting it, Gulchima careened into the top-rail of the boat. Her french-fry plopped into the water.

The river-hag chuckled, then slid toward her. It held up its overlong claw, ready to cut her throat. To kill her. It was angry, huffing air, growling. Magic didn't like a challenge.

Gulchima closed her eyes. She didn't want the last thing she saw to be its stupid magical weedy face.

From behind them, Gulchima heard Isolde. She was trying to say something.

"Mel-mow, moo-mu-ful," Isolde said.

"Rowg?" asked the river-hag. It turned.

Isolde was the last thing it would ever see.

Isolde mashed the last of the potato bits in her mouth, until her cheeks were full. She winked at Gulchima, then slapped her overfull cheeks. The mashed potatoes erupted like a volcano, spewing out of her mouth and into the river-hag's eyes.

The creature screamed, clawing at its face. It rebounded off of the steering oar.

Isolde threw the bag of potatoes to Gulchima.

She caught it, then swung the bag of potatoes like a war-hammer, connecting with a huge uppercut that sent the river-hag off its feet, and over the side of the boat.

Gulchima looked at the river-hag as it lay facedown in the water, its arms spasming.

"I always knew your big mouth would get me out of trouble," Gulchima said.

"I know," Isolde replied. She spat on the deck. "And don't you just *hate* cold mashed potatoes."

* * *

In a few minutes they righted the houseboat, and the river-hag slime was mopped from the deck. Tiktok was with the herbalist, getting a tincture of light acid applied to his face. Maybe it would improve his breath.

Isolde and Gulchima stood side by side, guiding the boat with the twin steering oars. The wind, the soft lapping of water, it was hard to believe they'd almost died a few minutes ago.

"You did good," Isolde said after a lengthy silence. "I mean well. But you look awful. Your hair . . ." She picked a twig out of it. A small insect that had been nesting there buzzed angrily and flew off.

Gulchima patter her hair. "We both did good. Those river-hags usually try to waylay sailors by enchanting them. They don't usually come *onto* your boat."

Isolde shrugged. "One more reason not to gird about with magic. Magic keeps changing the rules."

Gulchima pressed her lips together. If Isolde felt that way, then she didn't know everything about the next contract. Bayadev was overflowing with magic. Big problems meant big profits.

"So you heard about Bayadev," Gulchima said, pretending her heart wasn't beating in her throat.

"You told Uncle Roog," Isolde said sweetly. "You may as well have told us."

She hadn't told anyone. But Uncle Roog—who wasn't really her uncle—must have found out somehow. Like while cleaning her cubby where she slept. She pictured Roog tripping and falling, so that his hand accidentally felt underneath her sleep-sack. He'd try to look away, but his eyes would mistakenly read all the personal letters hidden there. For half-an-hour. All the while he'd be grumbling about the undead, the bad food, how nobody liked him. Still, he had saved the boat today. Uncle Roog had his uses.

"Am I running the Outfit or not?" Gulchima asked.

"Well, are you?" Isolde said. Her voice rose in pitch. The sweetness evaporated.

Gulchima crossed her arms. "Yes. And it would be a lot easier if you helped me."

"I am helping. You're the one throwing money overboard," Isolde yelled. "And throwing Novvy overboard too. Do you even care about him? He could have been killed today at the bridge."

Gulchima gripped the top rail, digging her fingers into the smooth wood. Her eyes traced the pattern of the grain, the swirls and knots. "That one hurt. Nice work. There's one point for you."

"I'm not keeping score," Isolde said.

"Are you sure?" Gulchima snapped. "Because every few minutes you tell me the score is Gulchima eleven, Isolde thirteen. You're two years older than me now. You're thirteen, I get it. You think I don't know? That I'm a freak to you?"

Neither girl said anything for a few minutes. They watched the lamps of the Barkers houseboat getting closer. No one followed them.

"Look, the giant's boulders," Isolde said quietly. "It's a good omen." She pointed skyward.

In the waning light, Gulchima saw one of Suur Töll's massive boulders, hurtling through the sky toward the enemies of the east. What was life like for Suur Töll, way out on Saaremaa island, in the center of the sea? What was that giant aiming at?

The return attack, boulders courtesy of the eastern giants, would soon follow. Neither side had very good aim. They'd been at it for centuries.

"A wasteful war," Gulchima said, absently.

Isolde reached out, and put her hand over Gulchima's. It felt warm in the cool spring air. She spoke slowly. "You're not a freak. I'm just scared. If we don't pay off our debts soon, we really will lose the Outfit." She started to tear up. "We could all be conscripted into the King's army. Not just Uncle Rattbone."

"Then help me," Gulchima said quietly.

"I want to." Isolde wiped a tear from the side of her nose.

"Wanting is not doing. *Doing* is doing."

"Now you sound like Mom," Isolde said.

Gulchima smiled, then imitated her mother's sing-song accent. "Now Isolde, moreover, one must remember: People who divide money in the mud are the lowest common denominators."

Isolde smiled. It wasn't the broad, confident one from before. "Do you think they worry about us?"

"Every day, and twice on Tiewsdays." Gulchima squeezed her hand. "Is Novvy really all right?"

Isolde breathed out. Somehow the tears made her more beautiful. "He's Novvy. I don't think he understands that bad things can happen." She wiped her nose with the back of her hand. "He's fine. He got sick because he ate twenty eggs. One of the older boys dared him."

Gulchima relaxed. She hadn't been worried. Not exactly.

"Twenty? Oh. Well. Good," Gulchima said. "Good-Good . . . Then, let me tell you about the contract."

This was as good a time as any. The contract at Bayadev wasn't just for re-construction of the town. It was to clean up magic. Lots of magic. That was why they offered so much money. Big Problems. Big Profits.

Gulchima paused. How would Dad say it? If he really

wanted things to go his way? If he needed people to do exactly what he wanted? He always would say:

"I'm excited to talk to you about Bayadev. Because I think I'm going to need your advice."

"Sure the prince was charming, but then I thought: Hold on . . . Is he shy or just plain weird? I mean, who goes around kissing sleeping girls? That's not exactly someone I'd want to marry. Imagine explaining to your friends how you met. 'Well I was asleep, and next thing I knew . . . .'

Plus, what if he kept doing it? You'd never get any rest."

-The Collected Lies of Gulchima Brixby
(15/100: **An Outlandish Story. Never Happened!**)

CHAPTER 10: GULCHIMA LANDS AT BAYADEV

THE SUNRISE WAS HIDDEN BEHIND THE MIST, and the stench of sulfur filled the air. It was Gulchima's first day in Bayadev. And it smelled.

Like rotten eggs. Like bad breath. Like Uncle Roog's cabin after a bean-bake. Did you get used to it after a few years, or could you always smell it? Would you bother to wash your clothes?

In the distance, a geyser erupted, shooting steam and water droplets twenty feet into the air. The closest gurgling mud pot quieted, as if listening. Then the geyser subsided with a thump and a hiss, and the mud pot started up again, twisting and bubbling. Gulchima could feel the heat coming off it, like a dirty sauna towel smothering her face.

She coughed. Bayadev smelled. Seriously, how did anyone live here?

Isolde and Novvy walked over to her, their faces red from heat and hurry. Gulchima noticed Isolde had wrapped a bit of rope around Novvy's waist and tied it to her wrist. Good idea. The soil was thin here in the geyser basin. Scalding death lay inches below them.

"Where's Uncle Rattbone?" Gulchima asked. "He was supposed to meet me here."

"At the alehouse with Roog and a few of the local burghers he knew," Isolde answered. "He told us to go ahead without him. We'll make a group decision on the contract this afternoon." She wrinkled her nose.

"Hot pot!" Novvy squealed. He yanked at the rope, but Isolde did not move.

"The alehouse already?" Gulchima asked. "Is there anybody those two don't know?"

Isolde shrugged. "Roog said it's 'normal and customary preliminary business'. Then Uncle Rattbone said buying a few rounds of ale for a customer was a 'good investment'. They'll come get us before they tour the town, so we can all size up the job together." She paused. "They said this looks like a *green arrow*. Nice work."

A *green arrow*—a large profit. And the compliment came from Isolde. Gulchima felt her pulse. Okay, she was still alive. And it smelled too bad to be a dream.

"So what, we sit around and wait for the adults to come get us?" Gulchima asked, sarcastically.

Isolde smiled. "No, we're supposed to go hob-knob with the local officials. They're waiting for you. They sent a message to the docks just after Uncle Rattbone left."

"Hot pot, not?" asked Novvy.

Gulchima turned to him. "No Novvy. That will burn all the skin off your body."

Novvy furrowed his brow. "Got lots of skin," he muttered. He looked at Isolde, hopefully. "Skin grows back."

She yanked him forward.

* * *

Bayadev called itself a burgh, but that was generous. It was just another town along the river, one of the few left standing after the war. The Sorcerer's Bastion lay beyond the mist, perhaps two days journey to the east, on high hills surrounded by mazes of ironwood. The Bastion wasn't one of the main fortresses, but rather the place where they'd finally caught and killed the Sorcerer. The *Sorcerer's Demise*, they called it now.

During the war, the larger burghs along the river were occupied, fought over and then destroyed in the final battles around the Bastion. Now that the *War of the Ribs* was over, everyone in Baltica was rebuilding. Since Bayadev had been damaged, but not ruined, it had a head start. With a functioning dock and warehouse system, Bayadev could establish itself as a major burgh on the river.

And they wanted it done quickly.

Gulchima walked from the geyser basin along the marked path. Isolde and Novvy followed, careful not to fall behind in the mist.

They passed a dense woods, a few hundred feet from the low burgh wall. The Maplespray trees along the edge were stunted and leafless, yet deeper in the woods the trees grew straight and tall and were starting to green out. And deeper still was a handsome white cottage, just visible behind the curl of smoke from a welcoming fire . . . .

Gulchima blinked.

No. That was a haunted woods. She knew it was haunted because someone had put up a sign that read, "Caution: Haunted". The incessant steam and calcium had eaten away at the wood of the sign, all but covering the letters.

It was haunted. Gulchima glimpsed the gauzy shapes of ghosts, gesturing to her, calling her name in her parents' voices. Her parents. That's what the ghosts *would* pretend to be. Ghosts were so heartless.

"Scratchy-Do-Dongs!" Novvy cried.

"No, just a magic trick," Gulchima said.

"I heard Scratchy-Do-Dongs, barking," Novvy said.

"Do you smell chocolate?" Isolde asked.

Gulchima sighed. She wasn't scared. Not exactly. "Keep moving. It's a magical trick in a magical woods. And if magic is trying to trick us to go there, then that's the last place we should go."

Isolde sniffed, shook her head as if clearing it. "Right. I thought for a moment, it was another mud pot. But one filled with chocolate. Wouldn't that be wonderful—"

"No. It wouldn't," Gulchima said flatly. "That much chocolate would spoil within hours. Plus the mud around it would mix with the chocolate, ruining it. Unless you like dirt in your food." She crossed her arms. "Which I don't."

Gulchima gestured at the ground between them and the haunted woods. "Plus, you'd boil alive in that mud pot. If you didn't fall into that geyser first. See it, bubbling there? That's hot scalding death." She turned to face her little brother. "Oh and Novvy, Scratchy-Do-Dongs is dead. He fell off the boat and drowned last fall. Sorry you were never told."

Novvy and Isolde stared at her. Gulchima stared back. Their shocked expressions were probably from realizing how right she was. She'd give them time to come to terms with it.

"You are so . . . odd," Isolde said. She put a protective arm around Novvy.

Odd? Isolde had thought of food, and Novvy of his dead pet dog. It *was* odd, and a little sad really. Of the three of them, Gulchima was the only one who had thought of their parents.

How could they be so heartless?

* * *

Gulchima, Isolde and Novvy headed to the burgh's main entry gate. The fields near the geyser basin were barren, but as they moved upwind, a few green shoots poked through the white pebbly soil. Not nearly enough crops for a burgh this size.

Near the burgh's wall, Gulchima passed through a tunnel that led under the dock ramp. The ramp was constructed of rammed earth and faced with flat rocks to stop it from collapsing. The ramp stretched from the top of the wall to the docks, but whoever had designed it was an idiot. Neither the ramp nor the tunnel was straight. The curves were random, not the systematic banked design that would slow cargo.

Gulchima would build two more ramps at least, she decided, then tear down this one and make it as straight as an arrow. That would triple the loading capacity of the burgh's warehouses, and ensure cargo could flow easily. And it would look better.

From the top of the wall, the wranglers slid boxes down the ramp to waiting cargo ships on the river. Each box sat on a sleigh with smooth wooden runners. A simple block attached to a drag line, slowed the cargo to manageable speeds. There was no need for hoists here, at least for the downward flow of goods. Gulchima liked that.

But half the time, the boxes got stuck at the second sharp angle of the ramp, scraping away the earth mounded up there. A wrangler stood on top of the ramp with a long pole, helping the boxes to move past that angle. Ridiculous. Gulchima decided she'd straighten that out on the very first day.

At last, Gulchima, Isolde and Novvy arrived at the riverside entry gate and found it largely destroyed. Two tall, muscular women stood guard over the rubble, which was smeared with the greasy green tinge of magical fire. The guards held identical pikes and both had cloth wrapped over their eyes. They snapped to attention when Gulchima approached.

An elegantly dressed man, with an embroidered maroon mantle on his shoulders waved lazily when he saw Gulchima. He gestured and the blindfolded guards moved out of his way.

"The final contractors, at last. I had all but given up hope," the man said. He introduced himself as Jaroo, the spiritual, economic, and fashion adviser for the burgh. "You received my letter?"

Jaroo was her father's age, but seemed younger. His lower lip protruded, giving him a permanent pout. His pot-belly and gangly arms and legs, reminded her of a bag of wet oats with sticks poking through it. Though he stood outside, the man wore neither boots nor sandals, but soft vermillion slippers, now soaked to a dark brown from the mud.

"We're here now," Gulchima said. Because as her father always said: Never give excuses to a customer.

"Correct," Jaroo said, rolling the word off his tongue. "I would show you around, but I assume you have already sized up the job. Today is the final day to do so, naturally. Are you ready to bid? The other contractors are waiting."

"Other contractors?" Isolde asked. "I thought you offered us the job."

"Oh I sincerely hope you hadn't journeyed under that assumption," Jaroo said in a brisk tone. "Well, nothing to do about it now but apologize, most deeply." He bowed to them, but Gulchima noticed he gave the guards a little smile when he did so. He wasn't sorry.

Jaroo continued: "There are several other companies interested in this contract, I'm afraid. They have tremendously impressive experience dealing with this sort of situation. Whereas your Outfit . . ." Jaroo shrugged. "Well, your Outfit was one of the lesser known choices. But since you are the only contractors from the local area—the rest are experienced foreigners—we thought it prudent to give you an opportunity." He looked around. "Now where is your Uncle? I understand he is really in charge."

"He works for me," Gulchima growled. She was fuming, bubbling, ready to explode like one of those geysers. She'd read that letter a hundred times. It clearly offered them the job. What kind of game was Jaroo playing?

Jaroo held out his hands, palms open. "Yes certainly, we must keep up appearances." He snapped his hands shut. "But I can't keep the other contractors waiting, children. Is your Uncle—your Outfit I mean—ready to bid? That is a yes-or-no question."

This would have been a great time for Uncle Rattbone to come barreling in, saying, "Now wait jest' a minute". But he didn't come. He was at the alehouse.

Gulchima rubbed her boot in the mud. There was something wrong about the situation, about Jaroo's smug little smile. But then again, the docks had been crowded. Maybe some of those boats really were from the foreign contractors. She had to stall.

"The ghosts at the geyser, that's a bid item isn't it?"

Gulchima asked. It was a reach, but it might work. "One part of the contract?"

Jaroo scratched his nose, irritated. "Yes. A bid item of minor importance."

"Someone thought enough of it to put up a sign," Gulchima said. "And they put it in the contract too. So I'll take care of that for free to show you what we can do. Don't start the bidding until then. If I fail, we'll leave on the boats we rode in on. What do you say?"

"That's also a yes-or-no question," Isolde added. She smiled at Gulchima.

Novvy pinched his nose, crossed his eyes and stuck out his lower lip, imitating Jaroo. "Whereas, naturally, well, children," he said, in a breathy voice. "Yes, certainly perhaps. Corrrrrrrrrrrrrrrrect."

Jaroo fussed with his mantle, drawing it over his chest. "Even if you get rid of the geyser ghosts, we can't hire you. We are on a tight schedule. You have no demonstrable experience."

Gulchima stared at him. They were in danger of losing this contract. It would take time to gather up the houseboats and find another job. By then, Brunhild would probably have found them. They'd be forced to join the army, or sent to prison.

"Ok, let's negotiate the terms," Gulchima said. "I assume actual *local* experience removing magic is worth a lot to you on this job. We have that, but you're right, we don't have a lot." This was another of her father's tricks. Agree with the customer. Or at least, appear to.

"Removing local magic *is* the job," Jaroo said. "We have big plans for Bayadev. A port for inland river barges, a takeoff point for trade routes through the Western Sea, an expansion of our 'certified non-magical fizz-water' products into new markets. To do that, the magic must be remediated."

"Wait. Magic is the job?" Isolde exclaimed.

Isolde grabbed Gulchima's arm, pulled her a few paces away from Jaroo. She wagged her finger in Gulchima's face. "You never told me the contract was for *removal* of magic. You said it was a rebuild."

"I didn't know," Gulchima said. She'd suspected it. Thought it was likely. Prepared for it. But she hadn't *known.* "But what's the difference. We remove dangerous walls and replace them with safe ones all the time. Who cares if the wall is dangerous because of an earthquake or because some dragon knocked it loose. Work is work."

"You said there was magic *hither-and-thither,*" Isolde said. Her face was tight, the cords on her neck stood out. "You did not say we had to remove it. I won't do it. I won't sign the contract."

Gulchima took a deep breath. She glanced at Jaroo who smiled faintly at their argument. What she wanted to do was to tell Isolde to go jump in the hot pot, then slap that smug smile off Jaroo's face. She didn't need Isolde's approval to sign the contract. Gulchima was the boss, applesauce.

No, she didn't *need* Isolde's signature, officially. But they were family. Gulchima needed her support. She needed her family.

"I've already put us on the spot," Gulchima said quietly. She looked over Isolde's shoulder, trying to sound calmer than she felt. "Let me try it. You don't have to help. But if we don't get this contract, we'll be heading to prison. So I'll take care of all the magic, alone, and you and Uncle Rattbone handle the standard construction work. Agreed?"

Isolde nodded once. "That makes sense," she said. "But

don't you go getting *zorged.* And don't get Novvy involved."

Gulchima reached out and squeezed Isolde's shoulder. "We got this. The Outfit can do anything." She turned and strode back to Jaroo. His smile soured.

"You are right to have concerns about our experience," Gulchima said. Again, she was agreeing with the customer. It was the best way to tell them they were wrong. "And so in addition to the geyser ghosts, I'd like to offer to remove all the magic from your burgh. For free."

Jaroo sputtered. He gestured to the two guards. "Frenja, Menja, go and fetch Lady Keyhide. She'll certainly be interested in this." One of the blindfolded guards walked confidently through the gate. The second guard spun on her heels to follow, but misjudged, and banged her knee into the pile of rubble.

Jaroo sighed. He turned his attention back to Gulchima. "All of it for free? Even the fizz fairies? The never-ending salt quern? The wonder worms? You'll remove all magic from all areas of the burgh? At zero cost?"

"Yep, you give us the contract to rebuild, and I'll remove the magic for free. You know you're not going to get a better deal than that."

Jaroo pulled a parchment contract out of his sleeve with a flourish. He scribbled on it with a *plumbago*, then showed Gulchima the changes he had made. She took his plumbago, made some additions of her own.

They went back and forth a few times. There was the standard contract items about rebuilding the walls, the gate, the oast house, the smith. They wanted a new port for sea-worthy ships, but Gulchima could see they had a terrible design in mind. In addition to the fizz fairies there were additional tasks about something called trangles, the haunted woods, and a clause that stated the soil must be certified magic-free and ready for farming.

Gulchima's eyes bulged when she saw the total amount they would be paid. The job was still a *green-arrow*. They could pay their debts with the rebuild alone. If things went well, they might make enough profit to free her parents from prison.

At last, Jaroo handed her a pot of red ocher paint. Gulchima dipped her thumb in the paint, then pressed it onto the contract. She'd signed it.

Jaroo took the contract, then carefully tore off a corner and gave it to her as proof. "And you understand you are forbidden to use magic? No left-over magical objects, enchanted doodads, or potions. All of these are forbidden."

Gulchima smiled. "We hate magic. We eat left-over magic for breakfast."

Novvy looked startled.

"Magic for breakfast?" Novvy whined. "Isolde! You told me those were eggs—"

A scream from inside the burgh startled Gulchima. She looked up.

Something green and flappy was in the air. It was dead. And huge. And headed straight for her.

Gulchima blinked, hoping she was seeing it wrong. But she wasn't.

It was a dragon.

CHAPTER 11: HUBWARD CATCHES HIS MONSTER

IT WAS *THE* DRAGON. Hubward slid down the earthen loading ramp, then leapt off just before he hit the river. Six shadows thudded to the ground around him. The seventh shadow had missed the message, and plopped into the water with a muffled curse that sounded like crickets. But that shadow pulled itself onto shore and then cartwheeled over to them. Only a spray of dripping water showed where it had erred.

The dragon was here. His dragon. The creature Hubward had been chasing, when it was alive. Now, it was a dead dragon. To the extent that a non-living magical nightmare could be dead.

And it was falling. And that meant . . . .

First, the dragon's tail smashed into the burgh's wall, turning it to powder. Its head dropped into the river, and the remnant fires in its gut spewed into the water, turning it to steam. Hubward leapt away, covering his mouth so as not to burn his throat.

A loud rumbling boom, like thunder inside a cave, shook the ramp, throwing piles of dirt and rocks onto him and his companions. Hubward dug himself out, patted the dust from his clothes. It was remarkable no one was hurt.

Actually, it was more than remarkable. It was *impossible.* That meant someone nearby had magic. Powerful, individualized, life-saving, magic.

It was someone close. Someone he could see.

Hubward's training kicked in, and he catalogued each person standing there, despite the steam. Jaroo stood with the three strangers from the houseboat: The bossy girl with the too-small mouth, her brother and her much more beautifuler older sister. Lady Keyhide, the Fizz-Meister and the two female guards with Seer-Slip blindfolds lurked suspiciously near the gate. But there were more people standing at the burgh wall, locals mostly. He'd have to remember each of them quickly, give each just one characteristic. The Alewife (tight dress), Ninestone (basket), WentWrong (a limp), and StickyBritches (obvious) were all watching too. Maybe twenty in total, including some newcomers he'd never seen before. He marked them all with some trait or tick. Eye-patch, no-teeth, weak beard—

A butterfly cleared its throat, interrupting him.

Then, remarkably, it spoke in human language. "Is the dragon dead?"

"Yeah, and I know what that means," Hubward said.

The seven shadows faded, melted, wavered, and rustled until at last they were people again. As they always had been. But they were no longer magically hidden. Hubward's most powerful spell had been stripped away!

He thought—he hoped—the change would continue. But they just stood there with those blank farseeing eyes.

Hubward looked at them: three boys, three girls and a man. All blue skin, and stooped shouldered. All undead. His former team, or *hand* as they were called.

Before the dragon killed them, they were one of the best

hands in the army. They were trained by the Sorcerer of course. The best hands always were.

"And I know what that means too," Hubward said. "There's only one person strong enough to bring down a dragon and remove my camouflaging spells . . . ."

The Sorcerer? Here? Alive?

The Sorcerer was banished to another dimension, or destroyed, or something. Certainly dead in any real sense of the word. But no one else could have cast that spell.

Hubward could see the magical signature, fading in the air. The spiked crenulations. The double-bottom of the first wave, a subtle coaxing down of magical defenses. This wasn't a forceful push of some clumsy power-mage. This was active, devious magic. And that flair at the tail end, like an extra nip of poison flicked in your eye. That was the Sorcerer's signature. It could be no one else.

The dragon—Hubward's quarry that he had been chasing for almost two years—was dead. But not like Hubward planned.

Hubward was supposed to do it. When the dragon killed his team, Hubward had sworn revenge. And now, even that was taken away from him.

He felt—what? Astonished? Sad? Guilty for taking his sweet buttery time. He'd hoped somehow the creature could change them back. A dragon can return what's stolen. That's why he'd waited. Wasn't it?

Yet, the Sorcerer was here!

Imagine that capture. Imagine the wonders Hubward could make the Sorcerer do. His team's lives would only be the start.

"Double promise. I'll avenge you," Hubward said. "This time I won't fail."

Hubward was suddenly grateful for butter. That spell would

have killed him, if he was magical. Since only the Sorcerer could have cast it, that meant the Sorcerer was here in Bayadev, pretending to be a normal person. That spell would have stripped even the Sorcerer's disguise.

But who was it?

A girl about his age walked out of the steam, rubbed her eyes in the bright noon sunlight. It was the one who ran the construction company, the one with the ridiculously tiny mouth. What was her name? Garlicka, Gulchima, Garanchala? Something like that.

The girl looked worried. She was pale, almost green, her hair straight as silk curtains. Her beautiful older sister looked liked angry was her favorite face, and the young boy with them had his mouth open in a Q of surprise—like an O of surprise, but with a lollipop in it.

A large bearded man, once a member of the Sorcerer's *federati* judging by his bawdy tattoos, stood with them. Their father maybe? He had bones tied in his beard, wards against puppetry. He kept them fresh, so he'd be a formidable opponent. Perhaps he was the Sorcerer in disguise.

How convenient! A boat of newcomers shows up, and on that day the Sorcerer is revealed. It could be any of them. It could be anyone in town.

The big man rumbled something to the girl, and she shook her head. He slapped his fist into his open palm, then dropped his head.

"You signed it," the big man said in a whisper. "You signed the contract!"

It was not a question.

END OF PART I

CHAPTER 12: HUBWARD MAKES A LIST

BY DELICIOUS LIGHT OF TALLOW CANDLE—tallow made of bacon fat—Hubward wrote:

The Sorcerer is here in Bayadev. I am SURE because:

-> I saw someone cast that spell in the ~~fog~~ steam AND

->That spell had the Sorcerer's fingerprints all over it AND

> -> Other people from the burgh saw that "someone" a few seconds later ~~BUT~~ AND
>
> -> The spell was so strong it would have **removed** all camouflage, even from the caster

SO . . .

-> They must know the spell-caster because they didn't run away

SO . . . . . .

THEY KNOW WHAT THE SORCERER LOOKS LIKE!!!

Who is the Sorcerer?

1. ~~The Dragon~~ - no because it is dead

2. Lady Keyhide - She's old. She's acting suspicious + Who hates magic that much?

3. Jaroo - Too much of a ~~pompous~~ ~~foozle~~ idiot, but Sorcerer could be pretending.

4. Is there a pompous idiot potion? <u>Look into it.</u>

5. ~~Bacon is delicious even in gas form.~~ FOCUS!!

6. Someone else in town? The Fizz-Meister? WentWrong the Wright? Ninestone?

7. StickyBritches, with that weird rash? The Alewife?

8. Someone on the houseboats? Strange it happened the day they arrived.

    a. Gulchima - Seems pretty lucky when magic attacks her. Convenient story about ~~disoppe disapar~~ going missing.

    b. Uncle Rattbone (you know what his tattoos mean!!)

    c. That little boy? Newvy? Novvy? (Parents missing = Where did he come from?)

    d. Lots of people on that boat (dot-dot-dot)

9. Note-> Add to play, a list of suspicious characters

    a. Have narrator read out loud to audience-> Who put lemon in lemonade mystery: (Butler, maid, stable-boy allergic to hay, evil sheep-shearer)

    b. + Don't forget the *oatmeal thing*.

Hubward paused, and then circled the last line, the one about the *oatmeal thing.*

Because it was important.

"Just kidding! None of what I told you was true. So here's what really happened those five years I was missing:

I travelled to this magical kingdom, and the people there called me 'Cinder'. They thought I was beautiful and elegant and had fabulous glass shoes, so it didn't matter that I was poor.

I think that's the most important thing: to be beautiful and elegant and always have nice shoes. Then, everyone can agree how great you are . . . I mean, if you're ugly, people will inquire further into your financial situation. Maybe ask you to sing a little."

-The Collected Lies of Gulchima Brixby
(33/100: **Unlikely**)

CHAPTER 13: GULCHIMA SURVEYS THE WORK AHEAD

TWO DAYS LATER, Uncle Rattbone woke Gulchima up early for a walkabout—a tour of Bayadev. It was the first time they'd been alone since the crash. Uncle Rattbone said little, just enough to point out the work that lay ahead.

Everywhere, Gulchima saw the beginnings of construction: The wall-makers raking rubble, the soil crew leaning on clean shovels, the wood for a gantry splayed near the damaged double-cylinder oast house. Isolde had been busy setting it all up.

But that's all it was: a beginning. About the only thing completed was the new geyser-powered sauna, and Uncle Roog has built that without telling anyone. Roog was crazy about taking sauna. So were most of the men.

Everywhere, too, Gulchima saw the mark of magic: Wonder worm silk floated from between cracked wallboards, red eyes glowered beneath rusted gates. Lights flashed and zigged in the bakery, accompanied by giggling too high-pitched to be children. A foul smell emanated from behind the alehouse, but Uncle Rattbone said that was just the normal stink.

Each magically infected area was painted with a red "M" in a circle. And almost every building was marked. Outside the burgh walls, more work waited. The pathway to the caverns which housed the fizz factory was also posted with signs, each bearing a red "M". She shuddered at the thought of going into a dark moist cavern infested with magic. She'd leave that one for last.

Gulchima knew that all of these preparations formed the frame of work, the skill before the labor. But taken as a whole, this mass of inaction looked bad. They needed some tangible progress (besides Roog's sauna). The Outfit needed a check mark somewhere on the contract. But where to begin?

They surveyed the remains of the inland entry gate, opposite the riverside gate. Not here, Uncle Rattbone said. This whole section would have to come out. The fortifications were smeared a greasy green-black, the stone and mortar melted like raked butter. Magical Fire. Some skinny old man had brought the gate down with a flick of his wrist.

The entire burgh had been touched by war, as had all of

Baltica. But here in Bayadev it was brief, a swipe of claw from a retreating beast. The Sorcerer's armies had fought a rearguard action on their way to the Bastion. A few hours, a few soldiers, a few magical hazards hastily thrown up to slow their pursuers. And Gulchima had to remove it. Somehow. The job seemed a lot more complicated now that she actually had to do it.

They passed by a cluster of crafthouses, on their way to the river. The air tasted of iron and sweat. The hostelry and smithy had been burned, the crumbled granaries plundered (in the name of good or evil, it amounted to the same), and most of the wattle-daub cottages inside the burgh had damage from the spray of arrows, projectile stones or haunted flame.

Gulchima pulled an arrow from a nearby wooden post. The feather fletching had rotted off, but the wood was springy, the metal tip sharp.

"So. You ready for the Festival of Rough Peter?" Uncle Rattbone asked casually. "Word is you're going to be planning it."

"Yep I got it handled," Gulchima said. "I won't forget."

Great, just what I need, another job to do for free. But she had a few weeks before the big holiday. She'd think of something for the kids on the boat to do.

Gulchima picked up a half buried metal helmet with a peaked cap. The inside felt sticky, and she saw a thin strand of goo on her fingers when she removed them. Magic?

"That's *Gumption*," Uncle Rattbone said. He didn't look at her when he spoke. "Makes sure your helmet don't fall off if you get knocked over."

"What's it made of?" Gulchima asked. This was the most words he'd spoken to her since the dragon crash, and she wanted to keep him talking.

Uncle Rattbone shrugged, then took the helmet from her.

His right sleeve slipped up, and Gulchima caught sight of one of his tattoos, a half-naked Swan Maiden draped over the word "SAAREMAA".

"Actually . . . it's not Gumption," Uncle Rattbone said. Some warmth returned to his voice. "See, when you melt a person's brain *too* quickly, it leaves a sticky residue like this." He rubbed his fingers together. "But to be honest, I suppose there's no right speed for brain meltin'."

A breakthrough! She had to keep him talking.

"Were they good guys or bad guys, do you think?" Gulchima asked. "Can you tell from the helmet?"

Uncle Rattbone's face drained. "Good or bad? What's that got to do with it?" He threw the helmet to the ground with a clang. "No such thing as good and bad in war. There's only 'us' and 'them'."

He stomped back toward the river, back to the docks. Gulchima followed.

"Maybe," she said, hurrying to catch up. "But Jaroo seems bad. If anybody is, I mean."

Uncle Rattbone spit. "Jaroo? When I met him, he was just Jax. A plumber. Used to work for your Dad before . . . Well, before your Dad threw him off the top of the houseboat for stealing lead."

Gulchima said nothing. Uncle Rattbone was on a roll, finally. She'd let him talk, let him blow off some steam.

"Changes his name, and expects us to bow to him," Uncle Rattbone muttered. He stopped walking, peered at a crack in the foundation of a cottage. "Now he's a politician. I suppose that's not too different from being a bad plumber."

"How's that?" Gulchima asked.

"Because he's used to being knee deep in other people's poo!"

Gulchima burst out laughing. Jaroo, a failed plumber! Now he called himself the spiritual-menu-and-fashion adviser for the burgh. What a joke! And she'd been intimidated by him.

Uncle Rattbone's anger softened, and then he smiled. "I was ticked with you Gulch, after you hauled off and signed that contract. You should have—"

Gulchima squeezed his forearm. "I messed up. I can give you all the reasons I messed up. All the things I should have done differently. But it boils down to the same thing: I messed up. I am responsible."

Uncle Rattbone tried not to, but he smiled again. He looked tired and relieved, as if being angry at her was hard work. "Just like your Dad with those straight speeches. That man could talk the scales off a dragon. Awful with money—that's where your Mom came in—but your Dad could be darn persuasive."

"I wish he was here," Gulchima said. "I could use his help with the dragon. If we can't use magical objects, and only magic can pierce a dragon's scales, then . . . ."

"Yeah I've been thinking about that too," Uncle Rattbone said. "About the dragon, and the ghosts, and all the other magical *nimbys* hanging around here. I got some ideas to run by you—boss."

He winked at her. "Let's go see your dragon."

* * *

It was worse than she'd hoped, but not as bad as it could be, because the dragon was still dead.

Gulchima counted two hundred paces, from the river where the dragon's neck was visible, to the iridescent tip of the dragon's tail. The end of the tail extended over the wall rubble, but stopped a dozen feet into the burgh's interior. It would be no problem to shift it, then finish the wall. Were people so afraid of magic that they wouldn't touch a dragon's tail?

The dragon had augured down when it fell from the sky. The wound that killed it, almost certainly to the underbelly of the creature via some magical object or spell, was now eight-feet below the topsoil. That wound was where you'd want to start cutting, if you were going to dismember a dragon. But because it was buried, it would be hard to reach.

The dragon's head, thankfully, bobbed under the water. Dragons emitted fire after death. No one knew why. Something to do with the scales probably.

It was the scales that stopped you, Gulchima thought. They retained magic. They could not be pierced, except by magic. And she couldn't use magic. Not even the kind of magic where everyone pretends it's not magic, so that the dragon goes away. Not even potions.

Uncle Rattbone handed her a crowbar. "Try this first," he said. He pointed at the dragon's hind leg. Just below the dragon's rump, a patch of scales were slightly lifted, like loose roof tiles.

Gulchima fitted the crowbar underneath a scale and levered down. But the crowbar's edge slipped off, as if the end of the scale was coated with grease. She ran her finger along the scales and they felt cold and hard, like stacked metal plates. If anything, the dragon scales were slightly rough to the touch, not slippery. Gulchima was surprised that up close, the dragon smelled like the Western Sea, all fish and salt and frigid water. She'd expected something foul, some unnatural rot.

"What about wood?" Gulchima asked. "Maybe it has special *nimby* powers against metal. Or maybe a stone wedge would work. Maybe potatoes?"

"That's smart, we'll try it later." Uncle Rattbone prodded underneath the dragon with an iron bar, levering against a rock.

Clunk. The rock fractured.

After they cut up the dragon, they'd still have problems moving it without magical assistance. But with a few pulleys, and a few trenches, they'd have the dragon bits removed. Could you eat dragon meat? That would be quite the party.

Gulchima examined her crowbar. It was heavy enough. She swung it over her head, then slammed the crowbar into the dragon. She'd expected sparks, or a ringing in her ears, like when your axe blade slips and you hit rocks. But that wasn't what happened. The dragon wasn't solid. Hitting the dragon was like pulling on a giant bow string the wrong way.

With an audible *Boing*, the crowbar rebounded off the dragon, flew out of her hands and embedded in the burgh wall behind her. It vibrated slightly.

"Oh right, sorry I forget tell you," Uncle Rattbone said. "Don't try to do that. We're still looking for Roog's splitting maul. I think it flew a good half-mile into the haunted woods."

Uncle Rattbone took out a knife with a sharp glittering blade. Obsidian? He started to saw at the dragon, but gave up after the stone blade spalled and then fractured. Uncle Rattbone blew on his hands.

"Hot?"

"Cold," Uncle Rattbone said. "Like frozen metal. Blade's ruined. Guess I'm out five thalers." He stood up straight and stretched his back. "Not sure what we're going to do with it. We'll find a way."

A cheerful voice interrupted them. "I say leave it where it is and use the dragon as a drift fence."

Gulchima looked up. A dirty chubby-cheeked boy, slightly younger than her, strode toward them. The boy wore a girded up tunic, torn and stained, and looked like he hadn't washed since before the war. He kept his hair annoyingly long at the front, and he flipped it up out of his eyes every few steps.

"He's a local war orphan," Uncle Rattbone whispered to Gulchima. "It always pays to hire a few on each job. Makes it harder for the local politicians to fire you."

Uncle Rattbone tugged at the bones in his beard. "Plus, orphans are good luck. Sure, sometimes they miss several weeks of work to go on some adventure, rescue a long-lost relative, find some *spotty* necklace or whatever. And yeah, there's a bit more *prophecy* associated with them than I'd like—" He rolled his eyes. "But overall, they're good workers if you treat them well."

"Okay, but what exactly will he be—" Gulchima started to ask.

"Hello again Hubwind!" Uncle Rattbone said, in an overly cheerful voice. He waved, though the boy was only a few feet from them now. Not really within waving distance.

"It's Hub-ward," the boy said. Hubward's smile faded, then his eyes focused on Gulchima and he smiled again, more brightly. "And I'm tremendously excited to be working for you today." He flipped his hair out of his eyes. "I'm an orphan. I'll drop everything to help interesting strangers."

How plucky, Gulchima thought.

"And this is Gulchima," Uncle Rattbone said. "Gulchima, I thought it best if I pair you with a local your own age. Always good to train others. And maybe you two could be friends. Hubward here, says he's got experience with magic."

"Experience?" Gulchima asked. "Polishing boots or cleaning dishes?"

"A messenger," Hubward said. He flipped his hair out of his eyes again. "For the Sorcerer." *Flip. Flip.*

Argh! That hair! Should she glue it in place? Or just yank it out?

"And he knows the burgh," Uncle Rattbone added. "And … he works at the fizz factory, which is another magical headache. So I'd thought you'd be good partners."

"So what's the plan, partner?" Hubward asked Gulchima. "I hear you like plans."

Gulchima held out her hands and counted on each finger. "Wonder worms, geyser ghosts, haunted woods, fizz fairies, salt-quern, trangles, and now, a dragon. Plus a few other things that are easy. Probably. And we're not partners or friends. You work for me."

"Uh-Hubward says he's got experience with dragons," Uncle Rattbone said.

"I've ridden them." *Flip.*

"Is that right?" Gulchima asked. "How exactly did you get a saddle to stay on a slippery dragon?"

Hubward shrugged. "Okay, I didn't exactly ride them. They carried me like a package, then dropped me off. Still, I learned a bit from the dragon handlers."

Gulchima's hand crept down to the bone knife on her belt. Not for protection. She needed to cut Hubward's hair. Immediately. She couldn't take another—

Flip.

"Yeah, but tell her about the weight thing," Uncle Rattbone said.

Hubward nodded, moved some dirt around on his face in a thoughtful gesture. "Well the thing about a dragon is: it can't fly. But it does fly. Even though all it has are those stubby little wings. So after it dies, the dragon has additional weight to it. It sort of . . . owes a debt . . . to gravity."

Gulchima snorted. "A debt to gravity! That's one of the stupidest ideas I've ever—"

"Just listen," Uncle Rattbone warned her.

Hubward continued. "Let's go over to the tip end of the tail, and I'll show you."

Without waiting for agreement—*Flip*—Hubward climbed over the remains of the wall, then stopped at the end of the dragon's tail.

"Orphans!" Uncle Rattbone said. He held his hand over his heart. "Don't you just love 'em."

Gulchima frowned. She followed Uncle Rattbone to where Hubward stood.

"Now lift the end of the dragon's tail," Hubward instructed her.

"What, with my bare hand?" Gulchima asked.

"You have bear hands?" Hubward said with a grin. "You're even tougher than I've heard."

Uncle Rattbone laughed, and even slapped his knee. "Good one Hubward!"

That was bit much. He's heard that joke a thousand times.

Gulchima reached down and tried to lift the tip of the dragon's tail. It was no thicker than a rope, easily gripped, and covered with swirly whorls that looked like smaller versions of the cold metal scales she'd felt earlier. But she couldn't lift it.

She couldn't even nudge it. The tail seemed glued to the ground.

Gulchima looked around and noticed that the nearby soil sloped inward, toward the tail, forming a shallow trench. "If the tail's that heavy, then the rest of the dragon's body must be immovable," she said. Her stomach felt like a block of ice.

"Yes, if you think about it logically," Hubward said. "But in this case, logic is wrong."

"Logic is wrong . . ." Gulchima said. She rocked back and forth on her heels as she mulled this over. "Logic is wrong. Logic is . . . Congratulations Hubwind. That definitely is the most ridiculous thing I've ever—"

"Gulch you need to listen," Uncle Rattbone said. He put his hand on her shoulder, a reassuring warmth. "You don't have to agree or like it. But you have to listen. Will you take him on for a week? For me?"

Gulchima nodded slowly. "For you."

Hubward continued, as if he hadn't been interrupted. "It helps if you think magically, not logically." *Flip*. "For a dragon, the debt-gravity runs uphill. So the tail is the heaviest part." He flipped his hair again.

Again!

"That's why the head floats," Uncle Rattbone added. "Kinda makes sense, if you don't think about it whatsoever."

Did it? Did it make any sense? Did partnering with Hubward make sense?

Flip.

A dragon owed a debt to gravity.

Flip.

The tail was heaviest.

Flip.

And old gravity ran uphill.

FlipFlip.

Plus, the scales couldn't be cut.

Flip. Flip. Flip.

Yes. It did make sense. As long as *zero sense* was allowed. But magic had rules. So there must be a way—

Suddenly, she had it! Gulchima wondered how many pulleys it would take.

She'd need more rope. But the solution was simple: Put the tail in the water and the dragon would sink!

She could get the dragon out of Bayadev. A few feet past its official boundaries anyway.

All she had to do was dump the dragon in the river!

FLIP.

CHAPTER 14: BRUNHILD LIVES

FROM BRUNHILD'S POINT OF VIEW, it was just bad luck. She'd only wanted to ruin Rattbone, ruin his company, ruin his niece and their boats. It wasn't about the money. The money was just how she kept score.

[If he were not evil, the gods would not have sent you to destroy him.]

They'd done the expected, Brunhild thought. Rattbone and the others had trundled to Bayadev in those ponderous river barges they lived on. The River-Hags had even slowed them, just as Brunhild had instructed.

Everything went to plan. She'd had Rattbone within her iron grip.

And then that *muckspout* had showed up with the potatoes!

Now, Brunhild lay in the delightfully brisk water on a stretch of gritty beach along the river. Her soldiers had abandoned her. And who could blame them? She had not been particularly kind.

She opened her eyes. It was mid-morning, and the sun traipsed just behind the trees, darting out playfully in squares and triangles of light on the beach.

[The world-mill grinds us all. But heroes break the pattern.]

Yes, heroes did break patterns, Brunhild reflected. And she knew for certain, that she was a hero. The very word was written on her heart. Brunhild knew this, because she'd torn it out and read it for herself.

That had been an afternoon to remember, she thought fondly. Brunhild's voices had guided her, as always. What wondrous teachers they were. And when had they led her astray?

[NEVER!]

Yes, never. She reflected that her voices had always told her the right path to take.

[ALWAYS!]

She paused.

Always? Perhaps, not always. For instance, her voices had a penchant for the *one-felled-swoop* approach to problems. Perhaps the attraction to singular swoop-felling was genetic. Her mother had been a tremendous swoop feller, after all.

[Bunch their game-pieces to clear the board.]

Brunhild chided the voices. That sort of thinking was exactly the problem. It occasionally led to trouble.

"*All flowers grow in blood*," Brunhild said. To her surprise, she spoke the words out loud. Sometimes this did happen, she lamented. The voices just bubbled out.

Brunhild shook her head. The din of some long forgotten battle rose in her ears. A woman sang-screamed instructions in an unknown language. That meant danger. She sat up.

A rough man stood over her, grinning. He had a nice, even, evil smile. Well practiced, imposing. Brunhild would tear out his teeth and make a necklace of them, she thought. A memento of that wonderful smile.

"That's some nice armor you got," the rough man said. "How about handing it over, then I'll let you go free."

"There is no freedom until the last sorcerer is strangled with the intestines of the last king," Brunhild's voices said.

That wasn't really within the context of the conversation,

Brunhild thought. But the voices had a limited vocabulary. Brunhild shook her head again. A warm wave of confusion passed over her as the voices took control.

There were others here, Brunhild saw. Perhaps two dozen rough men and women surrounded her. Not thieves, and certainly not beggars, judging by their clothes and weapons. Brigands, perhaps? Her eyes narrowed. Gold-teeth, eye-patches, leather jerkins . . . Bandits! She'd been abandoned to a band of bad bandits! Fortune had smiled on her this morning.

Brunhild catalogued their weapons, her eyes slashing across each bandit. They couldn't hurt her. They had no potatoes, today.

She got to her feet. Brunhild rotated her left arm until she heard a snap. Rattbone would pay for that injury. He'd pay for stabbing her through the chest. This band of bad bandits would help her.

"I said hand over the armor," the rough man said. "Or we can take it, and throw you back in the river." He brandished a bondsman's axe.

Questions fluttered across her mind like startled sparrows. The potato incident led one to consider: Had Rattbone finally guessed what she was? Was that why he'd annulled their marriage? Her mother was a River-Hag, her father was misled. Not a common pairing, but they'd made a shambling home of love for her and her siblings.

As if Rattbone's family was free from magic. Oh the things he had confessed to her. About his brother. About his brother's wife. And their daughter, Gulchima. Brunhild knew all about her too. Probably more than the girl knew about herself.

"*Kiss the arm you cannot break, then cut it off and eat it.*"

The rough man took a step back. "What?" he looked at his

fellow bandits. "That's not how it goes. Did you mean, 'kiss the arm you cannot break, and pray the gods will break it'?"

Brunhild paused. Had her voices been misquoting this entire time?

[Impossible! Crush his skull!]

"I've heard it both ways," Brunhild said, embarrassed. She started to giggle, then laugh, then cackle. The voices made her do this when they were confused or nervous.

The rough man took another step back. His axe was still in range, however.

"Last chance," he said.

Brunhild continued laughing. The man with the evil smile was correct. It was a last chance. But not for her.

She'd failed to destroy Rattbone on the river, but she had another chance. Rattbone needed to be signed to a valid contract. Without that, she could take him to debtor's prison to collect on his debts. Admittedly, a contract law technicality wasn't as dramatic as the chase and subsequent boat smashing she'd envisioned, but it would be effective. Rattbone would pay.

And even if Rattbone got the contract, Brunhild had an insider at Bayadev who would stop them from finishing the job. But perhaps, given their relationship, "insider" was not the correct word choice. They weren't really *inside.* Not exactly.

She could call the insider an "assistant", but that was too businesslike. Perhaps "puppet" was the most apt description. It paid to be apt, Brunhild knew. One could make a lot of money, if one maximized their levels of *apt.* Even with minimum aptness, her puppet could ruin the contract. If Rattbone even got that far.

Brunhild smiled.

The biggest and baddest of the band of bad bandits strode

forward. He was massive, bald, and had a long beard. The other bandits whispered his name: Kondo.

Kondo didn't want to talk. He raised his two-handed long sword, and grinned.

It was a nice sword, well balanced, cared for. Brunhild caught the blade in her hand, as he brought it down.

"It appears you intend to stab me through my chest," she said. She sprung up, flipping neatly in the air, then came down behind him.

Kondo turned his head to look at her, his mouth slack, his eyes bulging. She could smell what he ate for breakfast.

"You're . . . you're . . . ."

Brunhild's eyes flared a brighter purple.

"Oh, I'm not magic," Brunhild whispered. "But I am woman." She took a sip from her drinking horn, gargled, spit. "Do you want to hear me roar?"

Brunhild started to sing.

CHAPTER 15: HUBWARD GETS THE FIZZ

"SO I THINK JUST BEFORE THE CURTAIN OPENS, we'll have a narrated description of the weather," Hubward said to absolutely no one.

He sat, obviously alone, in the amphora storage room of the fizz factory. He was deep within the cavern, near the gas-baggery. A single wall torch provided light. Officially he was stacking cartons of the amphora, empty clay vases which were used to transport liquid fizz-water. But to an outsider it would appear the cartons of clay amphora were stacking themselves, while Hubward sat on the floor scribbling notes about the play he was writing. And, the shadows looked all wrong.

Hubward had done his best to restore the camouflaging magic for the seven undead members of his team. The haunted woods had some residual magic he could tap into, but the work was sloppy. He'd used second-hand magic, after all. What would you expect?

"When a scene has good things happening, it will be sunny and bright. But dramatic scenes will have dark and stormy weather: Drizzly disagreements, cold confrontations, misty mysteries, that sort of thing. We need to spend time establishing the weather. Where the sun is, how it is feeling that day. We'll just establish that in the first few minutes of every single scene in the play."

A dust mite sneezed.

"Oh so now you have a better idea? Ok . . . what else would work?" Hubward chewed on his chalk. "Breakfast! We'll start each scene with the actors eating breakfast, but *combine* it with the weather. Everything has to do two things, you guys know that. So we'll have rays of light on raisin-oatmeal, gray clouds on gruel. Before—I mean when we were all . . . well before your *incident*—people in the audience were always coming up to me and asking about the weather. And what the characters had for breakfast."

A cricket rubbed its legs together, once.

"Well they ought to have been," Hubward said, grumpily.

The door to the storage room creaked open. A middle-aged woman walked in, carrying a wide basket filled with fragrant leaves, foul ointments and clinking tinctures. She was Ninestone, the factory herbalist. She smelled of woodsmoke and lavender.

Hubward jumped up and pretended to stack the last of the amphora cartons, shoving it too hard. One of the clay containers clanked loudly.

Six of seven shadows darted away, flattening themselves against the wall, contorting into strange shapes. But the seventh shadow stood where it was.

Hertrude was stuck again? Zorgs! And he'd just fed her a pumpkin.

"Hubward, there you are," said Ninestone. "I see you're done already." Her smile faded. "And how did you manage to stack those cartons way on top?"

"Just good at jumping," Hubward said. "Normal boy games always involve jumping. Like, 'I got you', we yell and then pretend to cut off the other boy's leg with a sword. But then, that boy jumps over the pretend sword, and he's like, 'Aha, now I got you'." Hubward rubbed his nose with the back of his hand. "So that's how."

Ninestone narrowed her eyes. She poked Hubward in the stomach, but grunted with satisfaction when she felt the roll of fat on his midsection.

This time, the roll of fat was real. He'd been drinking butter.

Ninestone put down her basket. "Factory orders, you need a physical before you start working. But you've been here two weeks and I haven't seen you."

She was right. Two weeks since his job interview. Two weeks of spending his days working at the factory, his nights prowling around Bayadev. After the mysterious dragon murder, he'd started working a side job with the Outfit, helping that mean mumbly girl, Gulchima. He was exhausted.

The Sorcerer would slip up, eventually, and he could quit these jobs, capture the Sorcerer and finally (finally!) get some time to work on his play. But there was so much powerful magic in this place, it was hard to tell what was really going on. Of one thing he was certain. The heart of Bayadev's powerful magic was in the underground fizz factory.

Hubward glanced behind him.

Hertrude, his seventh shadow, was visible to him as the dusky outline of a teenage girl. She started shuffling backwards. Worse, she was headed directly for Ninestone's basket.

The other shadows protested, trying to get Hertrude's attention. But the cacophony of mouse muttering, cricket chirping and dew drops dripping, did not work. This was a small room, and though Ninestone could hear the strange noises, she didn't seem to notice.

Adults! Did they notice anything besides money, and who was kissing who?

"I've only been here since last Runesday," Hubward said.

"So *almost* two weeks." He slid his body between Hertrude and the basket. She bumped into him, and he leaned over the basket, pretending to study its contents.

Hertrude started slowly shuffling forward. But her steps were not magically obscured. Hubward could hear the shuffling, plain as oatmeal.

"*Almost* is too long," Ninestone said reproachfully. "Rub this on that rash on your arm." She handed him an ointment.

Hubward did as he was told. He tried to hand the small clay jar back to Ninestone.

"Keep it," she said. "Now open your mouth, let's see your teeth. We don't want any of your weird orphan diseases in our fizz-water." She smiled faintly. Hubward had a hard time not smiling back.

Ninestone placed a mint leaf on his tongue. To his surprise, it evaporated.

With one hand, Ninestone pulled and wriggled his teeth, with another, she ran a thin string between them, freeing the meat and kernels that were stuck there.

"Swish, but don't swallow," Ninestone commanded. She gave Hubward a small vial of fizz-water, but when he poured it in his mouth, he could tell it was laced with something sour. Green foam erupted from his mouth.

"Ma-mic?" he asked. He spit the foam onto a proffered cloth.

Ninestone laughed. It was a twittering sound, and it made her look young. She held her warm hand to his cheek. "Magic is illegal," she said, peering into his eyes. Her eyes were a non-descript faded blue, but she had a freckle in her left eye shaped like a diamond. She slapped his cheek, and he blinked.

"See, all done Hubward," Ninestone said. She fussed with something in her basket, then picked it up.

His face still felt warm from her touch, and he could smell lavender. "Not so bad," Hubward said.

But then he saw what Hertrude was doing.

Hertrude shuffled forward, then smacked into the wall of stacked amphora cartons. The wall started to waver. The uppermost carton tipped, started to fall.

Hubward grabbed Ninestone by the arm and spun her around, so that she was facing the door. At least she wouldn't see the sloppy shadows.

"I wanted to ask you—" Hubward started to say.

The other six shadows darted out from their hiding locations and caught the falling amphora, which rained down like a sudden hailstorm. The tallest shadow jumped onto the back of another, then tossed them back into the carton. Its throws were incredibly accurate. Two other shadows escorted Hertrude to the corner of the room, and hid her.

A ladybug buzzed, warning Hubward. He slapped out his hand, and caught a wayward amphora that spun wildly toward the back of Ninestone's head.

"—about this fizz-water," Hubward finished. "Is it healthy?" He showed her the empty amphora he had just caught. "Oh this one's empty. Never mind."

Ninestone paused, and narrowed her eyes. "You seem well fed, Hubward. Healthy. But why are you so jumpy all the time? Did something happen?" She lowered her voice. "In the war?"

It was still odd to Hubward. Ninestone was openly suspicious, and yet she couldn't see his companions. They stood only a few feet away. Seven people shared the room with them. All she had to do was stumble into one of them, and he'd be found out.

If that happened, what would he do? Hubward wouldn't hurt someone like Ninestone. Avenging the Sorcerer's atrocities did not give him permission to hurt innocent women that smelled like lavender and had a freckle in one eye.

"I move around a lot," Hubward said. "And I'm not much use in a fight. So when someone bigger comes along, I run. Every time I enter a room, I think of how I'm going to escape."

Ninestone tapped a finger to her lips. "Very believable," she said. She sighed. "And very predictable. Hubward, I'm going to advise you, as your herbalist, not to be so predictable. You can't *always* run."

"Why not?"

"Because predictable things get put on lists," Ninestone replied. "And do you know what happens to things on lists?"

She smiled, and Hubward found himself smiling back. "Eventually, things on lists get *crossed off.*"

Hubward paused, not certain how to respond. He suddenly wondered if Ninestone would let him stay with her, instead of sleeping rough in the forest. He could play with her other children, watch them, help around the house. Maybe the Sorcerer had already fled. Maybe Ninestone could be his . . . friend.

"Do you have children?" Hubward blurted.

Ninestone's lips trembled, and she held her hand up to her mouth, as if steadying them. "Yes. Once." She looked at him, and Hubward saw her faded eyes were starting to tear up. "Now, I am here."

Once, but now I am here. It was the common refrain for those who had lost someone in the war. It meant: Yes it happened, and yes, I do think about it. But not all the time. I have a life to get on living. "Now I am here," meant simply: I survived, and I live for those who didn't get the chance.

Hubward didn't press her. He saw the word was tattooed

on her inner forearm. He should have noticed it.

Ninestone paced forward, and the shadows, who Hubward could see as normal people, slid out of the way. She picked up an amphora, and the tall shadow contorted, bending backwards to avoid her touch. The shadows weren't magic. Only their camouflage made them appear so.

"Well you're quite the worker, I must say," Ninestone said, changing the subject. She turned to face Hubward. "The Fizz-Meister is impressed. He says you've filled twice as many containers of fizz-water as any other novice."

"Happy to have found work," Hubward replied.

Ninestone held her index fingers in front of her face, and stared over them for ten seconds. She shook her head, as if clearing it. "Apply the ointment twice a day. And I wonder if, and forgive me for questioning you, but I wonder if you couldn't do with some vegetables once in a while."

Hubward stiffened. Vegetables? Him?

"I just hate to see such a small boy—on his own, a young sir of course, but still small—I'd just hate to see him lose his teeth. Do you know what they say about teeth? Teeth are like girlfriends . . . ."

"Like girlfriends?" Hubward asked. He swallowed.

"Yes, ignore them and they'll go away. Can you promise me you'll eat a fruit or vegetable twice a week."

"You can't eat something twice," Hubward blurted out.

Ninestone frowned. She reached into her basket and pulled out a packet of seeds. She handed it to him. "Okay, try this. Sometimes the food you grow tastes better. It's time for you to put down some roots, Hubward. Time to stop running and hiding."

Hubward took the seeds. Vegetables, he thought. Yuck. Maybe he could feed them to a pig, and eat his vegetables indirectly.

"What kind are they?" he asked tremulously.

"Pumpkin, naturally," Ninestone said.

And she was startled, when, despite the clank and spray of the busy fizz factory, Ninestone clearly heard the sound of seven cats barking.

" . . . I mean, I was amazed. Who would build stairs that way, with no guardrails, or handholds, or anything. A gust of wind would knock you right off. I'm just saying if I had to carry laundry from one spot to another, a walkway over a gaping chasm would be my last choice."

-The Collected Lies of Gulchima Brixby
(70/100: **A Good Point**)

CHAPTER 16: GULCHIMA AND THE HEARTLESS GEYSER GHOSTS

ACCORDING TO HER PLAN, Gulchima was supposed to be defeating the wonder worms right now. That was first on her list.

They were *worms* after all. How hard could it be to capture silk worms—even *wonder worms,* whatever that meant? She'd brought spiders. She'd brought live carp. She had a barrel of frogs waiting.

Her master plan was to start with wonder worms, then the trangles, then the haunted woods. Rattbone and Isolde would take care of the regular construction jobs, while Gulchima figured things out.

Once she got the hang of things, Gulchima would move on to the more dangerous geyser ghosts, and the fizz fairies, and whatever else. Somebody had mentioned Bayadev had lunkers, but that would be easy, since she'd done those before at the bridge. The dragon would be last.

But Lady Keyhide had called a meeting, and Lady Keyhide ran the burgh. She was Jaroo's boss. So instead of following her plan, Gulchima was here, at the geysers with the ghosts, getting screamed at.

That's how it went with construction. If the client wanted a meeting, you had to go. They yelled, you listened. Then you went right back to doing whatever it was you were doing before. But you had to let them yell.

So Lady Keyhide had yelled, then Jaroo had lectured. They were "deeply concerned" about the progress. They couldn't cancel the contract yet, but they could make Gulchima's life "quite difficult, naturally". At last, Gulchima had convinced them to give her a chance. She'd gone off and grabbed the two people who had to help her: Isolde and Novvy.

Now, Gulchima, Isolde, and Novvy were back at the geysers.

But this time they had an audience.

"Gulchimaaa . . . joinnnn . . . usssssss," a ghost crooned. It was just visible in the spray of mist. The ghost looked like her mother. At least that's what Gulchima saw. Isolde saw something different.

"Quick, Isolde, stare at the ghost farthest on the left," Gulchima barked. "Do you see it?"

"I saw it last time. I see it now," Isolde said. "This is a stupid plan."

"It will work if you stop blinking," Gulchima said. She stumbled over a mound of mud as she sidled three steps to the right. But she didn't look down. She couldn't.

"I have hot stinky geyser gas wafting in my face," Isolde replied. "Why don't you come over here and 'stop blinking'."

The ghost screamed. Not the spooky, startling, come-hither-and-investigate kind of scream. The ghost was scared. It slid toward the geyser.

Almost there . . .

"See! It's working!" Gulchima said. "I figure the ghosts are people that got killed in the geysers. They *hate* geysers. Whenever one erupts, they scatter away from it."

"So?"

"So if the ghosts are afraid of something, it's dangerous to them. We'll use the geysers to get rid of the ghosts."

That was step two. Step one was capturing them.

As you moved toward a ghost, it slid away from you, luring you into danger. That was the geyser ghost rule, she supposed. It always slid *away* from you.

But what if three people looked at a ghost at the same time, from different directions? What if they circled around the ghost, and then opened their eyes? It wouldn't be able to slide away. It would be trapped.

In essence, your eyes were like frozen ropes, holding the ghost in place. You could push it ahead, by stepping forward. You could pull it towards you, by walking backwards.

But Gulchima didn't have three people, she only had two. And even if she had ten people, it was difficult to communicate in the geyser basin, and too dangerous to approach the ghosts from the opposite side. There was too much hot scalding death over there. So Gulchima had modified her plan. Now, it was all about triangles.

If Gulchima and Isolde stared at the ghost and walked toward it at the same pace, the ghost would have to slide away. But only in the direction they chose. They were three points of a triangle, after all. So Gulchima could make the ghost slide any direction she wanted. By stepping to her left or her right, she could move the ghost a few feet to either side. By stepping forward in unison, they could push the ghost back.

"This makes no sense whatsoever," Isolde said. "Triangles? Geysers? Just sub-contract this out like they want and we can—"

"We're almost there," Gulchima said.

Gulchima took one half step to her left. Then she smiled. She had maneuvered the ghost directly over the geyser. It struggled, waved its hands wildly.

Five, four, three, two . . .

Bloop. The ghost slid away from the edge of the geyser.

Isolde had blinked. Again. Another failure.

"Okay, let's take a break," Gulchima said in a chipper tone she did not really feel. Her face felt clammy from all the steam. And *Sweet Sorcerer* she was thirsty.

Isolde coughed theatrically. "Sounds good. But I thought you were going to take care of the magic alone, and I'll take care of the construction. That was what we agreed when you talked me into this contract."

"I need help this one time," Gulchima replied. "I can't ask anyone else."

"I thought Uncle Rattbone got you help," Isolde said. She wiped at her eyes. "That Hobart boy. The orphan."

"Hubward? He's working," Gulchima lied. She would not become bosom buddies with that helpful ragamuffin just because they were the same age. She would not let Uncle Rattbone hire a friend for her. "You know, this will go a lot faster if Novvy could help—"

"Novvy stays on the safe path," Isolde said flatly. "That's one promise I won't let you break."

"Suits me," Gulchima said, coldly. "I can do this all day."

Gulchima walked back over to the path marked with white rocks, then took a sip of water from her drinking horn. Novvy stood by Lady Keyhide and Jaroo. Novvy was babbling about something and holding Lady Keyhide's hand.

Lady Keyhide's face was painted with red cinnabar and ash. She was the Burgher-Meister, what a town would call a mayor, or what Novvy called, "the biggest spider in your apple cider".

The cape-like palla she wore was shredded evenly along one edge. Were the cuts in her clothes a sign of mourning? Or was that simply vermillion paint?

"—then, I almost fell on my maple tubs," Novvy finished.

"Your what?" Lady Keyhide asked. She was trying, desperately, not to smile. Her heavily painted face had developed a crack just below the left cheekbone.

"Maple tubs," Novvy repeated. He slapped his bottom with both hands.

"You mean your . . . butt?" Lady Keyhide asked.

"No! Isolde said I can only say 'butt' when I take a bath," Novvy explained. "Otherwise I have to say 'bottom' not 'butt'."

"But you said *maple tubs*," Lady Keyhide replied. Her mouth twitched.

"Yeah, I asked about 'ham-hock', but Isolde said that was naughty, so I asked about 'maple tubs' and she said it was ok, since most people wouldn't understand what I meant." He looked around, conspiratorially, then whispered, "It means butt."

Jaroo mopped his brow. "Lady Keyhide, I must insist we finalize our modifications on the contract—"

Lady Keyhide waved him into silence. She reached into her side satchel, then leaned over Novvy. "Would you like a lollipop?"

"Does a lion want to eat your face first?" Novvy asked.

"What?" Lady Keyhide asked, drawing back.

"He means yes," Gulchima explained. "Novvy, remember if

you talk too much, you'll drop your lolly."

Novvy took the candy with two hands, then focused intently on eating it.

Lady Keyhide took out a small ball of amber, cradling it to cool her hands. "How goes it?" she asked Gulchima, in an unfriendly voice.

"We had one ghost on the line, but I slipped and lost it," Gulchima said.

Lady Keyhide grunted. "I am a busy woman. What is your expected deadline?"

"Soon."

Jaroo broke in. "Soon before lunch? Soon in the next week? When is *soon*?"

Gulchima crossed her arms. "I had planned on the wonder worms first. That is all prepped and ready. You just need to wait and I'll get to it."

Jaroo started to speak, but Lady Keyhide shushed him.

"And those woods?" Lady Keyhide asked. "Why haven't they been burned? Or is lighting a fire not on your *list* either."

"I was just on my way to burn them, when I got your message," Gulchima replied. "I will take care of that next."

Jaroo sighed. "It has been over an hour, Lady Keyhide, and the ghosts remain. No work has been done. Perhaps now is the time to discuss renegotiating the contract?" He stuck out his lower lip. "As we discussed. Earlier."

Lady Keyhide passed the amber ball from hand to hand. She stared hard at Gulchima. "I understood you had experience with these things. Perhaps we can find you some help. I know a wonderful up-and-coming orphan. And what an inspiration he is." She smiled at Jaroo, who smiled back dutifully. When she turned from him, Jaroo scowled.

"Hubward is working today," Gulchima said.

"Unfortunately."

Lady Keyhide loosened her grip on the amber ball. "So you know him? Wondrous. I shall send Hubward over to help you. He is such an inspiring young man, don't you think?"

Gulchima swallowed her sarcastic reply. "Mmhm," she said.

"It's a shame *you're* not an orphan," Lady Keyhide said. "Isn't that a shame Jaroo?"

"Yes, Lady Keyhide," Jaroo said in a strained voice.

"Oh? How's that?" Gulchima asked coldly. This was not going well at all. Getting angry wouldn't help.

"Well orphans make for more interesting stories. More drama," Lady Keyhide said. "Whereas you, with your stable quasi-family, loving uncles, business prospects. I mean what's really at stake for you here? It's just a job. You don't seem too invested."

Just a job? What about Prison? Forced Conscription? Death?

"Well my parents are in prison," Gulchima said. "If we get this job done on time, I'd have enough money to bribe—I mean, *pay,* their restitution."

Lady Keyhide narrowed her eyes. "In prison for what?"

"Destroying magical objects," Gulchima lied.

"Really?" Lady Keyhide suddenly looked interested. "Destroying magic?"

"Sure. It's a family tradition dating back to my great-great-grandmother. She was a witch-hunter. Glinda-Eater-Of-Troll."

"A witch-hunter!" Lady Keyhide clapped. "Jaroo you didn't tell me they had a family tradition to *destroy* magic. That's much more inspiring. My paradigm has *shifted.* Absolutely! Gulchima, can you teach me how to do it? Let's set up a lunch meeting."

"Sure. You'll just have to wait until I take care of those worms—"

Lady Keyhide raised her eyebrows. "Wait? You understand

my grandson was lured into the woods by those wicked ghosts. The ghosts are still here, the woods are still here. Yet you tell me to *wait*."

Gulchima stammered. No wonder Lady Keyhide was angry. "Is he all right? Your grandson?"

Lady Keyhide turned toward her. "He hasn't spoken since. But he's alive. I thought if those woods were destroyed . . . " She gripped the ball of amber tightly, making her fingers white and pink. "He's Novvy's age."

Gulchima thought about it. Now Lady Keyhide's standoffishness made sense. So did her bubbling anger. She wanted to help her grandson. Or at least to destroy what had hurt him.

Sure, Jaroo had signed the contract, but Lady Keyhide *controlled* things. She wanted something *done-on-the-run*, but to do the job correctly, Gulchima needed one more person . . . Maybe she could kill two river-hags with one potato.

"Help us," Gulchima said.

"What?"

"Can you help us catch the ghosts? Avenge your grandson's injury? Destroy magic? We need a third, and I don't want to send my brother out there."

Lady Keyhide looked surprised. "I would . . . I would love that. I can hear those stupid things from my window at night."

"You said lunch meeting?" Gulchima threw a dried strip of fruit to her. "How about right now?"

Jaroo cleared his throat. "There are no reports of Gulchima's family destroying magical objects. Lady Keyhide, this negotiation may be compromised."

"I don't care," Lady Keyhide said. She bit into the fruit strip. "This Outfit has spunk. They hate magic. You heard the girl's story about growing up to be a witch-hunter. Trained since birth. Did you see that glint in her eye? It's inspiring. She is what we need, and you, Jaroo, you should focus on the fizz factory problems."

Jaroo frowned. "Yes, Lady Keyhide."

Lady Keyhide bustled away from him, and followed Gulchima into the geyser basin. There, they met up with Isolde.

Gulchima explained how it worked. To her surprise, Lady Keyhide understood the geometry immediately, and she jogged over into the mist without being told.

"Okay, let's start with that ghost in the center near the mud pot, do you see it?" Lady Keyhide asked.

Gulchima did. With Isolde on her left and Lady Keyhide on her right, it was much easier. As long as two of them stared at the ghost, it couldn't move.

After a minute of fine tuning, Gulchima took three large steps forward, and the ghost was shoved over the geyser opening. And just in time.

Five, four, three, two—

With a *fffff-thawump* the geyser cannoned the ghost high into the air, launching it into a cloud. The ghost moaned, then screamed, then waved its arms frantically. It looked like a mix of a devilishly handsome lumberjack, her mother, and a mug of hot chocolate.

But once it reached the cloud, the ghost dissipated.

"What happened?" Lady Keyhide yelled. "Is it dead? Can a ghost be dead?"

"Clouds are cages for ghosts," Gulchima explained. She had heard this once, and apparently, it was true. "Everyone knows that's what clouds are made of: Ghosts. I thought the geyser would kill it, but this is even better. Ghost jail."

Lady Keyhide clapped. "Ghost jail," she said. "I like that."

Her makeup had cracked along her eyes, the red on her cheeks ran down her face like warpaint. "And I really liked that part with the *thawump* sound, didn't you like it Jaroo."

"Yes, Lady Keyhide," Jaroo called from behind them.

After that, it went quickly. In a short time, Lady Keyhide, Gulchima and Isolde had wrangled all the ghosts, and sent them flying.

The last ghost was trying to hide, and all but refused to entice them. It wasn't waving, or saying, "Gulchimaaaaa, come joooooooin usssss." Instead, it crouched down, and said in a low, mumbling voice, "*Well, umm, not much for you to see here, really. May as well go away. Please. Go away now.*"

Then the geyser erupted and the last ghost flew up, into the air, and was gone.

"I like the noises they make," Lady Keyhide said again. "Just after they get hit." She stared out into the geyser basin, and did not blink. "I'm going to sleep *good* tonight."

Novvy wandered over to her. He reached out to grab hold of her hand, then asked, "Have I told you about how awesome I am?"

CHAPTER 17: HUBWARD MEETS A MAN-OF-ARMS

HUBWARD DIDN'T LIKE TO SNEAK AROUND the fizz factory by himself, but the rest of his magical team was acting up. The mention of pumpkins, and all the free magic floating around the fizz factory caverns, had them riled up. So he went it alone.

Officially, he had a note from Lady Keyhide telling him to gather some things, and then go to the haunted woods to meet Gulchima. Unofficially, he was snooping.

The hallway he'd wandered into was abandoned. Old hand-cranked fizz factory machines, cobwebbed and half repaired, were pushed up against the wall. Crates were stacked haphazardly, and a pair of old brooms covered a small deep hole in the floor. The hole smelled damp, and cool air whistled up through it. There were no torches, but—*flip*—Hubward didn't need torches to see.

He had magic hidden in his hair.

Everything was coated with dust, to the point that Hubward became suspicious. An abandoned hallway! Old machines? The Sorcerer was so predictable.

When he came to a dead-end, Hubward touched a brick with his elbow in the usual way, and a doorway appeared. It was obvious how to enter, so Hubward did, noting the door moved noiselessly. It had been oiled recently.

Hubward looked in and catalogued the room's interior. On the scorched wooden table were glass vials and powder-tins, each neatly aligned and arranged by size. Below the table were piles of mesh, some clean, some crammed with yellow cake-like mixture. On the far side of the room was a fireplace that heated a vat of bubbling inky black liquid, one shade darker than regular black. And there, against the wall, behind the growling green creature, was a red and white candy-striped overstuffed chair, holding a massive pile of books, each—

—But then Hubward stopped cataloguing. Green creature?

A horrible, headless, eight-armed creature towered over him. It held a hatchet in one hand, a metal ruler in the other, and it stood unsteadily on two legs.

A large broad nose, nearly two feet wide, protruded from the center of its chest. It had no eyes or mouth, and no head to put them in anyway, but each booger-caked nostril whistled foul air at him. Its green nose hairs were as long as Hubward's awesome haircut, the front-flip.

Hubward took a step back. His eyes widened.

"Man-of-Arms! I didn't expect to see you here," Hubward said with a grin. He approached the creature.

Two of the creature's arms bulged with muscle from beneath its stained white apron. It had cut a flap to allow its nose an unobstructed smell of the room. The rest of the green creature's arms—there were eight in all, and some sprouted where its head ought to be—lay feebly at its side, unmoving. Each of the dead arms had a metal clasp around the wrist, made of gold.

"It's me, Hubward. You might not remember me, but I put on that play for your son's birthday. The one about the arm-wrestler."

Man-of-Arms gestured wildly, clashing the hatchet against

the ruler. He did remember. And he was still angry.

Hubward grimaced. "Well I *did* apologize. How was I supposed to know that was a *real* cake."

Man-of-Arms dropped the weapon and the ruler with a clang. He sniffed at Hubward, theatrically, then banged his two free hands on the table. This meant: *I remember.* The other six arms swayed, but did not move. The golden handcuffs on each wrist sparked, emitting large wisps of magic. A dozen smaller *magitrons,* tiny particles of magic, pinged around the room in sprays of silver and magenta.

"Okay, calm down, that was like, two years ago," Hubward said. "What have you been up to?"

Man-of-Arms slapped his chest, his belly, his butt. Then he put his hand in his armpit, and made a farting sound.

"Sounds great. Glad you had nice weather. I did think she was the one for you, so yes, I'm very happy for you both."

Fart-fart-fart. Man-of-Arms made the armpit-fart sound three times, then waggled his fingers at Hubward.

"Me? Oh, not too much," Hubward said. "My team of magical assassins is all dead now and I'm avenging their deaths by chasing the Sorcerer. You know. Same old thing. Oh, and I'm writing a play."

Man-of-Arms slapped his palms together, then flicked a massive, pancake-sized booger at Hubward. It squished against the door behind him.

"Weirdly, no. It's not about magical assassins. My play is a murder mystery. It's about lemons."

Fart-booger-fart-fart, Man-of-Arms said. He made a lassoing motion.

"Well, a biography *could* work," Hubward replied. "But I'm bored with magic. Magic doesn't sell. Who wants to hear about a young orphan boy discovering magic? Nobody. Nobody would want that. But murders are hot right now. Mistaken identities. Rainy rooftops. The big reveal at the end. It's hot, you know?"

Man-of-Arms tried to make a motion that meant "exasperated". But the arm he needed to express it was not moving. So he flicked another massive booger at Hubward. This time, the pancake-sized booger stuck to Hubward's chest with a *thwack*. There were several nose hairs bristling out of it, like arrows.

"Well yeah, I guess it is the same thing," Hubward said, quickly. He brushed the booger from his chest, but it stuck to his hand like a glove. "Anyway, have you seen the Sorcerer? I'm due for some avenging."

Booger-bellyslap-booger-honk—

Surprisingly, Man-of-Arms said he had seen the Sorcerer. He saw the Sorcerer a lot. Because the Sorcerer was here, in the factory, almost every day. The Sorcerer worked here, but Man-of-Arms couldn't explain what job the Sorcerer did. And unfortunately, almost everybody in the burgh worked here.

"Ah, so it's not the Alewife, or StickyBritches?" Hubward asked. He'd followed them yesterday to Lake Pepsid, and neither had come to the factory. "And nobody on the houseboat is the Sorcerer I guess."

Man-of-Arms slapped the table, then slapped his belly.

He put a hand in his armpit. *Fa-fart-faaaart.*

"Right. We can't be sure," Hubward answered.

If only Hubward knew what the Sorcerer looked like! It was weird to admit, but despite all the years of training—his team had been trained by the Sorcerer before turning against him—Hubward had never seen the Sorcerer. The Sorcerer was always wearing the magical armor, so you couldn't describe him. If it was a him. The Sorcerer could have been a her. Or even, an it. And since Man-of-Arms could only smell/hear, and not see . . . this was going to take a while to describe.

A half hour later, Hubward was growing weary of interpreting the gestures. His face was sticky with flicked boogers, but that was how these things communicated. Who was he to judge?

"Okay, so the Sorcerer smells horrible, like sulfur or bad smoke is that right?"

Man-of-Arms made an impatient, armpit-fart noise.

"Okay not sulfur to you, but sulfur to me," Hubward said.

ShoulderSlap-booger-honk-stomp.

"So the Sorcerer is a fat man? No. A woman with—No. A pregnant man? No, of course not. It's hard to understand you with only two hands. If you'd just let me chop off your arms—"

Man-of-Arms growled at him. Hubward wondered how a creature without a mouth growled. Perhaps he sniffled in a menacing way.

"Okay, just a suggestion, calm down. Maybe you like golden handcuffs and being stuck in a lab with weird, inky, one-shade-darker-than-black liquid burning down the side of your cauldron. It's your life. I won't cut your arms off without permission. I was just offering to help."

Man-of-Arms started to respond.

But then, from behind the closed door, Hubward heard muffled voices.

Man-of-Arms gestured wildly for Hubward to hide.

He slipped behind a large pile of cake-covered mesh, then became very still. He was the camouflage expert. Hubward knew how to hide.

Jaroo entered the lab, his socks squishy and black. Menja and Frenja, the two large guards with Seer-Slip blindfolds, came in just behind him.

"Octo, we're moving you, now. You-Know-When's orders," Jaroo said.

From this position, Hubward could not see Man-of-Arms' reply.

Jaroo looked around, eyes narrowed in suspicion. "For your own protection of course Octo-Arm. The strangers on the houseboat are starting to investigate. We can't let them know about our . . . work. Unless . . . you want me to free your other arms. Is that what you want? To be divided?"

Man-of-Arms banged on the table twice. That meant: *No! Please No!*

Hubward watched as Jaroo clasped another golden handcuff around one of Man-of-Arms' wrists.

Then Jaroo removed a different golden handcuff, and put it on his own wrist. In a shaky voice, he said, "Frenja, Menja, gather up his notebooks. We'll put him in the Deep Place."

Frenja spoke, or maybe it was Menja. "What is it saying?" They had such high girlish voices for large women.

Jaroo answered. "He says he's working hard, and all is in readiness. Then he just repeated it. 'All is in readiness, the magic has been prepared.'"

Hubward flipped his hair down, so he could scan the room. Magitrons sparked from Jaroo's hand.

Was Jaroo the Sorcerer in disguise? He'd been at the docks the day the dragon crashed. And Jaroo was always sneaking about. Hubward's heart thudded in his chest.

"I will tell You-Know-When," Jaroo said. "You-Know-When was most concerned about the magic."

Hubward heard a symphony of banging, honking, armpit-fart-noises.

"Now what is it saying?" asked Frenja.

"He says he's worried that it will hurt the strangers in the burgh," Jaroo said. He flexed his fingers, as if they were stiff. The golden handcuff vibrated around his wrist.

"What strangers?" Menja asked.

"The Outfit," Jaroo laughed. "Rattbone, Gulchima and the rest. Well, we have to test it on *someone.* We're paying them good money after all. Why not try to get our money's worth?"

Jaroo snapped his fingers and a small magical flame blossomed in his open palm. "Maybe our little test won't hurt them."

He grinned, evilly. "But maybe, it will."

"That last one was an exaggeration. You knew I was joking, right? What really happened was that I learned love was the strongest magic of all.

Not quite strong enough to save any of the loyal soldiers who fought and died alongside us, but still pretty strong. Since I had all the love—just about everybody loves the chosen one—I was perfectly safe.

I think I learned that love really is powerful, as long as you're important enough. The dead loyal soldiers should have brought more love with them to the battlefield. That would have stopped the giants from crushing them with those big boulders. Probably."

-The Collected Lies of Gulchima Brixby
(22/100: **Preposterous!**)

CHAPTER 18: GULCHIMA SELLS HAUNTED WOOD

GULCHIMA WAS FEELING GOOD. Almost great. She'd taken on this magic problem step by step and things were going well, though not exactly in alphabetical order.

Lady Keyhide liked her, and Jaroo was in the doghouse (they'd been marked on her plan as "K" and "J"). The geyser ghosts were gone (that was "G"). And now she was looking at the haunted woods (that was "H").

So G and H, and, J and K, were handled. All that was missing was an "I", as in "I don't know how to deal with the dead dragon". Maybe that was cheating. Maybe that should be under D.

Hubward was late, and if she was paying him (Did he work for her? Or was he a volunteer? Or a paid playmate?), Gulchima decided she would dock his pay for lateness. After a half hour of waiting, Gulchima realized he wasn't coming, and she didn't mind. Her face still hurt from fake smiling at Lady Keyhide anyway.

Gulchima entered the haunted woods alone. On Uncle Rattbone's advice—which was as flexible as cement socks—Gulchima had agreed to contract this task out to a man named Soltanabad. She wouldn't have to do any adventuring here. She'd just pay someone and they would remove the problem. That's what subcontracting was all about.

As she walked across the carpet of needles, Gulchima heard the snaps of branches and the thumps of axes on wood. But she saw no smoke. That was a problem. According to the contract, the haunted woods had to be burned.

Mostly, burned.

All around her, Soltanabad's crew crawled likes bees in a hive, chopping wood, spraying safe paths, dropping the valuable lumber and piling up the slash for burning. It sounded like progress. But where was the smoke?

There had to be smoke. Sure most of the *cursed* wood was going to be resold in another town, but the people of Bayadev couldn't know that. Soltanabad had to burn some of it, to make it believable.

And the smoke made people like Jaroo stay indoors. That was the best way to build anything. Without an audience.

Gulchima stumbled over a vine. A few feet away, she saw

an unkempt chubby-cheeked boy standing on the side of the path, waving at her. He flipped his hair out of his eyes, and started to say "Gulchima! I have to warn you about—"

From a tree above her, a feller yelled, "Look out Hub!"

The boy spun around.

The first thing she noticed was the boy's orange cork boots, which jittered and tap-danced a few inches above the forest floor. His boots were easy to notice, but the rest of him proved more difficult to describe, because he was being eaten by a giant glowing red plant.

"Hubward!" Gulchima yelled.

Hubward had only been working for her for a few seconds, and she'd already killed him. How annoying!

She ran toward him, toward the giant pulsing plant mouth that was trying to swallow him. She needed fire. She needed an axe. She needed—

A plant's tendril snaked around her boots, almost tugging her off her feet. Gulchima already had her bone knife in her hand and she slashed at it, scraping the back of her hand on a thorn.

Brown syrupy liquid spurted from the plant's tendril, and she tore her leg free.

She looked up. Hubward was still being eaten, and only the bottom of his boots were now visible. It looked like he was struggling mightily against the attacking plant, but if it closed its mouth around him, he'd be—fertilizer.

Gulchima jumped forward, then struck at the plant's mouth with her knife. It had teeth made of thorns. The blade of her knife bounced off the glowing red plant. It left only a scratch.

Gulchima felt herself lifted up into the air and pulled back. But it wasn't the plant that held her. It was a man.

A heavily accented voice said, "Stop girl-boss. Latewise

arrive. My workers take care. I am tree-boss. Soltanabad."

She continued struggling, but looked up at the man pinning her in place, Soltanabad. He had one knitted eyebrow, and several gold teeth.

"That's Hubward. He works for me," Gulchima gasped.

"Not," Soltanabad replied. "Is my cousin's son, Hubek. Curious boy. Always mischief. Now? Not as much for a while."

Talking to Soltanabad was a linguistic adventure, Uncle Rattbone had warned her. It was as if the man continued to speak his native language, but used *Aestii* words so Gulchima could understand him.

"What? Is he going to die?" Gulchima asked. "That plant is eating him . . . we have to rescue him."

Soltanabad laughed, then frowned. "Maybe. We see. Everyone dies, girl-boss. I say this morning, 'Hubek stay on path'. He say, 'blah-blah'. Then he go off path. Now he is zorged." He pinched his fingers. "Small zorg. Tiny. Very painful. Boy filled with maple syrup now. Not die. Definite-Probably."

"What?" Gulchima asked. Her mind caught up to the conversation. That wasn't Hubward being eaten. Soltanabad knew what to do. And, though her heart thudded in her chest, she couldn't save that boy anyway. "What is that plant?"

Soltanabad gestured to two workers who had appeared at a run. Both sprayed the pulsing red plant mouth with bags of glacier water, and it withdrew, icy and shuddering, into the forest. The boy, Hubek, was covered with an orange dripping fluid, but otherwise unharmed. His face and neck looked abnormally swollen. His legs were the size of tree trunks. His clothing had split.

Soltanabad let her go. He wore the same style of sleeved chiton, leggings, and broad brimmed hat as the rest of his workers—though his brim was much wider, and he favored bright purple cork-covered boots. He adjusted his hat.

"Plant is Chomp Maple. Delicious. Dangerous. Bothways."

"What are you going to do to that boy?" Gulchima asked. *It wasn't Hubward.* But the boy was swollen to three times his normal size!

"We drain him," Soltanabad said, flashing his gold teeth. "Sell syrup for small profit only. Is problem. But is ant-problem to bear. Yes? We make money so is okay. Boy live. Not sleep because infected. But live. Lots of syrup in his bottom. Little syrup in his top." He scowled. "Face syrup no good. Bottom syrup is best. Maple tubs, we say them. Favorite brands to buy. Maple tubs. Good on pancakes."

The boy, Hubek rippled when he walked, like he was already full of maple syrup. The two workers escorted him back to their camp.

Soltanabad rubbed his hands together, and smiled. "Very strong infected. Lots of syrup from him! Maybe big profit after all!" He looked sideways at Gulchima, then adjusted his smile. "Use wrong words. Very *sorry* at boy. Big Sorry. I show you work girl-boss. You gladwise with eyes."

Gladwise with eyes. That meant she'd like what she'd see. And the boy, Hubek, he would be okay. Alive, anyway. He'd be tapped and the maple syrup could be drained.

Soltanabad gestured for her to follow him through the woods.

"How goes it?" Gulchima asked. She walked on the safe path, careful to keep well within the damp needles.

A tree fell a foot from him, but Soltanabad did not seem to hear it.

"The time passes, and trees pass, groundwise," Soltanabad said.

"Groundwise," Gulchima agreed. "I see the trees are dropping. But no smoke. You need to burn *some* of the trees. What if Jaroo's guards come in here?"

Soltanabad grinned broadly. "Stepwise? Into the cursed woods? They don't follow the path, and when later?" He clapped his hands. "Zorged. No problem, no problem. They stay outside."

Gulchima parsed these sentences, and after a few seconds the meaning arose: They stay outside because they do not know the path. Very smart.

Gulchima looked around the woods. She only made six-percent on the deal, but it was worth it to have someone else handle this task. Gulchima had no interest in this side of the business. Timber removal was just a form of extreme landscaping. And there were *things* in here. Gulchima didn't want to be Zorged.

"Stepwise is good," Gulchima said. "But you need to burn some at least. Put up smoke. Otherwise . . . ."

It was all a cover. They burned the slash and only the non-merchantable trees. But it had to look like they burned the whole cursed wood, so the burghers knew they were getting their money's worth. That had been Uncle Rattbone's idea too. It was a good one.

Soltanabad gestured to the fallen trees. "Good wood. Here, here, here. I have many family helpers all these evenings. I must take all that." He looked perplexed, then corrected himself. "That's my this."

"Smoke," Gulchima repeated. "Put up some smoke, so the burghers can't see you. No one can know you're reselling this cursed wood."

"Cursed?" Soltanabad waved this away. "Once we cut it, the cursed fly out, into the air, poof. Needwise, all the wood. Not enough wars near wood. All plains and horses now, even desert. Why fight over sand? Not enough cursing of woods, so I have time of roughness. We use magic of smoke. Samething, samething."

Gulchima didn't have time for this. She had a dragon to take care of, plus a million other things. She looked around. Even with the Sorcerer lost in some vortex, these cursed woods could grow back their power. Gulchima heard their whisperings.

"I need smoke in the air right now," Gulchima said. "I need some progress. One of the rich burghers lost her grandson here."

Soltanabad shrugged. "It is cursed wood, what did he think would happen? The name is in the name."

Gulchima's brain interpreted: They called it cursed for a reason.

"Okay," Gulchima said. She chewed her lower lip. "Then it's a problem of finances, I see that. You mobilized a lot of people out here, and there's not enough work, right?"

"Yes, now you see. Clearwise, with eyes."

"So reduce your cut, and I'll do the same. I'll reduce my take to three-percent. You leave more trees for the burn pile, and make more profit. For the honor."

Soltanabad frowned, dug his foot in the soft soil. A glowing red tendril crept around the ankle of his cork boot, reaching almost to the silver crescent at the top. Soltanabad took out a small pouch and sprinkled glacier water on it, covering the oozing thorns. The tendril stopped moving. Soltanabad picked it up, examined it closely, then threw it to the ground in disgust. "Worthless!"

"For the honor?" Gulchima said quietly.

Soltanabad embraced Gulchima, pulled her close with one

arm. He smelled like mint tea and garlic. "Okay okay. For the honor. But next time I need more product."

Gulchima agreed, noting how the man's grammar had improved after he got a better deal.

"Next time, you need less hungry cousins."

* * *

In a different part of the haunted wood, Brunhild waited. Her tooth necklace glinted in the sudden spread of sun between clouds.

Brunhild flashed her steel mirror, aiming for the upper right window of an abandoned warehouse in Bayadev. Immediately, she received a response, three flashes in quick succession. Her agent was eager. All was in readiness.

Brunhild started to giggle, but fought down her glee. One couldn't eat one's fairies before they hatched, she reminded herself. Still, all *was* in readiness. Brunhild could prepare for the next stage of her plan.

Would Rattbone predict it? Doubtful. He was busy with the blossoming problems which all work brought.

Could Rattbone stop it? Impossible. Rattbone had no experience with this sort of thing. Even Brunhild had needed help setting it up.

Yes, this time her plan would work. Brunhild's voices had led her to the correct point of attack, one which Rattbone would never see coming.

It could not be stopped.

The next person to touch the dragon would die.

Horribly.

"Well I was stressed out, so I did what adults do: I went to the beach for five years. I got mixed up with the wrong kind of lobsters, then a sea-witch stole my singing voice—

What do you mean, 'Now I'm just making this stuff up'? You've already heard that story? It's a popular fairy tale? Oh. Right. Then let me tell you what really happened . . . ."

-The Collected Lies of Gulchima Brixby
(12/100: **A Lazy Liar**)

CHAPTER 19: GULCHIMA SEARCHES FOR "TING WAFFLES"

A WEEK LATER, Gulchima was at the fizz factory, which was housed in the caves outside of Bayadev.

Gulchima wasn't exactly afraid of the cave. First of all, it was large enough to be called a cavern, and secondly, it was well-lit, contained fizz factory machinery, and had dozens of people scurrying around.

So she wasn't *exactly* afraid, and her hands weren't *exactly* sweaty, because it could have been condensation from the cave. And her heart wasn't exactly hammering in her chest, it was just thumping loudly, like a person frantic to get out of a damp enclosed space, where they were trapped, and the air was running out, and—

"Stop!" Gulchima said out loud.

Hubward looked up from his position at the bottle washing station. "Okay. So now you *don't* want me to finish up this last bottle?" He wiped a dripping forearm against his chin. "Because you just said you were fine with it."

"No, not you. I mean, yes, you. I mean . . . ."

Hubward put down the bottle. "It's okay, I get it, you're busy." He wiped his hands down his tunic, in that unthinking gesture that all boys had. "You're a magic removal expert and time is thalers. I can go now. I'm *red-to-goop-it*, as they say. I am a plucky orphan, remember, so I'll drop everything to help interesting strangers." He winked at her.

Gulchima felt a constriction in her chest, but it loosened as they walked deeper into the factory. Movement helped reduce her anxiety.

She didn't exactly dislike Hubward. He was entertaining. A little.

But Gulchima felt like they were being forced into a friendship. Just because he was about her age, and he existed, didn't mean they had to be *best* friends. They worked together to destroy magic. That was it.

"What do you know about the fairies in this factory?" Hubward asked.

He stretched his lower back. At least his hair was pulled back, and not flopping into his eyes.

"They're small."

Hubward nodded, but when Gulchima didn't continue, he said, "Yes, but I mean compared to the varieties you've faced before, how do they stack up? Have you trapped southern gold-smacks before?"

Gold-smacks? She'd never even seen a fairy. "No . . . um, just normal swamp fairies. They were green. And sparkly."

"Swamp fairies!" Hubward jumped. "Then these gold-smacks should be no problem for you. How did you handle the marshy-mallow they threw at you? I'm just wondering. Did it stick your eyes shut? I knew a guy, we called him 'no-brows' because his eyebrows had been so covered with the marshy-mallow stuff, they just fell off and never grew back." Hubward inspected Gulchima's eyebrows. "Anyway, how did you do it Gulch?"

"That's a trade secret," Gulchima said, keeping a straight face. "Tell me about these fairies. I don't know much about gold-smacks."

Hubward gave her the low down: The fizz factory produced certified non-magical fizz-water, so the fairies were an embarrassment. Under threat of losing their jobs, no factory worker spoke of them.

Or if they did, it was indirect: Our *little helpers*, they might say. The infestation. Ting waffles (those-T'ings-WhAt-FLy-around-uS). And always mentioned with a raised eyebrow, or a small nudge, that meant, "And it's just between us—understand?"

"That's dumb," Gulchima said. "Why would adults play pretend?"

"Well if pretending fairies don't exist makes adults sleep safer at night, who am I to say different?" Hubward said, with a dramatic wave of his arm. "You know how cranky adults are if they don't get the exact sleep they want, or drink the exact hot drink they want upon waking, or have the exact weather they want while lounging by the sea."

Gulchima snorted. *Adults!* Always wasting time on hot beverages and being sad about kissing.

Hubward led Gulchima onto the fizz factory floor. It was loud and busy and put Gulchima at ease.

Small bottles and clay amphora marched by them on moving walkways. Occasionally the bottles halted, and strange nozzles squirted bubbly liquid into them. From atop the cavern ceiling, enormous leather bags of gas wheezed, as if the factory had lungs. The clank and spray was a cauldron of confusion, and they had to shout to hear each other.

Gulchima pointed at the moving belts that carried the bottles through the filling station. "Magic?"

"No, it's all geyser powered," Hubward shouted. "Geysers turn the wheels, wheels turn the belts, belts move the bottles."

He led them through the sticky fizz factory, waving hello to the other workers. Hubward seemed to have a special handshake or elaborate greeting for each person he met. Near the bubble-laths, an older factory worker sat on the floor. He was bleeding from a large gash on his head.

The factory herbalist, Ninestone, was attending to the wound. The Fizz-Meister, the man who ran the factory, watched over the proceedings, while several fairies, visible as puffs of giggling light, zipped around them. The Fizz-Meister smelled strongly of sulfur. He seemed nervous.

The worker monotoned, "Oh how clumsy of me. It appears," he licked his lips, "that I have dropped this bottle, poured out its contents onto my head and then gently tapped the bottle against my skull several times until I fell into unconsciousness. Alas. This completely normal, non-magical accident hath ruined my day."

Ninestone grimaced. "Very believable," she said. She sprayed the air with lavender oil, and the fairies sped away.

A fairy zipped by Hubward's head, and he reached out as if to slap an invisible hand. Gulchima heard an indignant squeak, like a snail who stubbed its foot.

"How many fairies are there?" Gulchima whispered.

"Only a few dozen here, and another colony set up in the Bakery in the burgh," Hubward answered. "But they're all based out of the caverns. They've set up a fairy land." He waggled his eyebrows, ominously.

A fairy land? What was that?

The Fizz-Meister became agitated when he heard the word *fairy*. He was a thin nervous man, his eyes darting about, as if trying to see around corners. His clothes were baggy, and his arms seemed to be 90% elbow. She'd seen him at the docks the day the dragon had crashed, but he had only seemed concerned with the loading ramp.

"Those bats again," the Fizz-Meister said in a clipped tone. "Alas, it is common and completely normal to have bats inside a cavern such as this."

"Bats?" Gulchima asked. "But I saw light. Unless those bats were carrying lanterns, I think those were—"

"Bayadev bats are known to carry lanterns," Hubward said smoothly. He stepped on Gulchima's foot so she would stop talking. "Otherwise they'd get lost in the dark."

The Fizz-Meister grinned nervously. He spoke in an overly loud voice and said, "The factory is perfectly safe. This man was injured because he was clumsy. Terrible thing, that clumsiness. Why I've had three reports of extreme clumsiness and one just-plain-bad-luck in the gas-baggery this morning. Perhaps someone should visit it? Anyone up for it? Anyone?"

He didn't pretend to look around. He just pointed at Gulchima and Hubward. "You two. You're orphans. You both have inspiring life stories, with your post-war experience, and whatever. It's good for morale. You will go there, to the gas-baggery, and improve morale."

Gulchima understood. "And where would you say the morale is the worst?"

"I believe bad morale was almost at the top of the ceiling in the gas-baggery," the Fizz-Meister said. "Likely it is hidden behind a stalactite. That is where bad morale was. So go there and take care of it. Ninestone has some lavender bombs that are good for morale."

A pack of fairies dove down, pelting the Fizz-Meister with eggs. They whirled away, giggling.

"Eggs!" the Fizz-Meister exclaimed. "Where do they find eggs inside a cave?" He caught Gulchima's eye. "Those bats I mean; the ones that carry the lanterns."

Ninestone rolled her eyes, then started to clean the factory worker's wound again. "Birds have eggs," she muttered.

The factory worker licked at the goo on his face. "Alas. It must be bat eggs. Normal non-magical—"

A bag of flour fell onto his head, turning him white as a geyser ghost.

The factory worker smiled, looked up at Ninestone. "Oh that's sweet, actually. The *bats-carrying-lanterns* must have remembered: Today is my birthday."

He wiped the flour from his eyes. "They're making me a cake."

* * *

It was quieter in the gas-baggery. The cavern held several large stitched leather bags, some as big as a house, which captured the gas emanating from vents on the walls and floors. Smaller bags of sealskin, some deflated, lay near rainbow colored bubbling pools on the cavern floor. Thinner hand-stitched balloons floated off the ground, just above small lanterns which were cemented to the stalagmites. Buckets of glue, probably used to seal the bags, lay overturned on the floor. In one, Gulchima saw quite a bit of hair, and a pair of wooden false teeth.

"What is this place?" Gulchima asked. She pushed between two mid-sized balloons of gas and immediately regretted it. Her body didn't like tight spaces. She was okay with it mentally, but her body had other ideas. Her body wanted her to run into the blissful open air and forget all this cavern-fairy-magic stuff. Gulchima tried to take in a deep breath to steady herself and failed.

"This is the fizz in the fizz factory," Hubward said. "Different flavored gases come up out of these vents. Then, in the factory they put the gas back into the water."

"I thought the fizz-water just came out that way," Gulchima said. "What are the lanterns for?"

"Well they help separate the flavors of gas from the regular air," Hubward explained. "And if the lanterns go out, it's a warning to go find fresh air. Bad air doesn't burn."

Bad air? Like poison? Gulchima felt her chest constrict again. There was light here, which was good. But somehow, being away from the others made it hard to breathe. Was she getting nervous? No, not nervous. Just . . . ready. Ready to face the fairies. Ready to get the heck out of this cave!

Gulchima poked experimentally at one of the sealskin balloons that floated above the cavern floor. "I suppose you'll tell me this isn't magic either."

"Just gas," Hubward said. "That's the kind that goes into *Spring-Evening-Mist* fizz-water. They say it's a gas lighter than air."

"And what's that used for?" Gulchima asked. She pointed at an oily black sludge pool, that shimmered and popped. Several dead rats floated in it. The gas bag above it seemed corroded around the edges.

"That's *Pure Clean Snowmelt* fizz-water, 'fresh from the

mountain meadow,'" Hubward said with a laugh. "Which is technically true. The water came from the mountain meadow before all that sludge got into it. Tastes great though. Our top seller."

"And the rats?"

Hubward shrugged. "Why mess with the secret formula?"

* * *

Hubward yawned and watched Gulchima as she prodded the bags, and chewed her bottom lip, and thought smart thoughts.

She seemed interested in everything about the factory; everything except him. She hadn't asked about his orphanhood even once, or how he was getting along. She didn't feel sorry for him, or want to punch and rob him. She was indifferent. And she wasn't the Sorcerer.

Hubward flipped down his hair to cover his eyes, then scanned her once more, to be certain. Not one spec of magic, which was itself interesting. Weeks earlier, Hubward had hidden a Seer-Slip—a translucent cloth used to detect magic—in the front bangs of his hair. He couldn't walk around blindfolded like Jaroo's two guards, with their obvious Seer-Slips. That would draw too much attention. So instead he'd hidden the Seer-Slip in his hair.

Hubward flipped his hair, and the Seer-Slip, out of his eyes. Nothing here, except those fairies. But wait . . . there *was* something.

A white bone. That was nothing to wonder at, all bones were white, or yellow. But with his Seer-Slip on, there was more to see.

The bone was glowing with magic, even more than the fairy land where it was embedded. It was like staring at the sun.

Looking up, Hubward noticed bones scattered all over the cavern ceiling. They *darkled* with magic.

Suddenly, it all made sense: The Sorcerer, the fizz factory, the dragon. He understood the connection.

Hubward felt the exhaustion of the last few weeks flood over him. All the extra work had paid off. He'd figured it out, and now he understood. After he saved the world and captured the Sorcerer and avenged his team's deaths, then he could finally get back to writing his play. It would be epic.

There were a few other loose ends to tie up, but at least now he understood what Jaroo had been talking about . . . sort of. And now he was certain what Jaroo was planning to do to Gulchima and the Outfit.

He'd just have to find an excuse to go to the—

Gulchima groaned. She pointed up at the ceiling, forty feet above them. There beneath a mass of zipping lights, was the fairy land, a disgusting nest of villainy and stolen objects. "How are we supposed to get up there?"

A simple levitation spell could do it, Hubward thought. But of course, he couldn't do magic right now. He'd sacrificed magic for bacon.

"Do you have those lavender bombs Ninestone gave you?" Gulchima asked. "Maybe if we take out the fairy queen with the bomb, the rest will leave. Can you hit the fairy land from here? How far can you throw?"

Hubward picked up a small rock, then tossed it into the air. It did not come close to the fairy land, but even so, a fairy zipped over, caught it in mid-air, and then tried to drop it on his head.

"Okay, what else you got?" he asked.

"Let's trap one of the fairies. See if we can glue a lavender bomb onto its back."

That wasn't a bad idea, Hubward thought. And—he flipped his hair over his eyes, so he could scan for magic—if they could knock the fairy nest off the ceiling, he could take a sample. There was something else interesting inside.

A cave cricket blinked its eyes, sightlessly.

"Not now," Hubward muttered to one of the seven shadows around him. "You heard her. Get me a fairy . . . ."

One of the shadows leapt into action, bouncing off the nearest balloon. It caught two fairies in flight, somersaulted, then placed the wriggling fairies into Hubward's hands. A second shadow, distracted by the spectacle, fell into the black oily pool, the one with all the dead rats. The other shadows rushed over to help it get out.

Well, that was easy, Hubward thought.

"I caught two, they were fighting!" Hubward whooped.

Gulchima ran over to him. "Great! Now what? Can we attach the bomb—"

"I have another idea," Hubward said. Suddenly, he knew what to do. It would impress Gulchima, he thought. And then she'd have to be his friend. Maybe, she would even read his play.

It was a two part plan:

Firstly, he handed over one of the struggling fairies.

Then, he grabbed the second squealing fairy by its head.

Hubward started to pull.

* * *

"Don't kill it!" Gulchima yelled. "They're just . . . insects."

Gulchima had a hard time seeing what the fairies really were. They glowed brightly and always were in motion, like a hummingbird. They looked like miniature blurry babies clothed in white and gold feathers, except they had two sharp fangs and orange fiery eyes and they were so very angry.

The fairy slipped out of Gulchima's hand, but she caught it by the foot. The fairy started to fly away, but its leg stretched out as if it was made of rubber. It snapped back into her hand with a giggle that sounded like a curse.

"What! It's just a fairy. It can stretch, see." Hubward swung the fairy around by its head, like a fresh piece of taffy.

"Yes, but you don't have to grab it by the head, do you?"

Gulchima's fairy bit down on her hand, hard. Pain shot up her arm. It felt like a bee sting, but larger and itchier. Gulchima's hand began to swell.

"Oh come on, they're not supposed to live in caves," Hubward chided. "Once we knock down the fairy nest, they'll go back to the magic oak where they started. I didn't know you were a fan of fairies, Gulch. I didn't know you were a fae-weather fan."

Hubward held the fairy above him. He twisted the fairy, wringing it out like a wet towel. A single drop of sparkling liquid fell off the fairy and into his mouth.

His eyes crossed, and Hubward started to huff and puff.

"What was that? What did you just do?" Gulchima asked him. She punched him on the arm.

The fairy he'd just twisted had bounced against the wall and was buzzing in slow circles. It was dazed. But it was alive.

"Fairy Juice," Hubward grunted. "Fairy Juice—Juice—Juiiiiiiiice."

Gulchima wanted to ask what "fairy juice" did, but there wasn't time.

Hubward yanked Gulchima's hair, then pinched her ear and yelled:

"Fairy Juice makes you fly!"

* * *

"Ow! What was that for?" Gulchima yelled.

"Because you're such a big, mumbly, *cumberpatch*!" Hubward shook his head as if clearing it. "Sorry, Fairy Juice makes you mean, too."

"Then why did you just drink it?"

Hubward leapt up, and started levitating a few feet above the ground. "Because it also makes you fly." He took off his boot and threw it at Gulchima. "Sorry. I have to do it this way Gulch. I can't help it." His voice rose in pitch.

"Why?"

"Because if you want to fly like a fairy, you have to think of the meanest thing you've ever done to someone, the meanest thing you did for no reason."

"But . . . that's magic."

Hubward snorted. "It's not magic if you know how it works—you *stinkpot*. Sorry. Now take some. We'll get rid of the fairy land together and we'll be best friends. Best friends forever!"

He grabbed her wriggling fairy and shoved it under her nose.

Gulchima slapped it away. "Don't call me stinkpot! And I'm not going to use stupid magic. And I'm not going to squeeze a thing that looks like a baby with fangs."

"I'm sorry, did you want to destroy the fairy nest or not?" Hubward yelled. He flipped erratically in the air, crashing against a stitched gas bag. "Why are you being so difficult? Why are stupid girls so difficult? Why don't you drink Fairy Juice and fly and destroy the fairy nest and be my friend. Why won't you notice my cool front-flip haircut? I'm an orphan . . ." Hubward sank to the ground. His face was wet with tears. "I have a cool haircut and I help interesting strangers."

Hubward started weeping. He was embarrassed to cry in front of his new best friend.

"I don't hate your haircut," Gulchima said. She put her arm awkwardly around Hubward and patted him exactly twice. "But, did you say *nest*? I thought it was a fairy land?"

"Same thing," Hubward muttered.

He thought she knew about swamp fairies. How could she not know that?

* * *

Now that her eyes had adjusted to the low light, Gulchima saw the nest for what it was: Nothing more than a stinking pile of fairy droppings. It was a huge midden of random junk: bones, bracelets, candy wrappers, and two more sets of wooden false teeth, all encased in a steaming pile of poo.

"Just a nest," Gulchima said. "So all the stories where people are transported to a fairy land are fake. They're going to that pile of poo?"

Hubward nodded, wiping the tears from his face. "They're sticking their head in there. Fairy poo causes hallucinations. The other stuff covered with the poo are things they steal. The fairies are like pack rats."

"What's it like?" Gulchima asked.

"Did you ever eat so much candy that you threw up?"

Gulchima shook her head. "I don't like candy that much."

"Me neither," Hubward said brightly. "We have so much in common Gulch. We should be best friends. Can you put your arm around me again?"

Gulchima smiled faintly. "Maybe later. But what really happens, Hub. I mean . . . how would you know you were stuck in a fairy land? Say you disappeared for . . . a few years. Could it have been fairies that did it? And maybe you'd never know?"

"Oh, no chance!" Hubward slapped his knee. "The first thing fairies do is chop off your ears. They make fountains out of them."

"Actually I can see how that would look nice," Gulchima said quickly. "But most people say fairies are helpful."

Hubward shrugged. "Most people are dumb."

Gulchima laughed. That was a mean thing to say. Maybe her and Hubward could become friends after all.

But with that insult, Hubward started to huff and puff again.

"Uh oh," he said. "I never should have said that."

Hubward double over in pain. He pointed up at the ceiling of the cavern and started to cough, and then, to laugh.

A pack of fairies swarmed around the fairy nest on the cavern ceiling. Gulchima could hear them whispering.

"They're planning something," Gulchima said. "We'd better get out of here."

When Hubward didn't respond, she turned to look at him.

Hubward's eyes had turned a horrible glowing orange. His face was pale, and she watched as he hesitantly put a finger to his mouth.

Gulchima saw fangs. Hubward was turning into a fairy!

She jumped away from him.

"I told you to give me a hug," Hubward said in a strained voice.

Hubward rocketed into the air. "I told you Gulch. I just wanted to be your frienddddddd . . . ."

Hubward disappeared, flying up into the depths of the cavern.

And then, just to make sure Gulchima knew that things had turned worser, the pack of fairies attacked.

Giggling and screaming, they dove at her, pelting Gulchima with eggs and hot oil and rocks.

But the real problem wasn't the fairies, or even Hubward.

The real problem was that suddenly, the cavern had gone dark.

"It was weird. Five years of adventure and nobody took a potty break."

-The Collected Lies of Gulchima Brixby
(50/100: **A Biological Impossibility**)

CHAPTER 20: GULCHIMA LEARNS LEVITATION

THE FAIRIES KNOCKED OUT THE LANTERNS, either by crashing into them, or smashing them with rocks.

Gulchima stumbled forward, but somehow was lifted off the ground, and spun around, just as hot oil spattered across her path. The fairies hadn't thought this attack out, and some of the cooking oil ignited when it splashed against one of the sputtering lamps. Fire! At least Gulchima could see by firelight.

"Hubward!" she yelled. But Hubward was nowhere to be found.

She could leave him. The flames from the cooking oil raged, but Gulchima could see the exit door. She could see the escape route.

No. Gulchima wouldn't do it. She wouldn't leave him. Hubward was a friend. Well, not a friend—but Hubward was an employee. Well, not an employee, because she wasn't paying him. But, anyway, whatever he was, she wouldn't leave him.

Gulchima grabbed a deflated leather bag, coated it with glue from the bucket, and tossed that into the fire. The material caught instantly, in a *whoosh* of flame. Now, Gulchima could see much better. At the top of the cavern, a large figure floated near the fairy nest. It was Hubward.

Was he trying to disable the nest? Trying to use the lavender bombs and bring it down?

No. Hubward seemed to be talking to the fairies in a giggling whisper. One of the fairies zoomed by his left ear, as if inspecting it. Then, they shook hands.

He's going into fairy land!

The fairies dove at Gulchima again, swiping at her head with a pair of cutting shears. Somehow, she felt her arm moving up, felt the bucket of glue clanking into the attacking fairies. That was another stroke of luck.

How odd. It was almost as if her shadow had come to life and guided her hand. Could you have a guardian shadow, instead of a guardian angel? Or was she hallucinating from all the fairy poo flying around?

One of the nearby balloons, stretched tight by gas lighter than air, floated toward her. It had come unattached during the fairy attack. Just as Gulchima reached for it, the last strap broke, then somehow wrapped itself around her wrist. Gulchima was pulled upward.

The fairies zoomed around her, and Gulchima figured that in her helpless state, hanging from a balloon in mid-air, she was doomed. But she wasn't.

It seemed as if the fairies were fighting something. Some invisible force—or rather—seven invisible forces. The fairies dove and pelted at shadows, but sometimes they were slapped with torches, or hit with glue, or tossed into the bubbling vents. Had the Fizz-Meister come to her rescue? *What was going on?*

Gulchima's balloon floated her to the top of the cavern. Her wrist had started to hurt, but she was only a few feet away from the fairy nest. Hubward was sighing contentedly. He'd shoved his entire head into the fairy nest, and was up to his neck in poo.

"Yes, more bacon please, thank you minister," Hubward muttered. "*Mmm, yes it does go well with the other bacon. An excellent suggestion, if I do say so myself.*"

"Hubward, get your head out of that pile of fairy poo!" Gulchima ordered.

She tugged at him. But with only one free hand, she couldn't budge him.

"Leave me alone," Hubward pouted. His voice was muffled. "I want to live in fairy land. I can be great there! I can be a king!"

Two fairies were pulling at Gulchima's legs, a third tried to bite through her rabbit-skin leggings. The balloon bobbed away from the nest, but Gulchima spun around, then grabbed Hubward's foot.

"Hubward, that's not real. It's just imaginary," Gulchima pleaded. "Would you rather be good in the real world, or great in poo land? Choose real life!"

"I hate real life!" Hubward said. "Real life is hard. I'm tired of doing everything." He kicked at her.

The balloon was shoved violently away.

Gulchima had one last chance. She freed her hand, swung forward on the wrist strap, and then flew into the air. She thudded on top of the fairy nest, but her knees began to sink into the poo.

Gulchima knew she had only seconds to convince Hubward, before the fairy poo absorbed her too.

"Hubward please! You have so much to live for! I know you're an orphan and people don't like you very much, and you smell weird. But . . . I understand."

"No you don't," Hubward said. "Your parents are alive."

"They're in prison Hubward. My parents are in prison and I don't even know why!"

She had a sudden urge to confess everything. To tell the truth, for once, about what had happened those five years she was missing. To explain to Hubward why she was really afraid of the dark.

"I didn't just disappear for five years," Gulchima said. "And it wasn't any of those stupid adventure stories I tell people." Her knees sunk deeper into the fairy nest.

"So you've been lying this whole time? You told me it was mermaids on horses that stole you away! I thought we were friends!"

"Hubward, I was lying. But I . . . I don't have any friends either! I don't know how to have friends. I'm not good at it."

Hubward pulled his head out of the fairy poo nest. "You don't?" he asked.

"No! Everybody thinks I know what I'm doing, that I have it all together. But if I'm so great and so smart, then why don't I have any friends?" Now Gulchima had started to tear up. "My family hates me. I ruined the company. Now you're going to get your ears cut off, and I'll be alone in the dark. Again."

"You're not alone," Hubward said quietly. "You've got me."

"Great, I've got an orphan with fairy poo in his ears."

Hubward's eyes dimmed to a dull brown. His fangs receded. "Yuck," he said.

He reached into his pocket and pulled out several lavender bombs. Then he took out a spark-box and lit them.

"Sure I'll be your friend, but only because you need the practice," Hubward said. "The war messed up a lot of things in Baltica. War has echoes, you know? It doesn't end when the fighting is over."

Gulchima sobbed. Why was she crying? What was she crying about?

"C'mon Gulch." He reached out to her. "Grab my hand. I'll fly us back down."

Gulchima grabbed his hand and together they stepped off the fairy nest, and—

—Plummeted straight down.

"Whoops! I thought I could still fly—"

They splashed into the oily black sludge pool. It was warm, but not too hot, and it smelled worse than Gulchima had imagined. A dead rat floated nearby, inches from her face. They pulled themselves out of the pool, and started to laugh.

From above them, they heard the crash of the lavender bombs exploding. The fairy nest groaned, tipped sideways, and then fell with a *thwump* into the sludge pool.

Gulchima was doused a second time, when a wave of sludge splashed over her.

"So, you free tomorrow?" Hubward asked.

"I have a list of things to do," Gulchima said. She squeezed her leggings, trying to dry them. "Why?"

Hubward pointed at the destroyed gas bags, the fire, the mess. He coughed and waved the smoke from his face.

"Because after this, I don't think I'll be working here much longer," Hubward said.

Gulchima wiped at the sludge on her cheek, then tasted it with the tip of her tongue.

"Hmmm. I think it could use a bit more rat."

"I didn't just disappear for five years . . . And it wasn't any of those stupid adventure stories I tell people."
—A Breakthrough! Read the most recent report from our loyal spy. The girl admits to it.

". . . Now you're going to get your ears cut off, and I'll be alone in the dark. Again."
—Our suspicions are correct. She was awake the entire five years she was missing. She must know how to find what we seek. **Proceed with the plan**.

-The Collected Lies of Gulchima Brixby
(100/100: **Truth at last**)

CHAPTER 21: FESTIVAL OF ROUGH PETER

GULCHIMA TOURED THE BURGH ALONE, and this time she saw progress.

It was early morning, two days after the fairy fiasco, and the work crews hadn't started yet. The fizz factory fire had been put out, and Hubward was home sick again. They were friends now, whether or not Gulchima wanted them to be. You couldn't go through something like that and not be friends, Gulchima supposed. They were *fairy fire friends*, and that was forever.

In Bayadev, the riverside gate was finished, and one of the new loading ramps that she'd envisioned—banked properly to allow proper flow of cargo—was finished too. The oast house was fully repaired, and the stone walls for the new blacksmith shop were already half built. Isolde and Rattbone had done their part.

Gulchima had done her part too. A few of the red M's, the signs marking magical problems, had been painted over with green G's. Officially, it stood for the word "Good", but Gulchima secretly believed the letter meant that she'd personally taken care of it. As in, we "Gulched" that magic!

It would be awesome if her name became a verb.

Even the dragon was half prepared now. The hoists and pulleys and levers were all in place. None of the adults on the houseboat would help her with the work, but she knew she'd eventually find somebody who wanted to get paid. Perhaps Hubward knew some workers at the fizz factory. Or maybe Soltanabad and his crew were interested? They seemed comfortable with danger.

Things were looking pretty good. Her tour of Bayadev was almost complete, but for the first time that morning, Gulchima came to something that displeased her. Uncle Roog's work on the main burgh wall had stalled out. Actually, it looked like he had not started.

She decided to have a word with him. Or rather, three words. Those words would be: Get. To. Work.

As usual, she found Uncle Roog in his newly built sauna, located in a small courtyard near a cluster of abandoned shoe-repair shops.

There was a line of men waiting their turn. Uncle Roog had built his sauna using stones and mortar that were supposed to be used on the wall. Outside the long rounded stone sauna, a basket of birch branch whisks were being sold, for a very high price. A sign on the sauna read: "Uncle Roog's Dragon-Hot

Sauna. Entry two thalers, per person, per hour."

Between the entry price and the cost of the birch branches—which the men slapped against their backs to reduce tight muscles while in sauna—Uncle Roog was making a small fortune.

Gulchima bypassed the line and banged on the wooden door to the sauna. A wisp of steamy air floated out from the gap at the bottom of the door, but no one answered. She banged again.

At last, Uncle Roog poked his mass of white hair out from behind the door.

"What? I'm in sauna," he said in an irritated tone.

"Uncle Roog, I need to talk to you. Now."

"You can't come in, you're a girl," Uncle Roog said. "This is men's sauna time. Women's sauna time is later. Children's sauna time is after that. I don't know if you're a woman or a child, so I'm giving you your options."

"I'm not here for sauna!" Gulchima yelled. "I want that wall done."

Uncle Roog scowled at her. "Well that's nice to hear what *you* want. Finally you're speaking up! But I don't care what you want today."

"You should be working," Gulchima warned him.

"Working? Since when do we work on the Festival of Rough Peter?" Uncle Roog asked. "It's the Seasonal Planting celebration, mumblecrust. Or did you forget? And another thing—I'm not your uncle, but if I were, I'd tell you to stop dithering with that magic."

A small explosion rocked the sauna, shooting smoke, and not steam, through the cracked door.

"Roog! Are you using fire medicine in there?"

"Of course I'm using fire medicine in here. How else could

I claim the title of 'Baltica's Hottest Sauna'? You think people will pay for a measly steam bath? This sauna is Dragon-Hot. Dragon-Hot, Gulchima! And another thing—don't think I haven't heard about your plans to replace me with Soltanabad's crew. Sure they work harder and faster and expect less pay. But you owe me. I'm family."

"You just said you're not my uncle," Gulchima reminded him.

"I meant 'family' in the familiar sense, you *smellfeast*!" He slammed the sauna door in her face.

Gulchima took a deep breath, and started to walk back to the houseboats. She'd have to speak to Uncle Rattbone, get his advice on what to do. She wouldn't let Uncle Roog ruin her good mood this morning. But something he had said bothered her.

Not the insults or the threats; that was just Roog being Roog. No, it was the part about the festival!

Was that today? The Festival of Rough Peter!

Oh Sweet Sorcerer, Gulchima was supposed to be running it. She'd forgotten.

She was head of the Outfit. The children were all waiting for her. She had to—

"—We've been looking everywhere for you."

It was her sister, Isolde, and she was angry. As usual.

Isolde was with Tiktok, the boy from the boat, who had kissed the river-hags.

They stood in the tunnel through the old curved earthen ramp by the burgh's walls. Tiktok was eating chomp maple syrup out of a jar. He stood dangerously close to Isolde, who had her hands on her hips, in exaggerated anger. She'd done some curling thing to her hair, and she wore her best dress. They both looked out of breath, as if they'd been kissing.

"Why?" Gulchima asked.

"It's the Festival of Rough Peter," Isolde said. "You forgot didn't you? Gulchima! You had one thing to do for the boats. One thing!"

"One thing? What about the geyser ghosts? What about the fairies? What about all the free fizz-water, they sent over this morning? I got cases of it."

Isolde nodded, but wasn't listening. "Well this is all on you. You said you would handle it. You said you were the boss. So you figure it out. You're just lucky Uncle Rattbone took care of the adults' party."

"I was just finishing up my plan," Gulchima said. She tried not to look panicked.

What was she going to do? Gulchima had to entertain twenty or more kids, give them the time of their lives. Everyone on the houseboats loved festival days. And of all festival days, they loved the Festival of Rough Peter the most.

If only she could distract the kids, keep them busy for a few hours. She needed an idea, she needed a . . . *treasure hunt.*

I'll take them on a treasure hunt around town, she thought. At each spot, they'd uncover some mystery, some clue, then they'd get a small piece of candy. She could buy bags of the stuff at the bakery, write up the clues in a few minutes. But this was the most important festival. So the final pot of candy had to be somewhere amazing. It had to be . . . .

Gulchima thought about the dragon. All the kids wanted to see the dragon up close. So why not?

She would be a hero to the children. And, since she had everything ready, she could cross one more thing off her list too.

With that many people to help, the dragon could be moved. The older children knew how to use pulleys and equipment and so on. Wouldn't that be the best festival ever? The festival day when they got rid of a dragon?

It would work. Gulchima was certain.

"Well let's get back to the boats," Gulchima said. "I'm sure the children are waiting for me."

Isolde huffed and started walking too quickly ahead of them. Tiktok hung back.

"Want some maple syrup?" Tiktok asked. "Soltanabad is practically giving it away."

Gulchima shook her head. "No thanks," she said. "As a personal rule, I don't like butt juice."

* * *

The Festival of Rough Peter was here and despite the tight budget and Gulchima's well-crafted plan, no work would be done today.

Festival Days were important to the Outfit, and there were lots of them: Rough Peter, Jacks Knees, Woodman's Lots. This was in addition to Enders Day, the day off at the end of each week, and whatever the local holidays were at the town they were fixing. And occasionally a lesser-known festival day would pop up, like Lover's Moon, which occurred anytime a girl of a certain age declared love for the first time.

It was difficult to get any work done, especially since some young workers were known to date local girls and fall in love with them, just to ensure they could get a Lover's Moon day off, and have extra time for fishing.

But today's festival was important, even to Gulchima. It had been her favorite when she was younger, because it meant the end of the snow, and the brief spell of warm weather.

The Festival of Rough Peter occurred at the start of planting season, and Gulchima wasn't prepared. She, as head of the Outfit, was required to run the event, set the traps, put out the brandy and herring and rum-bread. She would help the children set their snares for the mystical figure, Rough Peter, and make sure that if he was not immediately generous (wink wink), the other adults could put out presents in his honor.

She wondered who or what Rough Peter really was. In the children's stories he was half-god, or half-magic, she knew. But what was his other half? He reminded her of Uncle Roog.

As the legend went, Rough Peter sowed the seeds, stole your gold, and ate your food. He was a god of spring, in a shabby sort of way. But he was simple. He was easily outsmarted.

Rough Peter stole your stuff, but then stored everything in his magic rucksack, a bag which he patched, but never really repaired. On his festival day, you just had to steal it back.

Rough Peter liked a drink or four, and his rucksack was torn. And so what you needed to do, the legend said, was to make sure he was *boozled* on rum-bread. Then, you had to set up a few obstacles for him to trip over: a chair in the wrong place, a loose log on the floor, maybe a sharp stick to tear his magic rucksack.

If you did it right, a few things he'd stolen from others may appear as presents for you (and they would get new things too, so it wasn't really stealing). The seeds would fall out of the holes in his bag too, and be spread in the field.

And if you were lucky, and you trapped him, you'd find a piece of gold in his place, because "gold opens doors," as even the smallest child knew.

Gulchima wasn't feeling up to the task today, but she had to take the younger children, Novvy included, on the Hunt for Rough Peter. They'd never find him, but when they returned all the adults would swear Rough Peter had just appeared.

The children would get the presents he left, the older children would get the gold, and the adults would eat and drink whatever Rough Peter had accidentally "dropped". It was a great feast.

So no work would get done today or tomorrow. But, nobody would walk off the job in a huff either.

Gulchima boarded the Biters houseboat, where she and all the junior craftsmen lived. She walked to the central plaza and found almost the entire Outfit waiting for her. Every man, woman and child seemed to be there, and they were all in a good mood, all drinking the free fizz-water Jaroo had dropped off. They were clapping and carrying on, and it took Gulchima a few seconds to push her way to the front of the crowd.

The air smelled of vinegar and salt and rum-bread. Tormo, a young boy about Novvy's age, stood near her, trying to eat a cheese rope. But he was struggling without his two front teeth.

"What's going on?" she asked.

"Deadly combat," Tormo said in a bored tone. He pulled hard on his cheese rope and managed to free a few strands.

Gulchima was about to ask *who* was having a deadly combat, but there, at the center of the crowd, she saw it.

Uncle Rattbone and Hubward were staring warily at one another across a table. Their faces were deadly serious, and each was waiting for the other to make a move.

Hubward picked up a knife.

Uncle Rattbone narrowed his eyes, and picked up a bigger knife.

They were locked in deadly combat.

And Hubward was winning.

CHAPTER 22: GULCHIMA FINDS AN UNFORTUNATE TREASURE

WELL, IT WAS DEADLY COMBAT OF A SORT, Gulchima thought.

It was an eel eating contest, and the eels were already dead. So while it wasn't deadly for Hubward or Uncle Rattbone, it had been deadly for the eels.

The eel eating contest was an important part of the Festival of Rough Peter, especially if you liked to gamble or watch people eat themselves sick. And no one had bet on Hubward to win.

Hubward jabbed his knife into the bucket of eels on the table between them. The eels were pickled, and even from this distance Gulchima could smell the vinegar and salt that did nothing to cover up the rubbery eel stench.

Hubward held up a dripping piece of eel on the tip of this knife. It was almost as long as his hand. He put it in his mouth, chewed, and swallowed.

"Yum," he said.

Hubward shoved the glass figure of an eel across the table, toward Uncle Rattbone. "You're next," he gagged.

Uncle Rattbone swayed on his feet. His face was green, and his overshirt was damp. He wiped at his beard, once then twice. "Orphans . . ." he mumbled.

Uncle Rattbone stabbed into the bucket of eels with his knife.

He pulled out an eel piece slightly larger than Hubward's, but this one was undercooked. It still had slime on it.

The crowd groaned.

"That one's still alive," Tormo whispered.

Uncle Rattbone held a fist up to his mouth, puffed out his cheeks. The eel trembled on the edge of his knife.

At long last, Uncle Rattbone held the uncooked eel in the air, inches from his lips. A strand of eel slime dribbled onto his beard, and then . . . .

He threw up.

A lot.

Everywhere.

Twice.

Hubward had won! The crowd went wild.

Anya from the Black Sea and a few of the other carpenters rushed in and threw sawdust across the vomit on the deck, shoveled that out of the way, and then tossed the rest of the eels overboard. Hubward received the prize, the glass eel figurine, and Uncle Rattbone, who had never lost as long as Gulchima could remember, gave Hubward a hug.

He caught Gulchima's eye. "Orphans! Don't you just—*blaaht.*"

Uncle Rattbone threw up again. Everywhere.

Gulchima grabbed the sawdust and helped to clean it up.

* * *

The Hunt for Rough Peter was fun, thanks to Hubward. He was good with kids, good at being silly, pretending to trip over things, pulling candy out of thin air.

Gulchima made it up as she went, and eventually the kids found the clues for the treasure hunt. They visited the bakery, the east wall, the sauna—where the clue was hidden in Uncle Roog's hair.

At last, they arrived at the dragon. All was in readiness. The ditches were ditched. The ropes and tackles and pulleys were prepared. The levers of un-cursed wood were waiting. If she could get the tail moving in the right direction, Gulchima knew she could throw the dragon in the river. And once it was off land, it was officially out of Bayadev. Checkbox checked. Money earned. This would be a festival to remember.

The day Rough Peter moved the dragon.

"So what's the plan?" Hubward asked. He flipped his hair out of his eyes. "Gonna tackle the problem, head on? Or should I say, 'tail on'?"

Gulchima sighed. "The next time you tell me a joke, hold up your left hand so I know I'm supposed to laugh." She paused, then said with a smile, "Just kidding."

Gulchima walked over to the group of children. "Do you think Rough Peter is hiding under the dragon?"

The children looked perplexed. They talked it over.

"That would be a good hiding place," said Tormo. He whistled through his missing teeth.

"A great hiding place," said Novvy. "But how do we get underneath it?"

Hubward was standing near the dragon, staring at it. "Hold on a minute Gulch . . ." He flipped his hair over his eyes.

"Maybe we could use this lever," Gulchima said. She held out a long piece of lumber. "Maybe we could use that to look under the dragon."

The children cheered. Some stood back, afraid to approach the magical beast. Using a lever would be much better, they thought. They would be safer at a distance.

"Don't touch that," Hubward called. "There's something wrong. The dragon is swelling with magic."

Gulchima thought he was being silly again. So did the rest of the children.

She held her hand near the dragon and said, "Oh, is this what I'm not supposed to touch—"

Gulchima felt her skin blister, then tear from her palm, as if she'd just grabbed a hot piece of iron from the fire.

A whoosh of green flame shot out from underneath the dragon, nearly blinding her.

She staggered backwards. The air smelled of singed hair, and iron and smoke.

Gulchima held her right hand up to her face, but it wouldn't move. Her hand was a mess of blood, and black skin curled away at the edges. She saw something white, poking out at the end of her ring finger, and realized it was bone. Her bone.

Gulchima threw up.

But this time there were no carpenters and sawdust and laughter. This time there was only the ringing in her ears and the children, screaming, screaming.

—The children! Gulchima had to find them.

Most of the other children were far back from the dragon, and—somehow—the flame had missed them. Somehow—

A group of seven shabby people she hadn't seen before, stood in front of the children. They had taken the brunt of the flame, and—somehow—had shown up to save the children just in time. Their faces were dark and ashy, almost blue, but she could see places where the magical flame had burned them too. In a way, they looked like older versions of Hubward.

But they were alive, and—somehow—the rest of the

children had dove at exactly the right time, and were unharmed.

Perhaps these seven strangers were the source of all her "somehows". Perhaps . . . .

Gulchima stumbled over to them, counted the children.

Two were missing. Novvy and Tormo. They had been the closest.

She heard a groan, and fought through the smoke toward it. Her pulleys and wooden levers were all on fire now. Her right arm felt cold, but her palm burned, as if she were holding a hot coal. She'd take care of that later. Right now, she had to find Novvy!

Hubward lay in a heap, his arms outstretched.

"Hubward!" she yelled. "Are you all right!"

For a moment he didn't respond, but then, he stirred.

He stood up and Gulchima saw Novvy blinking from somewhere underneath him. Novvy was all right, and Hubward had saved him.

Novvy looked fine. And Hubward?

His eyebrows were missing, but she'd tell him later. And his hair . . . his stupid haircut was gone too. At least that was an improvement.

Hubward was bald.

Novvy patted Hubward's smoking head. "Got lots of hair," Novvy said. "Hair grows back."

Hubward looked at him, bewildered. His eyes were wide with shock. "Did you find . . . everyone?" he asked.

Gulchima started to tell him that everyone was fine, that some mysterious strangers had shown up and saved the day. But then she saw—

It was Tormo. Tormo, who was a little older than Novvy, and liked to eat cheese rope. Tormo was not all right. Tormo was—

Tormo lay in the mud, face down, unmoving. His hair was burned off, but the skin on his neck looked okay. Gulchima rolled him over, saw his blood on her hands.

He was not okay. Tormo was definitely not okay. His eyes—his face. It looked like a popped blister. She could see his lips, drawn back, like he wanted to scream, had planned on it— but would never get the chance.

Gulchima screamed for help, tried to stop the blood leaking from a gash on his neck.

But nobody came. Nobody came to help her.

From atop the burgh wall, someone screamed, "Fire! Fire at the docks!"

The burgh was on fire too. First Tormo, now the burgh.

Gulchima had ruined it! Why had she been so stupid? Trying to move a dragon, by herself.

Inside the burgh, the fire had spread. She saw green flames licking at the oast house, all the fresh gleaming wood on the new roof was already burned off.

She heard a loud moaning, like a siren, from the wonder worms inside. They moaned as they burned, louder and louder: *waaaaaa-waaaaaa-waaaaaa.*

But the boy—Tormo. He wasn't moaning. He wasn't breathing. His blood seeped out.

Ninestone, the herbalist from the factory, was the first to find them.

"What happened?" she asked. She was out of breath, and dropped her wide basket to the ground beside them.

Gulchima blubbered something about the dragon, the green fire. She noticed small useless details: The freckle in Ninestone's eye, the sparkling white bone in the dirt beside them, the way the blood leaked out of Tormo's body, like water from a hidden spring.

Ninestone lay her body across Tormo, started to chant in an odd vowelly language. She placed a packet of crushed birch bark across Tormo's neck, and the bleeding slowed.

"Is he all right?" Gulchima asked.

"He's not breathing," Ninestone said grimly. She guided Gulchima's good hand to the wound. "Hold this compress, here. We have to stop the bleeding."

Ninestone grasped a golden ring that hung from a chain around her neck. In her other hand, a ball of purple light crackled into existence. The freckle in her eye glowed purple too, like a star in the middle of the night sky.

She was using magic. Ninestone was using magic!

Ninestone shoved the crackling light into Tormo's chest.

He gasped, then started to breathe again.

"That was magic," Gulchima whispered. "You can't use—"

Ninestone shook her head. The light in her eye had faded, and she looked pale, shaky. "No more death," she said. "I've seen enough children die."

"But magic . . . ."

"Then send me to prison for saving a boy's life!" Ninestone shouted. "Go ahead and report me. It's worth it!"

Gulchima shrunk back. "I won't," she said. "I won't ever tell."

Ninestone pointed at Gulchima's right hand, the one that had been burned by the dragon. "Your hand," Ninestone said. "Let me see it."

Gulchima pulled it away from her. It didn't hurt anymore. Was it the fear, keeping the pain away? Or was her hand . . . ruined?

"No. It's my hand, I . . . I understand what you're doing. But . . . no magic. I can't use magic."

"You might lose it," Ninestone said. The freckle in her eye began to glow.

"Save the children," Gulchima replied. "Don't worry about me." *Because I'm the one who caused this anyway. I don't deserve saving.*

Anya from the Black Sea ran over to them. She was Tormo's mother.

She scooped up Tormo in her arms. "What happened!" she wept. "Oh Tormo. Oh my boy. I told you to stay away from that dragon. I told you."

He mumbled something to her.

"It was my fault," Gulchima said. "I brought the children here. I told them it was safe." Her lower lip trembled. "I'm sorry."

Anya looked shocked.

"He may live, but I can't promise he will," Ninestone said. "Dragon fire smoke is dangerous too. Get him to the houseboats. We'll set up a hospital in the plaza there. And send someone to the fizz factory, ask for Man-of-Arms. I store my most important supplies with him."

"Thank you," Anya said to Ninestone. Then she ran off into the smoke, carrying Tormo.

Gulchima grimaced. "Do you have herbs, a salve, something? I can't feel my hand."

Ninestone rooted around in her basket. She took out a small green bottle of liquid that fizzed when she poured it on Gulchima's hand. Then Ninestone went off to help the other crying children.

Gulchima's hand throbbed, but that was better than feeling nothing. The white spot on her ring finger was just ash, not bone, she realized. Still, the burn would take weeks to heal.

The siren of the wonder worms deafened her. The flames grew higher. Bayadev burned.

Soon Uncle Rattbone was there, and the rest of the Outfit, both houseboats, came with him. The next few hours were full of panic and yelling, and buckets of water brought into the burgh. Gulchima helped with the fire fighting as best she could with one hand.

Soltanabad was there too, with his workers and their glacier water, which was doubly-effective against magical fire. Lady Keyhide, Jaroo, everyone in the burgh, everyone yelling, everyone trying to save what they could.

At last, the siren calls of the wonder worms faded, and Gulchima thought absently, that she wouldn't need to worry about them anymore. They were all burned up.

Perhaps, she wouldn't need to worry about anything else on the contract either.

Because this job was over.

END OF PART II

CHAPTER 23: BRUNHILD HAS SECOND THOUGHTS

BRUNHILD AND THE BANDITS had sauntered into the village of Boosh, just after breakfast.

"It's just, I love Rattbone. I see that now!" Brunhild yelled. She was punching a baker who had come at her with a rolling pin. The baker fell backwards, toppling a barrel of flour.

Kondo, the former bandit king, and current second-in-command to Brunhild, pulled at his long beard. His shaved head glistened from the fires they'd started. "Well naturally," Kondo said, in his deep rumbling voice. He picked up a small cow and threw it at a milkmaid. He grinned at the milkmaid's surprised *oomph*. "Love is like that."

"Love is like *what?*" Brunhild asked.

Now, she was shaking the mayor of Boosh, holding him upside down, by his foot. Coins poured out of his pockets like rain off a roof.

Kondo was not one for introspection. He scooped up three piglets. "Love is like . . . like sometimes you just have to burn down a burgh with magical dragon fire to find it. That's what love is like."

Kondo tossed the three little piglets at a gaggle of children, hitting them in their backs as they ran from him. They squealed. "How did you set that up, exactly? That thing with the dragon fire?"

Brunhild paused. She dropped the mayor of Boosh, and he tried to crawl away. How had she done it? She couldn't remember. Brunhild put her boot on the mayor's neck, contemplatively.

Brunhild could ensnare others with her singing; she was part River-Hag after all. And she was impossibly strong. Additionally, one could not ignore the magical scale armor she wore, which aided her in battles. But she didn't know dragon lore . . . She couldn't conjure that level of magic.

"It's all a bit of a blur," Brunhild said. And that was true.

The night of the fires at Bayadev, her voices had left her. She had set up the dragon fire trap indirectly—someone else had helped. Who was it? *She couldn't remember.*

But the trap had been for Rattbone and his family. Not those innocent children. Those children . . . she'd hurt them. How they'd screamed!

Brunhild couldn't get it out of her head.

The burgh had caught fire as well, and that wasn't the plan either.

Then Rattbone had shown up, barking orders, putting out fires, wonderful in the emergency. How she admired him in a clinch. Rattbone never started cackling when he got nervous. People followed his directions, even if he didn't pull out all their teeth.

So Brunhild had—

She released the mayor. The man had almost passed out anyway. What more could he give?

—The night of the fire at Bayadev, Brunhild had taken off her armor and went to help. In the smoke, and the darkness, nobody recognized her. Who was she, without her armor?

Did one exist, beyond one's job title?

Brunhild's voices had left her that night. Perhaps they were ashamed of hurting those children. Perhaps, she was better off without her voices.

"Well if you love him—" Kondo smashed the window of a cottage, threw in several flaming roosters. "I mean if you *really* love him, you gotta tell him. Get it off your chest."

Brunhild nodded, uncertain. She watched as Kondo continued to demolish the cottage wall. He did not touch the door.

She asked him why.

"I like to knock down the whole cottage, but leave the front door standing."

"That seems like a lot of work," Brunhild mused.

Kondo grinned. "The important things always are. Even a band of bad bandits needs to advertise. It's a form of social marketing, you see. Now they know *we* did it. I mean anybody could rob this village. They don't even have fortifications or protective walls."

"They *did* have walls," Brunhild reminded him. "You and Toothless knocked them down, using those magical weapons I gave you. Toothless dented his magic dentures. Remember?"

Kondo shrugged, but he blushed a bit in his pride. "I like what I do," he said. "And now with all the magical weapons you've supplied, we're going to be the best, strongest, richest band of bad bandits in Baltica."

A screaming farmer burst out of a nearby hay bale, brandishing a pitchfork.

"Surpr-i-ise," Kondo said, in a sing-song voice.

With his two-handed long sword, Kondo sliced the pitchfork into three neat pieces.

The farmer stopped his attack. His face dropped.

Kondo chuckled. He used his magical sword to pick up the bale of hay, then tossed it back onto the startled farmer. *Whumpf.*

One wishes for that level of job satisfaction, Brunhild mused. To enjoy what one does: Wouldn't that be a nice change?

Did she enjoy this anymore? The looting, the pillaging, the mayhem. It was exciting, naturally, but did she enjoy it?

[. . .]

There was space, where her voices ought to have reassured her. But they were missing.

Did she enjoy this anymore? Once, she had been a hero. The word was written on her heart.

A man came at her with an old sword, dull, stained where it was used to move the coals around the fireplace for several decades.

Brunhild sighed. "It appears you're trying to stab me through my chest," she said quietly. She gently headbutted the man, several times, until he went to sleep.

No, there was only one man who could stab her through her chest. Brunhild knew that now.

It was Rattbone.

And she *loved* him.

CHAPTER 24: HUBWARD PUTS DOWN ROOTS

THE PUMPKINS WERE ALMOST RIPE, though it was only nearing mid-summer. But then again, when had there been better care of pumpkins?

Seven devoted individuals cared for, watered, weeded, de-pested, and occasionally told bed-time stories to, these pumpkins. Grasshoppers were trapped mid-air. Bird traffic was redirected. The impossibly large squash and beets had been harvested early. But the pumpkins were left alone.

Hubward sat in the garden, with his seven undead helpers. He was utterly un-magical now. The fire had burned away more than his eyebrows. His magic was gone too. His team remained deadly, but still undead, and now they were visible.

And as healthy as he was—Hubward still drank a flagon of butter each morning—Hubward could not restore their magic camouflage. People would notice his helpers—his team—eventually. And then he'd have to move on.

"Pump-kin, p'mpkin," croaked the largest of his helpers.

"Pummmmkin," answered another. She held up an oak branch to shade the smallest pumpkin vine that was just starting to grow into a vegetable.

Now that he had some free time, Hubward should be chasing down the Sorcerer. Or at least, working on his play.

But he was doing neither. He was waiting.

He'd lost one job, at the factory. No surprise there. The Fizz-Meister was furious after finding the fairy poo in the fizz-water. And besides, after the small dragon fire mishap, the Fizz-Meister and Lady Keyhide and Jaroo had disappeared into the factory, locking the doors behind them. No one was admitted now.

That had been almost four weeks ago.

Hubward knew he should be digging up old magic to camouflage his team, but oddly, there was no more spare magic laying about. That had all disappeared the night of the fire too (along with his beautiful eyebrows and cool front-flip hairstyle).

A redbird landed on the fence, intending only to peck at a small bug near the pumpkin patch. It was ejected with a squawk, and a triumphant "PumpKIN!"

Two of his helpers exchanged high-fives, and then headbutted each other with a laugh. Laughing? Handshakes? When had they started doing that?

Hubward probably shouldn't muck about with magic. Ninestone had trusted him to manage her small farm, and she'd even given him a place to stay. He had to help her now. He was an orphan after all. And she was alone.

The good news was that Hubward had finally made a decision about his play.

He'd decided that the evil sheep-shearer hadn't done the murder after all. That was too obvious. *But who was it?* Someone less obvious . . . someone with a secret identity.

A Secret Identity.

Sorta, kinda, exactly like the situation with the Sorcerer. Except that was real life.

As for the Sorcerer, his final job—his real job—Hubward

knew he should be tracking down clues. He just needed time to think about it, just needed to make a list of suspects and narrow it . . . .

How can pumpkins grow so quickly?

The thought jumped out at him. It was odd, now that he noticed it. The handshakes and laughing from his team was odd too.

Hubward sniffed at the pumpkins, ignoring the warnings of his team. He wrinkled his nose. The pumpkins smelled like dirt. No clues there.

In Hubward's opinion, people who ate vegetables were really just eating dirt. Weird shaped, mushy, seed infested balls of dirt; that's what vegetables were. Dirt was the secret identity of vegetables.

The sound of footsteps startled him.

Hubward looked up, surprised. His team had scattered.

Ninestone was there. She was dressed in that modern style, wearing her patched dark blue skirt, white blouse buttoned to her neck, sleeves rolled up and pinned below her elbows. Her black felt hat tilted crazily on her head, which was how all the young women wore it.

She looked tired, but bright, as if she had finally managed to fight off a bad cold a few days ago. Ninestone had been caring for the children and adults burned in the dragon fire. There'd been many injuries, but somehow, nobody had died.

"I thought I saw you out here," Ninestone said. She glanced at the immaculate garden, and Hubward's clean tunic. "Been busy?"

"Sure! Busy doing normal boy things. Breaking sticks, looking at dirt, stretching worms. You know!" He waved his hand. "Worms are of a particular interest to a person like me."

Ninestone pressed her lips together. "Right. Well, I've got a soup on. Can you watch it? I have a new remedy for Tormo I want to try, and I'll have to run to the burgh. His beard is glowing now! It's bad enough that a five-year-old boy grows a beard, but Tormo's glows in the dark!"

"Did you say soup?" Hubward asked. His eyes narrowed. "What *kind* of soup?"

"The kind with squash, and beets, and a small bit of sausage," Ninestone said. "Now—"

"Yes but: What *kind* of sausage?" Hubward asked, suspiciously.

"Pork sausage. And—"

"Yes but: What *kind* of pork sausage?" Hubward interrupted.

"*Country spiced.* And no, you may not serve yourself, because you just spoon out all the vegetables and only eat the sausage. I've been watching you."

"Yes but—Well, okay," Hubward said. He sniffed. "Guess I'll eat that dirt then."

Ninestone squinted into the sun. She wiped her forehead with the back of her hand.

Hubward thought she was incredibly pretty, in that tired, half-worn way his mother had been pretty. Hubward missed his mother. It had been only her and him for a while before the war, and then . . . well, he really was an orphan now wasn't he? Because Hubward's mother was dead. Real dead, as in, her skin had never turned blue.

Just plain dead. Hubward wondered if that was worse or better than undead. Better, he thought. Better to be all the way something. Halfway would kill you.

"Are those mysterious foreign strangers going to eat too?" Ninestone asked, casually.

"Wha-What?" Hubward stammered.

"The seven strangers who showed up the night of the fire. I see them out here sometimes. I know you've been feeding them." She glanced around, but by now his team was hiding half a mile away in the forest.

"Old soldiers," Hubward lied. "I knew them during the war. I'm oath-bound to give them food and shelter. They didn't start that fire, I'll swear to—"

Ninestone held up her hand. "There's enough soup for them too. But can they please stop stealing my vegetables before they're ripe?"

"Good luck with that—" Hubward started to say. "I mean: I'll tell them. They like unripe vegetables. They're a different sort."

"I expect dragon fire does that to a person," Ninestone said. She toyed with the ring that hung on her necklace. It was cracked and tarnished. Probably from the night of the fire.

Hubward looked shocked. She knew? She knew the dragon had killed his team—made them un-dead anyway? Ninestone knew?

"Arp?" he blundered.

Ninestone turned to face him. "They were burned by the dragon fire, when the children were there. But they seem mostly unharmed."

She stepped forward. "Some say they caused it."

Ninestone stepped forward again; she was just a foot from Hubward now. He could smell her lavender soap. "Some say it's very *mysterious* to have foreign strangers show up in a place, and that very night, there is a magical accident."

"Eep?" he squeaked.

Ninestone leaned over, so her face was level with his. She stared into his eyes, searching. "Very. Strange."

"Ipe?"

"But nonsense," Ninestone said. She stood up straight. "Just a coincidence. And everyone knows they *saved* those children."

"Orp?" Hubward asked.

"Yes, utter nonsense," Ninestone assured him.

"Uuhp," he exhaled.

Ninestone lightly slapped his cheek, then spun away from him, twirling her skirt girlishly. She looked back at him and smiled over her shoulder, her eyes sparkling. "Take care of them Hubward, and don't fear. I won't tell anyone your secret."

"Yip," Hubward said.

"And Hubward! Don't burn our soup!"

CHAPTER 25: GULCHIMA SPLITS INTO TWO

IT WAS SUMMER, AND HE WAS LEAVING.

Gulchima found Uncle Rattbone on the dock near Lake Pepsid. The large briny lake was set back from Bayadev, in the hills above the fizz factory. The air smelled cleaner here, with a faint hint of apple blossoms, and for once, the sun was bright and shining. She could make out a small island in the center of the lake, where a few young men were laughing and bringing up nets filled with the small fish that the locals called *Suish-Swash*.

It was a happy scene, but not for her. Uncle Rattbone was leaving.

"Were you going to say goodbye?" Gulchima asked. She put down her bundle on the dock next to him. Her bandaged hand still bothered her. But it was healing.

Uncle Rattbone continued looking out at the lake. "Thought I'd make it easier on the both of us. Save you an argument." He gripped his war-axe, held it in his right hand as if testing its balance.

"I'm still running this Outfit." Gulchima said the words quietly. "You need my permission."

"Yeah," Uncle Rattbone said grimly. "That's why I was leaving without telling you. Between your disappearing act and

Isolde's screaming about the budgets every night at dinner, I'm almost happy to go to war. At least I'll finally get a decent night's rest."

"You don't have to go," Gulchima said. She kept her arms down at her side, her fists clenched. She stood next to Uncle Rattbone, but she couldn't look at him. She might start crying. Might beg him not to leave.

"As a matter of fact, I do," Uncle Rattbone said, with an edge in this voice. "I thought my killing days were behind me—ah, well." He rubbed his nose with the back of his hand.

"The war is over," Gulchima said firmly.

"Yeah but there's always another," Uncle Rattbone said. "Besides, I'm good at it. That doesn't mean I want to fight forever, but . . . we can use the money. Killing is what I'm good at, Gulch. That's what people pay me to do. What was I thinking, trying to be a guardian to you three kids? Trying to change who I was? I couldn't have done any worse, now could I?"

"You've been good—no, you've been great," Gulchima said. Her eyes were blurry with tears. "Better than we deserve. Don't leave."

"Am I? You and your sister won't talk, the Outfit is in shambles, and every other day your brother is almost burnt up or drowned. What good am I at this fill-in-fatherhood stuff? It's too hard! I guess when they were handing out brains, I was off training for war."

"It's not your fault!" Gulchima said. Her fingernails dug into her palms. Out on the lake a father and son were hugging each other, counting the fish they'd just caught. So, that was what a happy family looked like. "It's nobody's fault, really."

"Nobody? Huh." Uncle Rattbone stiffened. "Then *nobody* is the reason I gotta leave."

"So what? You're blaming me?"

"Gulch, I don't want to tell you that you're the reason, but yeah—you're the reason," Uncle Rattbone said. "You messed up. Epically."

"I did, huh. I really did mess up."

She felt better saying the words out loud. Not a whole lot better, but slightly better. Like one-minute-after-a-bee-sting better.

Gulchima started to giggle. "Oh, did I ever screw up. They're going to write songs about how bad I'm doing."

"They're going to write epic poems about it," Uncle Rattbone said, smiling. "I heard the locals talking about making a statue in your dishonor."

"Probably put it on a tapestry in the King's own fortress too," Gulchima said, giggling again. "Maybe hire a few dozen painters to record 'Gulchima's Greatest Flails and Fails'."

"How your father will laugh when we tell him!" Uncle Rattbone said, suddenly animated. "I mean to say, he'll feel bad about it, sure. But he'll laugh his head right off when he hears about the dragon. And who knows, Gulch? The King invited me to help fight the *Gutlanders*. The King himself! Who knows? Maybe all of this happened for a reason."

"Probably not," Gulchima said.

"Probably not," Uncle Rattbone agreed. "But it's just a small war. If I help out against the *Gutlanders*, maybe ransom a prince or two, we'll make enough to pay for the damage the dragon fire caused. Maybe Brunhild will follow me there, and you'll have a few months of peace."

"A few months?" Gulchima asked.

"Look, we're behind on this job. We won't break even now, with all the money we have to spend on repairs. We're lucky they didn't get rid of us, to be honest. Jaroo wanted to—"

"—And Lady Keyhide didn't," Gulchima added. She'd already had this argument with her sister.

"Yeah, she didn't," Uncle Rattbone said. "But I haven't seen her around much, have you? Some say she's been replaced, and Jaroo is the new Burgher-Meister."

"Maybe. But who knows? Since the night of the dragon fire, Lady Keyhide, Jaroo and the Fizz-Meister have been busy in that factory of theirs. They have it locked up tight. Hubward said nobody can enter."

They were both silent. White apple blossoms, carried by a breeze across the lake, floated down around them, covering her hair, and Uncle Rattbone's scale armor.

"I don't want to leave you either, to be honest," Uncle Rattbone said. His free hand covered hers, warm, softer than she expected, but with hard calluses just below his fingers. The hands of a skilled warrior. "Ah well," he said again, and this time the words were like weights on a fishing net, sinking her heart down, down, down to the bottom of the lake.

"What should I do now, Uncle Rattbone?" Gulchima whispered. "Nobody wants my help, and I've ruined everything. I don't want to do *nothing*. But what *should* I do?"

Uncle Rattbone pursed his lips. "Your back's against the wall. But sometimes, that's the best place to be."

He toyed with the new bones tied in his beard. These were larger and older than the ones he normally wore. Battle bones? "I'll tell you what your Dad would do: he'd find a way. He'd find a way to get rid of that dragon, by himself, and he'd be the hero. Your Dad was terrible with money once it came in, but he was always good at finding more of it. He just . . . he just wouldn't ever quit."

Gulchima started to speak, but Uncle Rattbone cut her off. "Look Gulch, here's what your Dad would say to you: So you screwed up! So what? That just makes your story more interesting. If you get rid of that dragon, people will believe in you again. If you do the impossible, you'll save the Outfit, you'll make the money, and then we can bribe the prison into letting us visit your parents. Maybe we find the right down-on-his-luck prison guard, and we bribe your parents right out of there. You know gold opens doors, right? Or did you forget the lesson of Rough Peter?"

"So just the impossible. Nothing else." Gulchima's tears had dried up. Uncle Rattbone was right.

"Gulch, you gotta find a way to move that dragon. And you gotta take care of the rest of the magical nimby stuff, to boot. And, you can't ask nobody for help."

"Nobody?"

"Well, Hubward of course. He's your best friend."

"My only friend," Gulchima said.

"Then that's how you know!" Uncle Rattbone said. "Your best friend isn't the one you like the best. Your best friend is the one that sticks by you, when everybody else walks away. Your best friend helps you wipe the ox poop off your boots."

He was right. She had Hubward. She'd burned all her other bridges, so to speak.

"You've been a good father to us," Gulchima said. "I understand. But I don't want you to leave."

"Yeah, and I don't *want* to go. But what's that got to do with anything? Ah well. It's better than being married to Brunhild. She sent me a letter, did you know that, an actual letter. Sayin' she changed her ways."

"Changed what? To a deeper shade of crazy?"

"I don't know, I'm thinking about it," Uncle Rattbone said. "We'll see how this side-war goes."

"Just be careful." Gulchima opened the sack she had

brought.

"I'm not worried about *Gutlanders*," Uncle Rattbone snorted. "I'm not about to be killed by men who put goat horns on their head and think it's scary."

"Good," Gulchima said. "But just in case, 'Luck for Journey'." She tossed thirty-seven kroons into the water. The seven lumpy coins disappeared into the clear water of the lake.

"Wastin' money," Uncle Rattbone muttered. "But I appreciate the gesture."

Gulchima gave him the sack of hard boiled eggs, the dark Muhu bread, the honey.

"Strength, for working," she said. Her hands trembled as she handed it over.

Uncle Rattbone looked at her, his face suddenly grim.

"Strength is needed," he said.

For both of us.

CHAPTER 26: HUBWARD HAS A PLAN FOR BUTTER

"WANT TO HEAR A JOKE?" Hubward asked nobody in particular. He adjusted the false eyebrows he'd glued on.

Gulchima grunted. She sat in front of a crackling fire, in the abandoned garden of a rundown cottage, halfway between Bayadev and the fizz factory.

It was several weeks after her Uncle Rattbone had left, and she was still grumpy.

"Nope," Gulchima said.

Gulchima stared into the fire, her head resting on her arms. Her burned hand seemed healed now, though she kept a small bandage on her finger. She was roasting her lunch on an oak branch and her eyes were red and rimmed with tears. Maybe it was from the smoke?

"What should you do with a green dragon?" Hubward asked, ignoring her.

Gulchima pressed her lips together. "I really don't know, Hubward," she said in a quiet voice.

"Wait until it gets ripe."

Gulchima's lips twitched. "Tell me another."

Hubward put down his spray bag of glacier water. Then he sat next to Gulchima by the fire, ignoring the afternoon heat. "Why is a dragon big and green and impossibly heavy?"

"I don't know: Why is a dragon big, and green, and impossibly heavy?"

"Because if it was small and yellow and easily squished, it would be a banana."

Gulchima laughed, then covered her mouth in surprise. "Wait. What's a banana?"

"A small fruit from the southern islands," Hubward said smoothly. "I saw them during one of my dragon flights in the war."

Gulchima wiped her eyes with one ash covered hand.

"Why do you have a bag sprayer full of glacier water?" Gulchima asked.

"I don't know: Why do I have a bag sprayer full of glacier water?"

"No. That's not a joke," Gulchima said, irritated. "I was just asking you. Are you working for Soltanabad now?"

Hubward smiled. "Oh no, I'm working for Ninestone actually. I'm using the glacier water to make butter popsicles."

"Butter popsicles, why?"

What kind of question was that? *Why wouldn't you want to make butter popsicles?*

"Because I tried bacon popsicles, and it didn't work."

Gulchima poked the fire. "Oh? Too crumbly?"

Hubward threw some dried grass into the flames. "Just a fundamental law of bacon: Bacon disappears faster than you can cook it."

Gulchima looked at him for the first time. "Explain."

"See, it's impossible to look at bacon without eating at least three pieces. So first I cook it: that's three pieces eaten. Then I wait for it to cool: that's another three pieces at least. I grind it up, three more. I forget what I was doing? That's three more. The wind blows . . . another three pieces. My pan only fits ten pieces, so—how many was that?"

"I think you have negative bacon," Gulchima said.

Good. She was being mean to him again, so that meant she was officially cheered up. Sometimes it was hard to be best friends with a grump.

"So what are you doing, exactly?" Hubward asked, pointing at the fire.

"Oh, you know. Just smashing these cute magical creatures with a hammer," Gulchima said. She pointed at the hundreds of small magical creatures swarming around the ruined cottage wall. "Of course, I burn the trangles first."

Hubward stood up. "Trangles! Here?"

Gulchima shrugged. "I couldn't find the salt quern. I was supposed to remove it, but the butcher keeps stealing it to salt the meat. So the only other thing in the contract I thought I couldn't screw up was: 'Remove Trangles from Gardens'."

The trangles were everywhere, spread across the garden like angry ants. They knew a lot of bad words, apparently, because they were constantly calling each other names. Horrible names. Even worse than the ones Hubward's brothers had taught him, before he was orphaned.

The trangles looked like gingerbread men cookies, except they were made of clay and animal poop and they were alive. They were only three inches high, and they had white buttons up the front of their bodies, but they used mouse droppings instead of icing. They were naked, not that it mattered, except for their sharp spiky hats constructed of broken snail shells and teacup shards.

The trangles looked innocent enough, until you saw their mean red eyes. And if you got in their way, they'd swarm and poke you with bent nails or glass. Sometimes they could kill you.

"Is it fun?" Hubward asked.

Gulchima took one of the trangles out of the fire. She had skewered it on her stick, like a marshmallow, and the trangle was burned black and hung limply. The stabbing would only annoy it. You couldn't kill trangles, unfortunately. You could only move them to another location. Covering them with honey and throwing them on an ants nest was the best solution.

"It was fun, at first," Gulchima said. "I grab one with these tongs I got from the blacksmith, then I put them into the fire. That's fun, but then they started squirming about, so I skewer them with the branch to keep them in place. After I roast them, they get hard as a rock, which I suppose they are, because they're just small clay monsters." She sniffed. "Then I smash them. With a hammer." She demonstrated.

"Remarkable," Hubward said, as a piece of shattered trangle hit him in the forehead.

"Yeah, but after I smash them into small pieces, they cool, go all soft and wiggly, and eventually come back together. It's not working! So now I just put them in a bag."

"No, I mean it's remarkable that one person could make so many bad decisions in a row," Hubward said. "You are doing, literally, everything wrong at once. Do you know *anything* about magic?"

Gulchima rounded on him, her hands on her hips. "Do *you* know anything about magic?"

"I do actually. I was in the war remember? I rode with dragons."

"Yes as a courier boy. You delivered packages."

"Not only that," Hubward said. He crossed his arms. "I know a little about magic."

"Yeah, you know how to spell it."

Now Hubward really was mad. He'd been trying to cheer her up. Girls! Once they decided to be grumpy there was nothing you could do about it.

"Actually, I used to do magic," Hubward said. *Whoops.* That had just slipped out.

"You never did. I don't believe you. Do some now," Gulchima said.

Hubward looked around. "Well I can't right now. I'm in disguise."

"Disguised as what, a boy with no eyebrows?"

Why not tell her? Hubward thought. They were best friends. He had to tell someone.

"I'm in disguise because I'm hunting the Sorcerer," Hubward said. "And I need your help."

"You can do magic. And you need my help? With the Sorcerer?" Gulchima snorted. "Is this part of that play you're writing? I've got enough problems without you joking around. Anyway, the Sorcerer's dead, so we can cross that one off the list."

Hubward cracked his neck. "Okay team, remove the threat!" he yelled.

Six blue-skinned strangers vaulted over the wall of the garden, then scooped up dozens of surprised trangles, before kicking and punching them into the air.

Hubward did a backflip, swung his spray bag onto his shoulders, and then squirted the swarming pile of trangles in mid-air with a spray of icy water.

The frozen trangles fell to the ground with a tinkle.

Gulchima looked at him, her mouth agape. "You can do backflips!" she said.

"And magic," Hubward reminded her.

"And magic!" Gulchima said. She closed her mouth. "But

now it makes sense. These were the people from the night of the fire, the same people who helped us in the fizz factory. But their skin. It's blue. That means they're . . . undead."

"Yeah for now," Hubward said, rolling his eyes. "This is my magical team, or hand, as we were known. We were assassins."

"For the Sorcerer or against?"

"Both. I was a *Gaunt* in the Sorcerer's army for a while. Then we switched sides and fought against the Sorcerer." He nodded to another group of trangles. They had organized themselves into straight lines and were marching at him, bent nails in their hands like swords. Kelsa, one of the undead girls in his team, scooped them up in her hat, then tossed the trangles into the air. Hubward sprayed them and they froze.

"A skinny little kid, doing magic," Gulchima shook her head. "I suppose you had to starve yourself."

Hubward shrugged. "Sometimes. But everybody does a little magic when things get seriously bad. Magic is another word for luck. Being a Gaunt, starving yourself, that was just a way to trick your body into having good luck. It makes every moment a crisis." Hubward sighed. "I was lucky, because candy made me thin. I'm allergic to it, so I swell up with water and can't keep anything down. But all that starving and magic, makes you really tired to be honest. I'd rather not do that again. Excuse me one second."

Hubward held both his arms up. Trumblebutt, the lone adult and former team leader, grabbed Hubward by his wrist and spun him around, just as several jagged teacup pieces slashed across the garden. They stuck in the wall behind him, vibrating slightly.

Hubward ran across the top of the wall, spraying the trangles with glacier water. The oldest boy in his team, Daaniel, swept the frozen trangles into the fire with a pine branch. They exploded.

"Anyway, not every team member did the same job," Hubward said from atop the wall. "I'm not much of a fighter. I was in charge of camouflage."

"But how—"

It was fun telling someone *everything*. You could interrupt them, just as they were starting to ask you a question. Maybe he wouldn't tell her *everything*-everything. Hubward would withhold one key piece of information. For instance, she couldn't know that his mother had been none other than—

"Oh and in addition to camouflage, I was the one that rescued the hostages," Hubward said. He leapt down off of the wall. "I'd go and sit with them, and it was pretty boring and they were nervous, so I'd . . . entertain them. When my team got turned undead, that's what I was doing. Guarding the hostages."

"That's why you're writing—"

—that play yes. I write plays now," Hubward said. "I suppose, in a way, the audience is my hostage. If I do it right, they can't leave no matter how terrible my work is."

"Oh, how's that?"

"Well you just leave a few things unanswered until the very end. Withhold one piece of information, and then distract the audience."

Just then Hertrude, the seventh member of the team, burst through the garden wall. She had a chicken stuck in her hair, and a loaf of bread on each foot. A small dog hung from her left arm, gnawing and growling. She spoke quickly, telling him the bad news. "PumpkinpumkinP'mkin! Pumppumppumpity, pumpkin!"

"Pumpkin?" asked the lone adult, Trumblebutt, in his dry croaking voice.

"Uh oh," Hubward said "We have a *bog* problem. Two *bog* problems actually."

"A *bog* problem?" Gulchima asked.

"Yeah, like a big problem, but harder to get out of."

"What problem?" Gulchima asked.

"One, my butter popsicles are melting."

Gulchima threw a frozen trangle at him. "And two?"

Hubward looked worried. "And two: They say the Sorcerer is coming. Right. Now."

CHAPTER 27: GULCHIMA FINDS THE SORCERER AND EVERYTHING

BUT IT WASN'T TWO PROBLEMS, it was four that came walking down the path from the fizz factory towards Gulchima's hiding place. First came Lady Keyhide and the Fizz-Meister. Two other people followed behind them.

"Which one is it?" Gulchima asked. "Is one of them the Sorcerer?"

She peered at the figures, barely visible in the mist from the geysers. As if her life wasn't complicated enough, with Uncle Rattbone gone, and the company failing, and her sister mad at her. Now this.

Still, if there ever was a valid excuse to cancel a bad construction contract, an all-powerful necromancer of unspeakable evil would probably do the trick. But Gulchima would have to prove the Sorcerer was actually here. Without being killed. Or turned into a toad. Or whatever.

"Hubward, ask them which one is the Sorcerer," she whispered.

"Can any of you talk?" Hubward asked his undead team. They seemed frozen in place. Now they were acting like the undead Gulchima had always heard about, just shuffling around, bumping into walls, staring at the ground vaguely. A minute ago they had been flying through the air, like magical assassins.

"The Sorcerer must be interfering with them," Hubward explained.

He snapped his fingers. "Do you have any pumpkin?"

"Hmm let me check in my pocket," Gulchima said "Nope, turns out I don't have a giant orange vegetable that won't grow for another month in my pocket. It's summer, what are you talking about?"

"Pumpkins help the undead to come back to life, temporarily," Hubward said quietly. "Everybody thinks they eat brains, but that's mostly not true."

Gulchima felt very cold. She turned to find one of the undead, breathing on the back of her neck. She poked it in the eye with a trembling finger, and it went *squish*. "Mostly?"

"Sometimes, the undead just get confused and think your head is a jack-o-lantern or something. So they might try to eat your brains a little." He patted Gulchima on the back, and shooed away his undead team. "But don't worry. They only enjoy eating pumpkin."

That actually made a bit of sense, Gulchima thought. She watched as Lady Keyhide, the Fizz-Meister and the other two figures approached. They were all dressed in red cloaks of varying shades, and each wore golden metal bracelets up and down their arms.

She heard a voice speak up. "Well, actually, Lady Keyhide, apparently, the problem cannot be reduced to such simple terms. Complications are complicated, naturally."

That many commas in one sentence? It had to be Jaroo.

"That's Jaroo!" Gulchima said. "So the Fizz-Meister, Lady Keyhide, Jaroo . . . who's the fourth person?"

Hubward peered at them. The last figure laughed gaily. "Very believable Jaroo."

"Ninestone," Hubward whispered. He frowned. "So one of those four is the Sorcerer."

Gulchima looked at the stumbling undead behind them. "Are you sure you can trust the information from your . . . team?"

"Yeah that just proves my point," Hubward replied. "Why, all of a sudden, are they confused? The Sorcerer caused it. Why did the dragon emit fire? The Sorcerer caused it. Why is the magic so strong at Bayadev? The Sorcerer *caused* it."

He slid down behind the garden wall as the four figures passed. Gulchima did the same.

"The Sorcerer works at the factory," Hubward whispered. "An old friend, Man-of-Arms, told me the same thing."

"Then it's the Fizz-Meister?" Gulchima asked. She felt a pinch on her leg as a fly bit her.

"I think so," Hubward said. But he seemed unsure.

"What about Ninestone?" Gulchima asked.

She'd seen Ninestone do magic to save Tormo, and Ninestone worked at the factory. But then again, she'd just seen Hubward use magic, or at least, a cool backflip with his magical team. And he wasn't the Sorcerer was he?

Hubward shook his head. "I scanned her, checked her out, with a Seer-Slip." Noticing Gulchima's confused stare, he added, "It's a cloth that lets you see magic. Jaroo's guards wear them all the time . . . Anyway, it's not her. My Seer-Slip would have detected something."

"Did you scan Jaroo?"

"Partially, but I never got the chance to finish. I never scanned the Fizz-Meister either. And come to think of it, Lady Keyhide never got scanned either. I thought I was charmed by her, and I forgot to do it, but I wonder . . . ."

"Then go get your Seer-Slip, and scan those three,"

Gulchima said impatiently.

"Can't. I lost it when I lost my eyebrows."

"Typical."

"Hey, there were a lot of people I did scan. You, for instance."

"Me?" Gulchima asked. She slapped at another fly bite.

"Yeah: A mysterious stranger shows up and a dragon dies. It could have been you or Rattbone, or anybody on your boat. It could have been your Not-Uncle Roog."

That was a good point too. Gulchima reached out and straightened one of Hubward's false eyebrows. "Then what are we going to do?"

"Gulch, we found it! The solution to both of our problems," Hubward said suddenly.

She noticed he still had a smudge of fairy poo behind his ears. Did he ever wash?

Hubward said, "If we defeat the Sorcerer, and we stay best friends, then the magic will disappear, your contract will be easy, and I'll avenge my team's deaths. That's a Win-Win-Win-Win-Win-Win situation, Gulch!"

"That's one 'win' too many," Gulchima said. "And I don't remember agreeing on that nickname with you, *Hub*."

Hubward smiled. "Listen Gulch. All we have to do is find the Sorcerer's secret hideout. I already checked the fizz factory, so it's not there."

He fiddled with one of his fake eyebrows, moving it up and down. "Aha! Hertrude mentioned something about going *inside* the dragon. If the Sorcerer wants us to stay away from the dragon, then that's exactly where we *should* go. Maybe we'll find proof, or a secret weapon . . . ."

He was right about that too. Gulchima sighed. As usual, the solution to her problems lay in a dark, smelly, enclosed place, filled with magic and dread, or at best, some rotting carcasses.

"Yeah, but we can't cut into it. Unless there's a secret door," Gulchima said.

"Not secret. But yeah there's a door." Hubward tapped his mouth.

"Nope," Gulchima said. "No way."

Hubward smiled. "Once we swim down to the bottom of the river, and get by the deadly fire, and bypass the sharp teeth, the rest should be easy. All we have to do is crawl in through the dragon's mouth."

"That's all?" Gulchima said. Her heart thudded in her chest. *Just that horrible impossible thing?*

Gulchima bit her thumbnail, trying to think of a way out of this. There was no way she was going.

But then, four trangles jumped up and bit the rest of her fingers. She shook her hand trying to get them off.

"Well actually, no," Hubward said. "We forgot about the trangles." He pointed at her feet.

Gulchima's legs were covered with a swarm of trangles.

They were carrying sharp twigs and nails and pieces of tea cups. And they were mad.

As usual.

CHAPTER 28: SOMEBODY IS PLANNING SOMETHING

The Collected Lies of Gulchima Brixby (A FINAL Entry):

> Everything is going to plan. Gulchima was drawn to Bayadev, and she holds the information we seek. She's isolated, alone, mopey: She's ready for our big finale. With Rattbone out of the way, we can't be stopped.
>
> Our little ruse has tricked the boy and his seven spies too. Now Gulchima will come to us. Our power will return, and we can be born. Back into time, back into place.
>
> Gulchima will enter the dragon gateway. And **she will be ours.**
>
> —A Voice Out Of Time

CHAPTER 29: GULCHIMA MEETS THE POTIONS MASTER

THEY TOOK CARE OF THE TRANGLES FIRST, rounding them up and then freezing them before placing the creatures in bottles. Hubward's team was no longer a help, since the run-in with the Sorcerer had taken away their ability to think clearly. He left them in the garden of the abandoned cottage, with clear instructions that they were to hide, and not dig for pumpkins.

It was a tiring evening. The sun had started to set as Gulchima and Hubward sealed the last frozen trangle piece into the last empty fizz bottle, and then tossed it into Lake Pepsid. The salty lake water would melt away the ice eventually, but it would also coat the bottles, trapping the trangles so they could neither escape nor bond back together.

Gulchima's lower back was stiff from rowing around the lake. But now that the trangles were defeated, she realized what was next.

Next on the list, was, oh, let's see. Yes. There it was.

Next was the dragon.

* * *

They walked down to find Jaroo there, alone, concentrating on the dragon and muttering in some strange language. In one hand, he held up a small amber ball, which he waved in front of him in a repeating figure-eight pattern. In the other hand, he held a small velvet-covered book.

Jaroo was oblivious to their presence. Gulchima thought he looked tired, especially around the eyes, where he had applied black kohl markings, like makeup. He wore a ridiculous sausage-shaped headpiece, bright red with gold piping. It looked like it would blow off if a butterfly sneezed.

"Hey Jaroo! Trying to bring the dragon back to life?" Gulchima asked, her voice loud and accusing.

Jaroo was startled. He stepped into a mud puddle, soaking his open toed sandals. She noticed he had painted his toenails red and gold, and that he wore several gold bracelets on each wrist. Jaroo quickly hid the amber ball underneath his robe.

"Ah the savior!" Jaroo said with a smirk. "And look, she's brought a pet orphan." He scowled at them both.

"What were you doing just then?" Hubward asked. "What was that amber ball?"

Jaroo's scowl deepened. He touched his black eye makeup. "That's fizz factory business," he said. "And that's all I'll say." He turned to Gulchima. "Shouldn't you be working? Or have you come to tell me you're giving up?"

"I'm here to measure the dragon," Gulchima lied. "We're going to get rid of it next week, using some of Roog's explosives. Then I'm going to save the family business. Then, after that, I'm going to tell Lady Keyhide to fire you, and hire Hubward instead. Now get out of the way. I'm doing this for my family."

She pushed past him.

"Oh you're 'doing it for your family'," Jaroo said. He stuck out his lower lip. "Well, whoopidy-doo-da for you. You're doing it 'for your family', aren't you so noble, and so deserving of a second, third, fourth, fifth, and sixth chance to get it right?" He smiled down at her. "But eventually, you'll run out of chances. And then, I'll take your other houseboat and be rid of you pests."

"What is your problem?" Hubward yelled. "Don't you want that dragon gone? Seems like you *want* us to fail."

"Oh and here's the inspiring orphan, who just wants to find a family to love him," Jaroo wiped away a fake tear. He looked around, pretending to be shocked. "Oh. Wait. Looks like there's no one interested. I suppose you're all alone Hubward. Again."

Gulchima stalked over to Jaroo, and pointed her fist right in his face. "Why don't *you* quit? Uncle Rattbone said you were a bad plumber. But you're a worse leader."

"Rattbeard said that?" Jaroo chuckled. "Yes. A shame he had to run off isn't it. I suppose he ran away 'for his family' too. And your parents . . . are they in jail 'for your family', Gulch? Oh don't worry. Soon you will join them. You can have a nice family reunion. In prison."

"I guess we'll see you there," Gulchima replied coolly. "You should hope we don't tell Lady Keyhide about the fizz-water you've been stealing."

This was just a rumor. But judging from Jaroo's face, it was true.

Jaroo flapped his arms. His face grew red, and he adjusted the golden bracelets he wore. "You're just lucky Lady Keyhide is enamored with you—" A horn sounded, echoing down the canyon from the fizz factory.

Jaroo straightened up. "Already?" He blew out a puff of bad breath, then spun, and stalked away. "Good luck on your impossible quest, you *whiffle-waffles*."

Gulchima watched him walk away. "Was he doing . . .

magic?"

"I'm not sure," Hubward said. "Is he really stealing—"

Then, a small voice interrupted them.

"Emm. 'Scuse me Gulch . . . Is the bad-man gone?"

The words came from the dragon.

* * *

A figure slid off of the dragon. It was Novvy, her four-year-old brother. What was he doing here?

"Emm. I want to help with the dragon removal stuff," Novvy said.

"Novvy, it's too dangerous for you," Gulchima said. Why him of all people?

"Emmm, but I get a vote right?"

"What?"

"Isolde said, I was part owner," Novvy said. He squinted his eyes, as if trying to remember how to spell a difficult word. "Because I'm a new kid, and Rattbone is gone. So I get a vote. She had me sign the papers. Now I can say butt."

"Sign what papers?" Gulchima asked.

"The papers . . . emmm, to get rid of the contract," Novvy said. "The papers to sell one of our houseboats to Jaroo, and put this stinky butt place behind us. She said those words, so I'm allowed to say *butt.* Oh, and I was to get some candy, if I signed it. Butt-butt-bottom-butt."

"You signed it," Gulchima said. It was not a question.

"She said with the two of us signing, you would be our-elephant," Novvy said.

"Irrelevant?" Gulchima asked.

Novvy whispered to her: "It means you don't matter."

"I know what it means!" Gulchima snapped at him.

So that's why Isolde was avoiding her. She was going to

cancel the contract by selling one of the houseboats. And since she had Novvy's signature, she probably could do it. Now Jaroo's comment about getting the houseboat made sense. That seemed like a terrible deal.

"So can I help? To get rid of the dragon. Pull-lease? I'll tear up the paper Isolde had me sign. I know where she hides that, next to her kissy letters from Tiktok."

Hubward said, "Dragon? No we said we're going to get rid of the *wagon*."

Novvy smiled. "Nope. I haven't been alive long enough to forget things. You're going to move the dragon."

"What were you doing out here anyway?" Gulchima asked.

"Potions," Novvy said. "I make potions then dump them on the dragon to see what happens." He pointed at a puddle of soap suds. "This one made the dragon wet."

"You can't come," Gulchima said. She crossed her arms.

"I am," Novvy insisted. "Tormo got burned, and everybody gives him candy. Now he can grow a beard, and the beard glows in the dark, and he has a cool scar. I want that too. I want candy."

"It's too dangerous. We're going inside the dragon," Hubward said. "Past the terrible fire, into the depths, over the sharp teeth . . . ."

"Hubward, that's not going to work," Gulchima exclaimed. "He doesn't get scared."

"Inside!" Novvy jumped for joy. "I've always wanted to get eaten!"

"Isn't that scary?" Hubward asked.

"Nope."

"Whaaat, iff I taaaalk, like thisss?" Hubward asked.

"Nope."

Gulchima thought this bad plan was suddenly getting

worse. But if Novvy came with them, he would tear up the paper he signed. And she couldn't let Isolde give away their houseboats. The Outfit would be ruined. What choice did she have?

"Okay Novvy you can come, but under one condition: You're not allowed to get hurt."

Novvy shook his head.

"Not hurt Gulch, never hurt," Novvy said. "I just want to get eaten by the dragon."

CHAPTER 30: GULCHIMA ENTERS THE DRAGON

GETTING RID OF THE DRAGON had seemed like a good idea to Gulchima. But that had been weeks ago, in the full sunlight, with her uncle standing next to her, and the apple blossoms falling gently around them.

Now, adrift on the dark steaming river, it seemed like certain death.

They were just above the dead dragon. And it was still breathing fire.

Flames erupted, spraying boiling water and steam up over the side of their skin boat. It was dark and moonless, and except for the occasional green dragon fire flame, Gulchima could not see Hubward or Novvy in the boat next to her. The boat fought to stay in place in the scalding waters above the dragon's head.

"Did you say certain *depth*?" Hubward joked. He struggled with the oars, attempting to keep the boat in place. But the river pushed them toward the pocket of boiling water.

"No, certain *death*," Gulchima said. "That's what this plan is. Certain death. Why are we doing this again?"

"One felled swoop!" Hubward yelled. "If we can surprise and capture the Sorcerer, our problems will be over. Your magic problem will disappear, and I'll force the Sorcerer to restore my team back to life."

"Okay!" Gulchima said, yelling to be heard above the hiss. She pulled Novvy away from the side of the boat just as a plume of steam shot up like a geyser. "But how exactly are you going to trap the Sorcerer? Do you have some magical assassin's weapon?"

"Yeah sort of," Hubward said. In the flash of flame she could see him patting his rucksack. "Except it's not magical, and it's made of soft, yellow, cake."

Well that certainly made no sense whatsoever. Just like this plan.

"How do we get down?" Novvy asked. "Without getting boiled like an egg."

"We'll just use the ice spray," Hubward said, pointing at his spray bag. They had refilled it before getting in the boat. "That will weigh us down."

"Hubward! Ice floats, it doesn't sink."

Gulchima grabbed the anchor. She looked at Novvy, his face painted green by the sickly dragon fire. "We'll all go down together. I'll hold the anchor, then Novvy, then Hubward. We'll swim down, and scout out the situation. Then we'll meet back on the boat and come up with a plan. If you get in trouble, find the rope, and pull yourself back up to the boat. Okay?"

They all agreed.

Back into the dark, Gulchima thought. At least she had dragon fire from a dead dragon this time. That was comforting. Still, it would be better than what had really happened those five years she'd been missing. At least she wouldn't be alone.

They locked arms and stood, almost flipping their small boat over. Gulchima counted to three, then jumped off the boat, with Novvy and Hubward. In mid-air, Gulchima tossed the anchor toward the back of the dragon's head, so they wouldn't hit the dragon fire. She'd timed it just right, and the anchor pulled them down, into the depths.

* * *

The dead dragon emitted an almost continuous plume of fire, in colors ranging from bluish black, to a pale red. The fire warmed the water, and quite a few animals had taken up residence nearby to enjoy it. It was like swimming in a large bath. Apparently only the very strong green bursts of flame came to the surface. It was as if fire was slowly draining from the creature.

The anchor landed in the silt on the side of the dragon's mouth, just below its jawline. She could see the mouth lolled open, the tongue unfurled, the giant head bobbing slightly in the river's current. She stared, expecting the slit of yellow eyes to open, but the dragon really was dead. And luckily, fire emitted from a dragon's nostrils, not its mouth.

The teeth were as long as her body, gleaming white even in the murky water. And the tongue that lay inside was covered with rough scales.

Gulchima fought a moment of panic, as her lungs started to complain. She felt a pressure in her chest. Okay, she'd scouted it out. No need to rush into things. They'd climb back up the rope and come up with a plan. She tugged at Novvy's hand.

But Novvy pushed away from her, and started to pull himself into the dragon's mouth. She yelled, unthinkingly, but all that came out was a *blurp* of air. Novvy did not look back.

Hubward followed Novvy into the dragon. He paused, hand resting on the dragon's tooth, and then turned to look at her, blowing out bubbles from his chipmunk-like cheeks in an effort to communicate. Then he too entered the dragon.

Now what?

The dragon's jaws moved in the water, but the creature was dead, and Gulchima could see deep inside its mouth there was a shimmering circle, like a small coin flickering in the torch light. She had no real choice, she had to follow Novvy and Hubward.

Gulchima pulled herself past the row of sharp unbroken teeth, her heart hammering in her chest. That was where she had to go. *She had to.*

Gulchima swam deeper into the dragon.

As she swam toward it, the coin she had noticed grew larger, and the water grew cold, impossibly cold, making her arms and legs sluggish, her eyes burn.

At last she came to the shimmering top of a pool of water. A glowing light zigged across it, as if beckoning her. Gulchima kicked in the water, shoving herself forward, and then, she burst through the top of the water and took a gasping breath, eyes wide open.

Gulchima had entered the dragon.

And it was not at all the way it should have been.

CHAPTER 31: GULCHIMA ENCOUNTERS STRANGE GRAVITIES

"STRANGE GRAVITIES INDEED," Hubward said.

They were standing in a dark cavern which stretched miles in all directions. It could not possibly be the inside of the dragon's mouth, and yet behind her, Gulchima could see the real world, stretched out in the pool of water, the dragon's teeth impossibly long and wide, lit by the rainbow flicker of flame.

Novvy's cough echoed around them. He'd swallowed a lot of water on the swim here, but was otherwise unharmed.

"The gravity debt must warp this place," Hubward said. "Make it seem bigger."

Gulchima sighed. A debt to gravity, and a dribbling flame. What ridiculous things dragons were. Now she was expected to believe that the dragon had a mouth ten miles wide?

The floor was slightly soft, like half-thawed ice, yet it rasped at her boots like the tongue of a cat. An icy cat tongue? Gulchima decided she must be standing on a dragon's tongue inside of its mouth. Her imagination wasn't this good.

"Finally! Eaten by a dragon," Novvy said. He looked around. "But where's its guts? Where's the gold?"

"And how are we seeing?" Hubward asked. The cavern was illuminated, but they couldn't tell where the light was coming from.

"And where do we go?" Gulchima asked. But she already suspected where. They had to go deeper into the dragon.

"Okay, let's figure out what we have to work with," Gulchima said.

Hubward opened his rucksack and took out a fishing net, and a platter with a half-smashed soft yellow cake. He slung on his spray bag, which sloshed with glacier water.

"I'm fortified," Hubward said. "What did you bring?"

Novvy held out a small potion bottle. "I've got this soap."

"So that's cake, soap, and fishing equipment," Gulchima said. "Hmmm, what else would we need to capture the most powerful magician in Baltica? I can't think of even one thing."

Hubward crossed his arms. "And you Gulch? What did you bring?"

She had a metal spear, a woodsman-axe, roofers tar, food and water, a jar of Quite Honorable Taciturn's melting powder, a packet of Uncle Roog's explosive fire medicine, and a dozen other things . . . in her backpack on the boat. She'd planned on returning to the boat after scouting things out. She'd planned on planning.

"I've got a knife, some ironstem rope, and a whole bucketful of surprise," Gulchima said. "Now where do we go?"

In the distance, she saw a flash of a maroon robe. A figure spun away from them, as if surprised.

"The Sorcerer!" Hubward yelled.

He took out his fishing net, and held the yellow cake in front of him like a shield. "Let's go!"

"That seems like a trap," Gulchima said. "We shouldn't split—"

But Hubward had already started running after the figure. Away and into the dark, like a dog chasing a skunk-bat. And with just as much luck of succeeding.

"Okay, we'll split up then," Gulchima yelled after him. The *foozle*. She turned to Novvy. "I want you to stay near me," she said. She held out her rope. "Do I have to tie you up?"

Novvy yawned, held up his arms. "Pickyback?"

Gulchima crouched down, so that Novvy could climb onto her back. A piggyback ride would be the easiest way to keep track of him. And her legs were strong.

She walked for a long time, but when Gulchima turned around to check her progress, they were only a few feet from the pool at the dragon's mouth. How could that be?

Simple. Magic had bad timing. It was too exciting when you didn't want it to be, but the rest of the time it was really dull.

Strange gravities must warp distance, Gulchima thought. And maybe, time too. Gulchima wondered if this was what happened to her during the five years she had gone missing. She remembered the sound of it, the dripping water, the waiting. It hadn't felt like five years for her. But it had felt like a few months at least. And what had she eaten? And what had she seen? Gulchima remembered little, except for the last part. But she'd sworn never to speak of that.

She'd been warned what would happen if she did.

They came at last to a small room. Which was interesting, because the previous second Gulchima was in the open cavern, walking across the squishy tongue. And now, she was in a small room, with a lit fire in the fireplace, and a single high-backed chair with a velvet seat. She didn't remember walking through the door, and Novvy had been snoozing, so she couldn't ask him.

The room was sparsely furnished, with only the chair and a scarred work table. A woman's hairbrush lay on the table, the hair white or light blond. Next to it, lay over a hundred small metal links, some cracked, others gleaming. Tools were scattered around the metal links, as if they were being repaired. On the velvet seat of the chair was a large water-stained book.

The title was "The Collected Lies of Gulchima Brixby".

"Hey, that's your name," Novvy said from just over her shoulder.

Gulchima snorted. "What kind of *mumblecrust* would write a book about me?"

"Lemme down," Novvy said, squirming against her. "There could be candy in here, or clues."

She knelt down and Novvy jumped off her back.

Clues? Clues about what? She picked up the hairbrush, examining the thin whitish hair wrapped around the bristles. What kind of nimby magic was this?

A hairbrush and a fire? A workshop to repair metal? This was the Sorcerer's secret lair? She expected bubbling inky-black cauldrons, and horrific things floating in jars. Maybe a skeleton or two, to give the place the right ambiance.

And if there was a book with her name on it, she certainly wouldn't open it. That's what the magic *wanted* her to do. What if, instead, she threw the chair into the fireplace, and stole some of the metal pieces. Wouldn't *magic* be surprised about that?

But no, that would give away that she had visited this place.

Gulchima touched one of the metal links on the table, and it gave her a shock, like when she walked across a bearskin rug. Then it crumbled to dust.

"That's weird," Gulchima muttered.

"What's weird? Novvy asked. There was a hissing sound.

Gulchima looked up and saw that Novvy had lifted up his tunic and was peeing into the fire. She looked away.

"Sorry, I had to go," Novvy said. The hissing of the fire

grew louder. "What did you think was weird?"

"What's weird, is this whole place, really," Gulchima said. She bit her lip. "But what are these metal links? They look like the bracelets Jaroo was wearing. The bracelets all four of them were wearing. Jaroo, Ninestone, the Fizz-Meister and . . ." She glanced at the hairbrush, and the white hair it contained. "And Lady Keyhide!"

Lady Keyhide was the Sorcerer!

The hairbrush with the white hair had to be hers. And the room seemed like her style. Outdated, red, expensive furniture. And Hubward had said he'd never scanned her.

It was so obvious.

Gulchima couldn't believe she'd been working with the Sorcerer. No wonder Bayadev was infested with magic! The person running the burgh was the Sorcerer.

"Emm Gulch. I think I found something else that's weird," Novvy said, almost yelling to be heard over the hissing of the fire.

"Are you decent?" Gulchima asked, without looking over at him.

"Emmm, yeah but . . . I think I found . . . It."

Gulchima looked up.

At first it looked like a puff of dark smoke had risen up from the fire and just hung around Novvy.

Then she saw its eyes.

A shadowy snake had wound its way around Novvy. Its eyes burned like coals in a fire, but the snake's body was partly invisible, like it was a cloud of ash.

It was magic, but something about the eyes told her this magic was smart.

The snake squeezed tighter.

Novvy whimpered. His clothes had started to smoke, and

brown scorch marks appeared across his chest. "Hot!" Novvy cried.

The snake smiled at her, baring its fangs.

"At last, we meet the famous Gulchima Brixsssby," the shadowy snake hissed. "Have a seat Gulchima. We've been expecting you."

"Let him go!" Gulchima demanded.

"We shall," the snake said, narrowing its glowing eyes. "But first, we want to asssk you for one sssmall favor."

The snake wound tighter around Novvy, then snapped at Novvy's left hand. This time, he screamed out in pain.

Gulchima saw his blood dripping onto the grating near the fireplace. It bubbled from the heat.

The ring finger on Novvy's left hand was missing. The snake had bitten it off!

"Let him go," Gulchima pleaded.

The snake spoke in a cold, taunting voice:

"Just one small favor Gulchima. That is all we ask."

CHAPTER 32: THE COLLECTED LIES . . .

THE ROOM SMELLED LIKE BLOOD.

"Just tell us what we want to know," the snake said. "He has nine more fingers you know. Or should we start with his toes?"

Novvy grew pale. He looked down at his hand. "Got lots of fingers . . . fingers grow back." He passed out.

"I don't even know who you are," Gulchima said in a loud voice. She was stalling. "You didn't have to hurt him, you what are you? Are you the Sorcerer?"

"We sometimes work for her," the snake said. "You may call us Ash, for we are the Ash of Empires. But truly, we are the Zeitgeist."

For her? The Sorcerer was a woman!

Ash flicked its tail, and opened the book to a blank page near the back. Gulchima's words were written there. "*I don't even know who you are . . . .*"

"Another lie!" Ash accused. "You know who we are. Out of place, out of time." It slammed the book shut. "And time is short. You must tell us what you saw," Ash said.

"What?"

Ash shook Novvy's unconscious body like a rattle, lifting him into the air. "You must tell us what really happened during those five years you were missing! You must come into the belly of the beast, and tell us there, so that no others can hear it. You mussst!"

The lie came easily to her lips. "Okay I'll tell you what really happened: There was this dirty sewing needle, I mean, it was gross. So I got infected by it, caught some disease, coughed all over everybody, and then we all fell asleep for five years. Everybody had a good sleeping, I mean, a beauty of a sleep. And when I woke up, everything was taken care of: the dragon was dead, the witch was watered, and they had this awesome rose garden maze just outside my window—"

Ash glowered at her. "Another lie . . . Here let us help you to decide."

The wall behind her disappeared. Gulchima was standing at the edge of the pool, near the entrance to the dragon. The comfortable room was still there in front of her. The book with her name on it was on the chair. And Ash was still wrapped around her unconscious brother.

But Gulchima's back felt warm.

In the light of the dragon flame, Ash looked thinner, less menacing. She could hear the rumbling, feel the heat as the fire erupted from the dragon. It wasn't just any fire. This was full-on bright-white dragon flame. The pool behind her started to boil. The air temperature jumped, sending sweat down her back.

Novvy moaned, then started to cough. The wet air had a chemical taste to it, like geyser smoke. It was getting hard to breathe.

"I can keep this up all day," Ash said. Its flaming eyes flashed at her. "So tell me what you really know and I'll turn off the fire. Give me what I want and your brother will live!"

Gulchima's eyes burned. She started to gag. She would do it. She would tell Ash what it wanted. No matter the warning, no matter her oath. She had to save her brother. She opened her mouth to speak, but she started to cough. Gulchima breathed in deeply. She had to tell Ash. She had to save—

"Hey, you old campfire!" said a voice.

Gulchima started to laugh and cough at the same time.

That would be Hubward. It had to be.

Nobody else would make such a stupid joke.

CHAPTER 33: HUBWARD SAVES THE NIGHT

AT THE SIGHT OF NOVVY'S BLOODY HAND, Hubward grew incredibly angry.

The phantom he'd been chasing had gone, so he'd returned to the pool where he'd started. Then he saw Novvy, and Gulchima's tense showdown with the ash creature, and the blood.

The blood was the problem.

Torturing hostages was against the rules. Hubward understood how hostage situations worked. He had been in charge of rescuing hostages, as part of his duties with the magical assassin team, or hand, as they were known.

He understood of course, that you sometimes had to kidnap a bad guy to rescue other people, and to make sure the other side knew you were really serious, you occasionally had to hold a knife to their throats, or make a threat. But then, one side or the other would drop their weapons, or poof into a cloud of magic, or something. That was how the game was played.

But, to actually go and chop off a finger! That was . . . well, that was just wrong.

Hubward was so, very, angry. He started to sweat, and naturally, his sweating would lead to weight loss. And weight loss would lead to magic, or its younger cousin: luck.

"Hey, you old campfire!" Hubward yelled. "Get away from my two best friends."

Hubward knew that the element of surprise was pretty useless on its own. His net, covered with the yellow cakey substance he'd found in the fizz factory, was already in the air, headed for the ash monster.

He'd meant to startle it, and it had worked.

But by yelling the insult, he'd also let Ash know he was there. That was stupid. Why had he given away his tactical advantage like that?

Ash flicked a fire ball at his net, and it *whoomphed* into flame mid-air. The cakey stuff absorbed the magical flame easily, no surprise there. But he hadn't covered the net entirely, and the exposed strands burned in an instant.

His net fell apart.

Hubward snapped his fingers. "Oh, right. Magical fire. Creature of ash. Makes sense."

Ash started to laugh, which was good. That gave Hubward time to come up with another plan. Evil creatures of the shadows were known to laugh for inappropriate amounts of time. *If they would just kill you immediately, they wouldn't have to hide in the shadows so much.*

But without the net . . . .

"Hubward, pee on the fire!" Gulchima yelled, through a coughing fit.

"But I don't have to go!" Hubward said. Then he understood what she really meant.

The air was hot and smoggy, and he had a hard time seeing. But the stupid ash creature had glowing eyes, so that made it easy. That was another problem with evil creatures of the shadows. If they were trying to hide, why wouldn't they cover up their glowing eyes?

Hubward grabbed the sprayer from his spray bag. He squirted at Ash's glowing eyes, an easy target.

Ash screamed in pain, which Hubward thought was a good sign. It dropped Novvy, then whirled away into the darkness.

The place where he'd hit Ash formed a small frozen cocoon around Novvy—like half an eggshell—supporting him. Hubward had sprayed a bit too much, and a small ice block had started to form beneath Novvy, on the dragon's tongue. Novvy's tunic was coated with ice too, giving him a silvery appearance. But he was still alive.

One of Ash's eyes dropped to the ground, and skittered across the floor toward him. Hubward picked it up, then, on instinct, rolled to his right. The spot where he had stood, was a smoking crater.

Now Hubward was sure the dragon wasn't alive. It would have felt that on its tongue, and would have come to life at this worst possible time.

But the dragon was dead. And Ash was—

It charged at him, fangs raised. Hubward shot another spray of glacier water, and it cut through Ash's neck with a hiss. It screamed again, but looped around him, slashing with its tail. Another line of fire came at him, and he had to backflip to get out of the way.

"He can do backflipsss!" Ash exclaimed. "A chubby boy like that?"

"I'm very limber," Hubward said, defensively.

But Hubward was going to get hit eventually. He had to turn down the steam so he could see better. But how?

"Gulchima, grab Novvy!" he yelled. Novvy was still lying on his icy eggshell.

Gulchima started to crawl forward. The steam from the

boiling pool was thickest near her, and much hotter than any sauna Hubward had ever been in. He had to turn down the heat. But how? Should he swim out and spray the dragon in the nose?

If he tried that, he'd be boiled like an egg. No there had to be a secret switch somewhere . . . .

The fire in the fireplace roared, flames licking out, burning the wooden mantelpiece. The flames almost hit the book that sat on the chair, and he had a second to read what it said. The book had Gulchima's name on it!

He reached out to grab the book, but his hand passed right through it. A simple enough *untouchable* spell, but Hubward had too much sausage in his system to perform the counter spell.

Ash rushed at him.

Hubward pretended to aim at it, but at the last second, he dove and fired his glacier water into the fireplace. The fire sputtered, the flames drooped, but it did not go out.

Ash swam above him, slowed, then looped back to face him. It glared with its one remaining eye, then disappeared into the dark of the dragon's throat.

The dragon flame had gone down too, the color shifting from bright white to a dark green. The pool had stopped bubbling, but it was still steaming. Gulchima gasped in a lungful of air.

"We can go and finish it off," Hubward said.

"We have to leave, now," Gulchima said.

"No!" Hubward yelled. "We have to kill this creature. This might be the Sorcerer. This might be the thing that killed my family!"

"Your who?"

Hubward grimaced. "My team . . . the magical team of assassins . . . That's my family. That's my dad, and my three brothers and three sisters. I thought the dragon killed them, but maybe it was this ash creature."

"And your mom . . . ."

"She's just regular dead," Hubward said. He sighed. "Not undead like the rest of my family. I have to go chase down Ash and defeat it. For once, I won't be just camouflage, I'll be the hero. I can avenge my family. Maybe cure them. You go ahead, save Novvy."

"No," Gulchima said, she put her hands on her hips. "That's what it wants. It wanted me to go into the belly of the beast, and so that's the last place I'll go. It's weaker out here. It's isolated. And . . . I need your help Hubward. I need a friend."

"We can kill it!" Hubward said. He took a step toward the dragon's throat.

"And we will, at the right time," Gulchima said, quietly. "That's what I learned. You gotta have a plan if you're going to fight magical chaos. Planning is our best weapon against it."

"So we let it live?" Hubward asked.

"No, we make Ash come into our world, and we fight it there. Now that we know about it, it's only a matter of time before we can kill it. Ash knows that. It's desperate."

Hubward licked his lips, his eyes bounced from Gulchima to the dark. From the fireplace, to the pool, and their escape route. At last, he dropped his sprayer.

"Ok, but at least grab the book," Hubward said. "We're kids, dealing with magic. We need to research something at the library before all of this is over."

"What's a *library*?" Gulchima asked. She slipped on the ice, where Hubward had missed. The dragon's tongue was as smooth as an ice-pond.

"Just grab the book," Hubward said, in an annoyed tone. "It

contains arcane knowledge."

"What's an *arcane*?"

"It means magical and old," Hubward said. "But listen, if you grab that book, it will get you out of the contract. It's proof you are being sabotaged."

Gulchima shook her head. "Too easy. Magic wants me to read the spooky book? I don't read the spooky book. Magic wants me to go into the spooky woods? I don't go into the spooky woods. I'm the boss, applesauce. Magic works for me."

Girls! They never listened when you told them what they should be doing!

"I just compromised earlier," Hubward said. "Now you have to compromise. And your compromise will be to get that book!"

"You're right," Gulchima replied coolly. She walked toward the high-backed chair with the velvet seat.

In the distance, Hubward saw a single glowing eye, open and watching.

But instead of grabbing the book, instead of even touching it, Gulchima kicked over the chair, and the book fell into the fire.

The fireplace exploded, shooting coals across the entire room, igniting the chair and the book and the hairbrush.

"Nooooo!" Ash screamed. It twisted out of the darkness, then dove for the book, trying to extinguish the flames. Gulchima had been right, the book was a trap.

Gulchima slid Novvy away from the fire. He still sat on his eggshell, but the fire had melted it into an elongated oval, almost like a boat made of ice.

"Hubward, let's go sledding. Spray the floor."

It made sense. They could make a boat of ice. They could sled out of the dragon's mouth.

First he sprayed all around Novvy, enlarging his "boat", making sure it was big enough for the three of them. Once that was done, he sprayed the floor, making a small icy ramp.

But ice would float. He needed a piece of the dragon. He needed excess gravity from the dragon, or they'd just bob around on the surface of the pool. And the water was still too hot.

"We're not heavy enough," Hubward yelled. "Ice floats, remember?"

Gulchima took out her knife and started jabbing at the only part of the dragon she could get to. Its tongue.

"It's not working!" Gulchima said. Her knife was just bouncing off the tongue, like it was made of stone.

Its tongue! Hubward knew what to do. "Isn't it annoying when you get your tongue stuck to butter popsicles in the winter—"

"Why are you eating butter popsicles in the winter?" Gulchima asked.

Why aren't you?

Hubward sprayed the dragon's tongue in a small controlled burst. The ice thickened, and he chipped a piece of it off. A small flap of the dragon's tongue tore loose. It was heavy, and would be much heavier in the real world, so he dragged it to the ice boat. Gulchima helped him to lift it into the boat.

"Okay, now we're heavy enough."

Gulchima and Hubward jumped in the ice boat, Novvy between them.

"*Yes I would like another candy*," Novvy mumbled. "*And two for my sick cat at home.*"

They rocked forward. The ice boat started to build up speed, like a sled heading downhill.

Ash bellowed, rocketing out of the smoke after them.

Hubward spun in time to see its fangs, its one good eye, and the look of shock as he unloaded the last of his glacial spray water into its head.

Ash's frozen body smashed into them, forming a roof that completely covered the top of their ice boat.

"Hey we're an egg!" Hubward said.

"I hope this egg is strong enough to—" Gulchima started to say.

They splashed into the pool and immediately sank, as regular gravity took hold.

Something about the transformation gave them great speed. They shot through the dragon's mouth, jarred against one of the teeth, then spun crazily through the boiling hot water, luckily (or perhaps magi-luckily) avoiding the worst of the dragon fire.

Then they reached the top of the water.

They bobbed to the surface of the river. The piece of dragon tongue dropped through the bottom of their boat, and the top of their ice egg cracked apart. It was still nighttime. Perhaps only a few minutes had passed for the rest of Baltica.

They floated in silence in the open shell of their ice ball. The dragon was behind them.

Gulchima, Novvy and Hubward. All alive. All unhurt except for Novvy's hand.

They breathed heavily but said little, as they drifted back to shore.

Gulchima reached out and pulled a white bone out of the ice. It was the tip of a dragon tooth. She hid it inside her rabbit-skin leggings.

"I'm gonna make a necklace out of it," Gulchima said.

Hubward patted his own pocket. He still had Ash's eye. It felt like a smooth cold stone.

It was dark now, no moon, but the locals were out on the burgh's wall watching them. As they drifted to shore, Hubward saw a solitary figure there, waiting for them.

It was Isolde. She had her hands on her hips. She looked like angry was her permanent face.

"Hello Gulchima, I think I'd like to have a word with you, if you don't mind," Isolde said in icy-cold politeness.

Just then, Novvy popped up from the middle of the boat, and smiled brightly at Isolde.

"Hey Isolde! Guess what?" He held up his bloody hand. "A dragon ate my finger!"

CHAPTER 34: BRUNHILD HEARS VOICES

"I KNOW WHAT I SAW, and I saw Rattbone kissing her!"

Brunhild lifted her chief spy like a bag of dried moss and tossed him into the bog with a tremendous splash. The man had dared to disagree with her.

Brunhild was not angry. Saying that she was angry would be like calling a volcano warm. Brunhild was *molten*.

Brunhild corrected herself. No, one could not be molten. Magmatic perhaps? Fuming?

For the sake of clarity, after Brunhild saw Rattbone kissing that Scythian princess, she merely felt *as if* she were liquefied rock, spewing from the center of the world with such heat and force that it would burn everything in its path. Brunhild would have to burn everything, she realized. *Everything*. Everything Rattbone loved. But she wasn't angry.

Her spy paddled around in the center of the bog pool, just visible in the torchlight. A few of her River-Hag sisters helped him to get out. Her youngest River-Hag sister, SwampWeed, had taken a shine to her spy, she noted. Perhaps they would entangle romantically, and SwampWeed would enchant him, and they'd be married, and have children, and Brunhild would sit all alone at a table during their wedding feast, and eat each of the six pieces of cake set there, before leaving early because of a stomach ache.

Perhaps. Perhaps one's future was unalterable. But first, she had to burn everything. And Bayadev would burn first.

[The world mill grinds us all.]

"Brunhild I assure you," the spy said from the edge of the bog pool. "Rattbone is merely working day-and-night with the younger exotically-beautiful Scythian princess, in order to find a traitor in the Soldier-King's inner circle." The spy smiled appreciatively at SwampWeed, whom he saw as a tall fair young woman with striking blue eyes, and not the short wart-covered monster with black oily eyes that she really was. "The war against the Gutlanders is going well, but there is a mystery at the Soldier-King's camp which must be unraveled."

"He dared—HE DARED—to kiss another woman!" Brunhild screamed. She picked up her scale armor, and started to slip it on. "A Scythian princess! Our sworn enemies from the east!"

She'd been spying on Rattbone, waiting for her chance to entreat him to rejoin her, and put all of this debt business behind them. But what a faithless man! To think she had almost allowed herself to be impressed by him, by his strength in the clinch. Now Rattbone had shown his true colors. Cavorting with Gutlanders, drinking ale from those horns they wore on their heads? Befriending an exotic princess, with olive complexion and fluttering eyelashes? Whose side was he even on? The Soldier-King would hear about this.

"It's merely the heart-pounding adventure of a lifetime shared by two extremely attractive people," her spy said. "There's nothing romantic about that, I assure you." He was toweling off, and SwampWeed just happened to be close enough to help him. Brunhild could almost taste their wedding cake.

Brunhild snapped up the last ties on her magical scale armor. It was a bit snugger than usual, she noted.

[A moth to the flame!]

Yes. She would make sure Rattbone had a reason to come to her. He'd be a moth to her flame, when she burned Bayadev and the houseboats.

That's why she had assembled this army. She started to cackle.

Brunhild walked down the wooden platform in the center of the bog, inspecting her army in the torchlight. Her sisters, the River-Hags were ready for revenge. They'd armored themselves against potatoes. Tonight, the white haired Uncle Roog would pay for what he did to them.

Her brothers-in-arms, the bad bandits, were ready for the plunder. They stood in a slouching line, dangerous glints flashing off the magical weaponry and enchanted armor she had given them. They were ready to rob and pillage a bigger burgh. Villages were just too easy.

The River-Hags on her right, and the bandits on her left, represented the two sides of Brunhild's nature. Worse and Worser. Magic and magically enhanced.

The torchlight flickered. Kondo, former leader of the band of bad bandits, finished his speech. "Now on to wealth and victory!" he yelled, waving his magical sword in the air. The bandits, with their odd assortment of magical gloves, boots, weapons, and even a magic diaper, hooted.

BogStench the oldest River-Hag finished her speech. "Rowg wrog, tiew rerth rand rirooorrry!" she screeched. The River-Hags sang in unison, but a bit off-key to avoid enchanting anyone. They flailed their weedy arms in excitement.

But that was not all.

Rattbone and his family had angered many creatures these past months.

A dozen angry fairies buzzed about, saying the naughty things they'd like to do to ears, and a lone wonder worm sat in a cocoon of glowing silk, doing whatever it was that those things did.

The lunkers were here too. Hundreds of long furry fingers reached out from underneath the walkway, slapping at the wood to show they were ready for the fight. One of the lunkers accidentally touched the bandit with the magic diaper, causing him to lose his pin, drop his diaper, and show his bare bottom to the night air, much to his embarrassment. He covered up.

But Brunhild would not cover up. Brunhild would not be ignored. She put on her *Strondem* helm, feeling the weight of it, the tingling as it fused to her skull.

She would not be ignored.

[No, we will not!] her voices rejoiced. *[We will not be ignored!]*

There! Even her old friends had returned, along with her fury. Her voices . . . her one constant in a world of uncertainty.

What was she to do now, Brunhild wondered.

[Use a body for a soul's return] her voices told her.

But whose body should she take? Whom should she kidnap? Whom was most dear to Rattbone?

[The girl] her voices answered.

Yes. Brunhild would kidnap Gulchima. Gulchima was Rattbone's favorite.

And then she'd burn Bayadev until it was ash. Until it was hot as the magmatic molten fuming volcano of fury in her heart.

[The volcanic ash of revenge is a meal best served with pumice on the side.]

Brunhild grimaced. She itched the back of her head. That one needed a bit of work. Still, one could not ignore their good advice.

[No . . . you cannot ignore our good advice] her voices agreed.

[Go now Brunhild, get the girl and bring her to us. We await you. Out of Time. Out of Place.]

"Can you be a bit more specific as to the address," Brunhild whispered.

[Bring Gulchima back to the dragon. Where we wait.]

CHAPTER 35: GULCHIMA LIES, TIES, AND BINDS

GULCHIMA WAS BEYOND TIRED. It was close to midnight, and she wanted nothing more than to find her sleep sack on the houseboat, and close her eyes. But sleep was not on tonight's schedule.

Tonight she had to argue.

Isolde had asked to meet her up at Lake Pepsid, so that they might have some privacy, and not have to be near the darned dragon. Gulchima had agreed. She was glad to get away from Ash, that horrible thing that lived inside.

So Gulchima, Hubward, and an injured Novvy, had walked up the path to the rundown cottage, where Hubward's team waited for them.

On the walk up, she and Hubward had exchanged notes and came to some conclusions. Lady Keyhide was the Sorcerer, though any real proof was back inside the dragon. Gulchima had a dragon tooth, and Hubward had stolen Ash's eye. But neither of those things seemed very useful right now.

Together, they had decided that Ash, the creature they'd encountered, was a magically powerful being called a Zeitgeist, but it wasn't the Sorcerer. If anything, it may be worse than the Sorcerer, Hubward had told her.

They had laid Novvy down in the garden next to the

abandoned cottage. Hubward worked on cleaning Novvy's wound, and he promised to go and find Ninestone the herbalist once he was done. Novvy would be safest with Hubward's family of magical assassins, for now. Gulchima had agreed.

Novvy had done as he'd promised, as well. He'd written a short note on a piece of birch bark. It read, "Isolde. Don't sell our boats, and I am a pickle. Signed tootday, Novvvvy."

He gave the note to Gulchima before lying down to rest.

Now, as Gulchima approached her sister on the dock overlooking Lake Pepsid, she felt her stomach fluttering. But her anxiety was blunted by her tiredness.

She's going to try to convince me to sell the houseboats. She'll be polite at first. I'll say something mean. Then we'll fight and I'll show her Novvy's note. I'll win the argument.

Was losing her sister worth it?

Isolde stood at the end of the dock, staring out at the island. Gulchima joined her, the boards creaking underneath her feet. The first glimpse of moonlight illuminated the water.

"So, you wanted to yell at me . . ." Gulchima said, attempting a joke.

"I wanted to thank you," Isolde said. Her mouth was set in a tight line.

"What?"

Was this a trick?

"Novvy told everybody what happened, after you first landed. About the dragon, about the monster inside, about using *non-magical* glacier water."

"You forgot the Sorcerer," Gulchima said. "Though I don't have any proof of that."

Isolde looked at Gulchima out of the corner of her eye. "Novvy said he snuck onto your boat."

So, this was it. Maybe Isolde was forgiving her. It would be easy enough to lie, or just say nothing. But then what? Isolde would find out the truth eventually.

Gulchima had broken one promise already, she wasn't going to cover it up with lying. She was too tired.

"Novvy didn't sneak," Gulchima said. "He asked, and I let him come. His finger—"

Isolde looked at her, surprised. "The truth?" She shook her head. "Uncle Rattbone was right about you. You have changed. I was just about to catch you in a lie."

"I thought you'd be mad," Gulchima said.

Isolde put her arm around her sister. "Mad at what? Doing whatever it takes to save the family business?" She sighed. "That's what I'm doing, that's what Uncle Rattbone's doing too. We're all fighting about *how* to do it. But magic—" she spat into the water. "Magic keeps changing the rules."

Gulchima said nothing. She was too tired to do anything tricky. She didn't have the energy to confront her sister about the houseboat sale. She didn't want to show her Novvy's note.

"Did you kill that ash thing that attacked Novvy?" Isolde asked.

"No, but we took its eye," Gulchima said. "We'll find a way to draw it out. We'll kill it in this world." Gulchima yawned. "Ice water should work. Or maybe we'll just blow it away with a big gust of air."

Isolde smiled. "I'd like to help with that." She sighed again. "But there's something I've been meaning to tell you. Maybe it will help explain some things. About me, and about Uncle Rattbone."

"Of course," Gulchima said, absently.

"Mom and Dad are not in prison for debt." Isolde closed her eyes. "Mom and Dad are in prison for using magic."

Gulchima took a step back. If Isolde hadn't grabbed her arm, Gulchima may have fallen into the water. *Mom and Dad, using magic!*

"But they hate magic!"

Isolde nodded. "But you were gone—disappeared—and after a while they started to . . . they started to go a little crazy. Dad, always out looking for you. Mom, always reading books, and following up on *leads*. It was hard, and then a year after Novvy was born . . . they were locked up."

"But—"

"Uncle Rattbone kept it quiet of course," Isolde said. "He spent most of our savings making sure nobody talked. You can't tell anyone Gulch."

"I won't," Gulchima replied. She steadied herself. She was good at keeping secrets.

"Do you know the last thing I said to Mom, just before I disappeared?" Gulchima asked.

Isolde shook her head.

"We had a big fight about a dress I didn't want to wear," Gulchima whispered. "I told her that I hated her and I never wanted to see her again."

Isolde looked at her, eyes filled with tears. "And then?"

"And then, my wish came true."

They both cried then, sobs for everyone and everything that had gone wrong. They cried together in the moonlight, and at the end of it, they were closer.

A rift had healed.

"Promise me, no matter what, you won't use magic," Isolde said

"Of course."

"Promise me!"

"I promise I won't use magic," Gulchima said. "I swear on

us. I swear on the family. I won't use magic no matter how tough things get. Not even magical objects."

"Not even potions?" Isolde reminded her.

"Not even potions." Gulchima laughed. "But you might want to check your soap supplies because Novvy has other ideas."

Isolde laughed too. She wiped her nose with the back of her hand. "I tore up the contract with Jaroo. We're not selling the houseboats."

Isolde grabbed her sister's hand. "We're going to get out of this mess *together*."

In the distance, they heard someone yelling. It grew louder. So did the sound of slapping footsteps.

Someone was running toward them.

Hubward came into view. He bent over, trying to suck in a breath.

"Sorry! I must have . . . started . . . yelling . . . too . . . early," Hubward said.

"What's happening?" both girls asked.

"Brunhild's here! That tax-collector you told me about . . . Brunhild's attacking Bayadev! She's burning your houseboats! She brought bandits with her."

"What bandits?" both girls asked.

"She said you owe her, and tonight you're going to pay," Hubward told them. "Then she started laughing and had an asthma attack. So I thought I had time to warn you."

"But we're under contract, she can't just do that," Isolde said.

"I think Brunhild's gone crazy," Hubward said, his face solemn. "She brought an army of magical allies with her: river-hags, lunkers, fairies, and some worm thing that just floats there."

"Where's Novvy?" Isolde asked.

"He's safe. I left him with my family," Hubward said. "We're undercover assassins. They'll protect him at all costs."

Isolde raised her eyebrows. "You're an undercover assassin?"

"Just show her," Gulchima said.

Hubward jumped into the air, did a backflip, then as he landed, he threw a dagger, sticking it into the boards between Isolde's feet.

"Undercover assassins," Hubward said. He wiped the sweat from his forehead, and one of his eyebrows fell off.

Isolde nodded. "Your story checks out. But you're so chubby, I didn't think—"

A powerful arm reached out from underneath the dock. It gripped Hubward's foot.

"Hubward, look out!" Gulchima warned him.

But it was too late.

Hubward was lifted into the air, then tossed into the lake, thirty feet from the dock. The back of his head slapped into the surface of the water, and he did not come back up.

Two figures jumped out of the water, and onto the dock. It was Frenja and Menja, Jaroo's two giant guards. They no longer wore their Seer-Slips, and now their eyes glowed a bright orange.

"Their eyes!" Isolde said, terrified.

"I think they're possessed by Ash," Gulchima said. "That creature we fought inside the dragon. His eyes looked just like that."

The two giant women grabbed Isolde and Gulchima and picked them up by their hair.

"Which one is the girl?" asked Menja. Her voice was high-pitched and girlish. But her muscles rippled in the moonlight.

"Voices said 'bring the girl'."

"Brunhild said 'bring the girl' too," Frenja replied. She sniffed at Gulchima. "This one smells like rabbit poo. What yours smell like?"

Menja sniffed. "This one smells like soap and kissing."

"You have girl, I have forest creature," Frenja said. She picked an insect out of Gulchima's hair. It buzzed angrily. "Forest creature needs bath."

Frenja tossed Gulchima into the cold water of the lake.

She landed in an awkward dive, and when she came back up to the surface she saw Hubward bobbing in the water, looking dazed.

Menja picked up Isolde and threw her over her shoulder. Then Menja did an impossible thing. Menja walked out across the surface of the water.

Without sinking.

The other guard, Frenja, followed her.

Frenja pulled out a small teapot shaped object. She threw it into the water.

The smell of salt filled the air. The lake bubbled.

"That's the salt quern!" Hubward said. "That's where it got to."

"So?" Gulchima asked. She started to swim toward her sister. "We can just cross that off the list too."

The surface of the lake started to fizz and roil.

"Oh no!" Hubward groaned. "The caverns!"

There was a sound like a thunderclap. The water rushed past her and suddenly, Gulchima was no longer in water. The water had disappeared. A giant sinkhole had appeared in the center of the lake!

Gulchima was lying in the muddy lake bottom. Thousands of fish flapped around her. The moonlight glinted off of the bottles she and Hubward had sunk earlier, the bottles filled with trangles.

"The salt ate away the lake bottom!" Hubward yelled. "The lake is above the caverns that house the fizz factory. Well, it used to be. Now the lake is flooding *through* the fizz factory caverns."

"My sister is down there," Gulchima said quietly. She stood up. "I'm going to go after her."

"Yeah, but what about Brunhild's attack? And what about . . . ."

Hubward pointed at the lake bed. The small fish were flapping about, but that wasn't the worst of it.

A few of the bottles that held the trangles had smashed open. The clay creatures were pulling themselves out, and smashing all the bottles they could find, freeing the others. They rolled themselves into one ball of clay.

"Oh no," Gulchima said. "Why did we put all the trangles in one place?"

Each time a group of trangles got together, they rolled themselves into a larger ball, then smashed more bottles, then rolled around the lake bottom, picking up more and more power, until one massive, fish-filled, muddy mountain was formed.

Then, the mountain of broken trangles started to grow arms, and legs, and horrible mean red eyes.

A giant trangle stood above them, blocking the entrance to the caverns. It was at least a hundred feet tall. And it was angry.

The giant trangle bellowed, shaking the leaves off the trees.

Behind it, closer to the sinkhole, an odd green creature leapt onto the muddy lake bottom. It had eight arms, no head, and one very large nose.

In one of its hands, the green creature held a sword. The other seven arms did not move.

"That's Man-of-Arms," Hubward said. "The best swordsman in Baltica." He swallowed. "I think we're in serious rabbit poo here Gulch."

"I never said you could use that nickname," Gulchima replied. A shadow crossed her face. "But yeah *Hub*, this is some serious rabbit poo right now."

A tree hurtled toward her, and she jumped out of the way.

END OF PART III

CHAPTER 36: BRUNHILD ATTACKS

BRUNHILD DID NOT KNOCK. She stood in front of the gate to Bayadev and hummed.

She could see the inhabitants of Bayadev atop the wall, could see their torchlight behind the main gate at the riverside entrance. Brunhild smelled unsheathed metal, heard the hasty clunks of wood being chopped. She knew what to expect. They were ready to fight.

This was rather fortunate, Brunhild surmised. Her army was ready to fight too, and she wouldn't have wanted to deprive them. She glanced behind her at the waiting River-Hags, the fairies, the bandits and lunkers. They were girded for battle as well.

It wouldn't be terribly difficult.

She'd sent her fairies in first, and they'd dropped firebombs around the burgh, little packets of flame to keep the inhabitants busy. Perhaps half of the defenders were now putting out fires.

Certainly, Rattbone's Outfit had done a stellar job rebuilding the fortifications around Bayadev. She'd found no weaknesses. Thus the firebomb distraction, and the showdown at the main riverside gate. It was better that one kept things simple, given the communication problems between magical creatures.

The houseboats were already overrun by her army, though she had found them abandoned. It was a shame she had to burn everything. She liked the houseboats immensely. But her sister River-Hags would not abide them. They simply would not.

A few arrows pattered harmlessly against Brunhild's gleaming scale armor. Arrows? *How ridiculous these Bayadev people were.* A potato dropped on her head. Brunhild picked it up, and threw it back over the wall.

"As I suspected," Brunhild said to Kondo, former leader of the band of bad bandits. "They've been told about the potatoes." She held up a small birdcage, as if showing it the front gate.

Kondo grinned, evilly. "Too bad they won't work no more on you." A spear whistled toward Kondo's head, but he seemed not to notice. A blue-white bolt of magic shot out from his sword handle, evaporating the spear half-a-second before it impacted him. The ash fell harmlessly to the ground.

"I presume you've sent some of your bandits to secure the fizz factory?" Brunhild asked. She swung her birdcage slowly back and forth.

"Oh yeah," Kondo replied. "Sent my best fighters. This is a big score for us, Brun-bun. We're gonna take over the fizz factory and get ourselves some real commerce. Even more than the *you-give-us-your-money-or-we'll-burn-it-all-down* variety. I mean a real business. Selling fizz-water will be a steady income, especially if we make all the workers become slaves. "

Brun-bun? Hmmm. She did not remember agreeing to that nickname. She would have a word with Kondo. Perhaps two words. The second word would be *now*.

"One must not put the cart before the oxen," she reminded him.

Her voices agreed.

"First we must get into the burgh," Brunhild recited, "then defeat the burghers, then kidnap Rattbone's nieces and then burn it all. Then heap it all up, and burn it again."

"Except the fizz factory," Kondo reminded her.

"Yes, excepting the fizz factory which is yours," Brunhild said.

A pot of boiling oil was tossed on her and Kondo. Brunhild noticed it in the way a person in a raincoat notices a light drizzle. The oil cooled instantly on her scale armor, then fell to the ground. "There's no need for such frippery," she called to her attackers.

Something inside of her birdcage rattled. Brunhild held it up.

"About time those furry layabouts did something," Kondo muttered.

A single furry hand darted out of the birdcage. Its fingers were as long as her hand. Brunhild had not realized how shy the lunkers were. Still, she'd accommodated them, and they had come through.

The hand paused as if considering, then pulled on a single nail in the center of the fortified gate. The gate collapsed inward with a crash.

She waved her sword in a circular motion. Her army of magical creatures charged into Bayadev.

The bandits would loot. The fairies would firebomb. The River-Hags would destroy. Brunhild hoped the lunkers would scurry inside eventually and cause mayhem. Right now they waited at the back and hid in the trees.

Brunhild looked behind her. The lone wonder worm was just sitting there on the dock where she'd placed it. No, wait. She saw motion.

This was it!

The wonder worm swelled up, then extruded a small puff of noxious gas. A nearby leaf turned brown and wilted. Then the wonder worm light went out.

That was it?

"Must be stronger in large numbers," Brunhild said to Kondo.

But he was busy smashing down the wall to the bakery, and didn't seem to hear her.

CHAPTER 37: HUBWARD GETS A PEP TALK

"I NEED TO GET TO THAT SINKHOLE," Gulchima barked. "Hubward, you need to get me past the giant clay trangle, then past the green creature. And you can't use magic."

"Oh is that all?" Hubward asked. He eyed the giant trangle. It was tearing out more trees along the lake shore.

"No actually," Gulchima said. "After I rescue my sister from the caverns, you'll need to save Bayadev and defeat Brunhild and all the magical monsters too. Plus take care of the giant trangle here."

"Oh, and nothing else after that, right?" Hubward asked, nervously.

"Wrong. Then I'll need you to meet me at the dragon, and we'll defeat that Ash creature once and for all," Gulchima said. "So that's the plan. In the short term. For tonight." Gulchima smiled. "There's lots more to do after that of course. But I don't want to overwhelm you."

"Ummm, thanks." Hubward swallowed. "At least things can't possibly get worse."

He was right. Things got *impossibly* worse.

The fish had stopped jumping into the air. As each fish gasped its last breath, the mud of the lake engulfed its body, bubbled up, and then . . . came back to life.

Each dead fish formed into another trangle. Except these were almost four feet tall, had the head of a fish, the body of a man, and swirling blue eyes. They were made of hardened mud, except for their teeth, which were barbed fishing hooks and sharp yellow bone.

These fish-trangles wandered around the mucky lake bottom like zombies. They bit anything that moved, which meant they spent a lot of time biting each other. There were thousands of them.

Gulchima put her hand on Hubward's shoulder. "Can you *please* stop saying that."

"Let me see if I can do magic." Hubward stepped back, pointed his pinky finger at the four closest fish-trangles. A sudden gust of wind hit them, and they exploded apart with a screeching *Rawrp*. One of the fish-trangle heads wriggled on the ground near his feet.

"Better than nothing. I'm at about one-third of my normal magical power," Hubward said. "The sauna in the dragon and all the running must have made me lose some weight." He snapped his fingers. "I know, I'll just make you invisible."

Hubward pointed his pinky at Gulchima.

Gulchima cringed away, slipping over a large white bone buried in the lake bottom. "You can't use magic on me! I promised my sister." She started to scrape the mud off of her lower legs.

"Ok. Hold on one minute." Hubward walked over to the closest fish-trangle head, and picked it up. He held it wriggling, under one arm.

"Can you walk like a trangle?" Hubward asked.

He explained what he wanted her to do. Gulchima covered herself with mud. When at last she was properly coated, Hubward put the fish-trangle head on top of her own head, like a helmet. She was a bit taller than the others, but could pass for one of them. He watched her walk.

"No, choppier steps," he said.

Gulchima did what he said. "*Rawrp*, I'm a clay monster that hates everything. Rawrp, rawrp, rawrp. I have the clay head of a fish but the clay body of a man for no explainable reason. *Rawrp*."

"That's pretty good," Hubward said. "Okay, so this is our stupid-awesome non-magical plan. I'll create a distraction, you lay here in the mud, then stand up and trangle-trot until you get to the sinkhole."

"And the green thing?" Gulchima asked.

"You should smell like a trangle to him. So it should work out."

"Back into the dark, alone," Gulchima said. "That's always where the monsters go. Do you have any advice for me in there?"

"Yeah, don't eat the yellow cake," Hubward said.

Gulchima stared at him. Her eyes were visible just below the swirling blue eyes of the fish-trangle. "I'm jumping into a sinkhole to fight who knows what, and you have dessert advice?"

"It's the most dangerous thing down there," Hubward said. "If you see any loose yellow cake, don't touch it. Especially if you're around magic."

"Anything else?" Gulchima asked. "Anything that will actually help me to survive."

"Yeah, tell the truth. It's the best chance you have. A lot of the people you're fighting are enchanted or bamboozled or hypnotized. So just don't forget to tell the truth. Help them to see what's really going on."

Hubward looked at the monsters, the giant trangle, and

Man-of-Arms. *That was only the first part?* He took a few steps back. "This is crazy. It won't work."

"Hubward, I don't have time for a pep talk," Gulchima said. "You have to do this."

Hubward nodded. "I will . . . but I need my family. I never was much of a fighter. I'll just run back and get them."

"There's no time for that," Gulchima yelled. "You have to defeat these thousand monsters by yourself. I'm going to save my sister. That's the plan."

"But . . . ."

She grabbed Hubward by the ears. "Hubward: Dragon Bacon."

"What?"

"Dragon Bacon." She kissed him on the cheek, leaving a trail of mud on his chin. "That's for luck."

Hubward felt incredibly warm, especially his cheek. His heart thudded wildly in his chest. *Had she just kissed him? A girl? Gulchima?*

But then again, Gulchima was covered in stinking mud and was wearing a dead fish on her head. Hubward sighed.

He'd always suspected his first kiss would involve a dead fish.

"We'll meet at the dragon and turn it into bacon. Okay?" Gulchima said.

Dragon Bacon!

Hubward turned to face the green monster, and the giant clay trangle in front of him, and the thousands of little fish head monsters in front of them.

He cracked his neck and sparks flew from his fingers.

"You know, I've always wanted to eat a dragon."

CHAPTER 38: GULCHIMA IS A NERVOUS TRANGLE

RAWRP. Gulchima started walking through the crowd of fish-trangles.

Rawrp. The creatures smelled like rotting fish. They pulled at her, and bit her arms, and made that ridiculous *Rawrp* noise.

She felt sad for the dead fish. They hadn't wanted to become magical. They had just been doing whatever fish do. Drinking water, she supposed. Did fish drink water? How did they breathe? Shouldn't they breathe better in the air? Or did they breathe water, and drink air?

Her mind spun. *Rawrp*.

There were too many of these things. She tried to walk like they did, but every few steps she was jostled aside, or bitten. It was almost impossible to walk a straight line. She had to get to the sinkhole and rescue her sister.

Rawrp.

Their swirling blue eyes never blinked or closed or showed alarm. They just stumbled around, with no particular aim, except to bite and be bitten.

Rawrp. A fish-trangle got a good hold of her shoulder with its sharp fishhook teeth. Gulchima felt the bite, like a stab of hot metal. She cried out, then covered her mouth.

Rawrp, rawrp, rawrp. The trangle on her head barked a

warning.

The other fish-trangles turned to look at her. They started to close in.

Gulchima was nowhere near the entrance to the sinkhole. She needed a miracle.

Not magic. Not exactly. She needed luck. Extreme luck.

And she hoped Hubward understood what she meant. Of course she wanted nothing to do with magic, but . . . she hadn't told Hubward not to use magic. She'd just told him not to use magic *on her.*

So technically she wasn't breaking her promise to her sister. After all, if you used magic against itself, that wasn't magic, right? If a magical monster breathed fire, and you reflected that fire back onto it, you weren't using magic. You were just . . . redirecting the magic.

You had to turn magic inside out. You had to make the dragon bite its own tail. Had to make the giant bash itself on the head. That was how you defeated magic.

So technically, a few seconds later, when Hubward performed amazingly impressive magic, it wasn't magic. Not exactly.

It was just extremely *lucky* that the lightning bolt appeared out of the clear night sky and hit the gathered group of trangles.

Rawrp.

Because the fish-trangles had been closing in. *Rawrp.*

And now, they were distracted.

They swarmed toward Hubward, and away from her.

CHAPTER 39: NOVVY IN THE GARDEN OF GOOD AND EVIL

"MY WORD! THIS FOOD IS DELICIOUS," said Father Trumblebutt. "What exactly do you call it again Novvy?"

"Emmm, pumpkin seeds," said Novvy.

Novvy thought it was weird. He'd been in the dragon with Gulch and Hubward. Then he'd coughed. Then something ate his finger. Then he'd been on the water. Then he'd been in the garden. Then the weird blue-skinned people kept talking about pumpkins. Then he'd been asleep. Then a bag of seeds came over the wall and hit him on the head. Then he ate a seed. Then he gave a seed to the weird blue-skinned people. Then they started talking. Then they started talking *sense.*

"Hmm, delightful," said Father Trumblebutt, leader of these blue-skinned people. The rest of them were just kids that looked like older versions of Hubward. "And I see PUMPKIN you've lost a finger recently."

"A dragon bited it," Novvy said proudly.

"What a coincidence. We were PUMPKIN killed by a dragon," said Father Trumblebutt. "Just PUMPKIN, of course. Hubward will PUMPKIN us in good time."

"Emmm, yep," Novvy said.

"It is PUMPKIN," said Father Trumblebutt. "There are

PUMPKINS when I've felt not quite PUMPKIN over the last few PUMPKINS."

This was fun. If Novvy gave them a seed they could talk regular for a few minutes. But eventually they went back to moaning and slobbering. It was fun and boring. Was there a word for that? *Foring?*

A loud explosion, like a thunderclap, echoed down the canyon. Something had happened at Lake Pepsid.

The seven blue-skinned strangers leapt into action. But Father Trumblebutt held up his hand.

"Hold on a moment . . . ."

They waited.

Novvy got bored.

He wondered about the seeds. The bag had said "Magic Seeds" on it. Somebody had writed it.

Novvy put a few seeds under the ground. Then he waited. Then he got bored again. Then a small green vine grew up out of the ground. Then the blue-skinned boys and girls stared solemnly at the ground. Then the flowers popped out, then sunk in, then plumped into green balls, then grew orange, then got eaten by the blue-skinned boys and girls and man.

"A magic pumpkin patch!" said Novvy, excitedly. The vines grew thicker around him. Then he got bored again. "What else do it do?"

A flash of lightning cracked across the sky. The head of a giant clay monster was visible. It roared fiercely.

"Ah see!" said Father Trumblebutt. He had just eaten three largish pumpkins and spoke clearly. His skin was pink now, almost orange. "That's your brother up there, fighting some magical creature."

"He always over-uses lightning when he gets nervous," Hertrude said, with a sigh. She was one of the formerly blue-skinned girls. "Should we go help him papa?"

Father Trumblebutt shook his head. "Hubward Trumblebutt has to fight his own battles, Hertrude. He's not ten anymore, he's eleven. I think an eleven-year-old boy can handle something like a giant clay monster, don't you? It's not like he's fighting hundreds of them."

"Yes papa. You're right papa," said Hertrude quietly.

Novvy got bored again. He wanted to go-see the giant monster.

And there were fires down below in the burgh. He wanted to go-see those too.

He was interrupted by the bad men.

"Oh look, a smallish boy guarding a pumpkin patch," said a cruel voice.

Three large men had entered the garden. They looked like mean ones. They looked like bandits. They had a lot of weapons.

"He's small. Maybe we can sell him to the diamond mines," said one of the bad men.

They walked toward Novvy, a large sack in their hand. They didn't notice the other people in the garden. It was like they couldn't see Father Trumblebutt, and Hertrude, and the others.

"I see they have a magical axe. That's a stupid weapon, isn't it papa?" whispered Hertrude.

"The handle isn't even magic," scoffed Daaniel, the largest boy.

"Don't they know how easy it is to defeat a magical axe on a non-magical axe handle?" asked another.

"Are they stupid papa? Are they?" asked Kelsa, the thinnest girl.

Father Trumblebutt cracked his neck. "We don't use the word 'stupid' in this family. But yes, stupidity and misuse of magic go hand and hand."

He moved toward the bad men, then stopped.

"Novvy, it appears we need your permission," said Father Trumblebutt.

"Emm what?"

"We need your permission to use our magic. Just the rules of being undead you see."

Novvy heard a scream from the burgh. It looked like Bayadev was on fire. The bad men laughed.

Hmmm.

"Did you bad men make that screaming?" Novvy asked.

"Yus," smirked the first bad man.

"Did you bad men start that fire?"

"Yar," growled the second bad man.

"Did you bad men see the other people in the garden?"

"Ney," said the third bad man.

Novvy experimentally punched the air. The first bad man went away.

Novvy kicked the air. The second bad man went away.

Novvy jumped in the air. The third bad man went away.

Novvy saw a lot of fighting. Punching and kicking and running and yelling. Then the three bad men were lined up neatly on the ground. They were wrapped in pumpkin vines and all their magical clothes and weapons were stripped away.

Novvy put on one of the bad men's things. It was a magical eye patch. It made the world look purple and tickly. He took it off.

He liked magic now. Magic was not boring. Magic was fun.

"Novvy, do you think we should go down to Bayadev and see what else needs a good kicking?" asked Father Trumblebutt. There was an edge of excitement beneath his politeness.

Novvy heard another scream. It sounded like a kid screaming. It sounded like his friends.

"Emmm, yes."

"And shall we engage them in battle if they are behaving inappropriately?"

"Emmm . . . ."

Hertrude spoke. "Should we hit them, if they are being mean?"

"Yeah, let's get the mean ones." Novvy touched where his finger used to be.

"Let's punch them like this. Then like that. Then like this." He punched the air, and parts of the garden wall exploded outward.

Gulchima was wrong. Magic wasn't boring at all, Novvy thought.

Magic was *fun.*

And punching bad guys was going to be fun, too.

CHAPTER 40: HUBWARD DOES A LITTLE LIGHT PRUNING

HUBWARD SQUEEZED THE EYEBALL until it shriveled. The eyeball juice was salty—no surprise there—Hubward had certainly eaten his fair share of eyeballs over the years. But it tasted slightly of peppermint.

Yuck.

The candy taste made him want to vomit.

Hubward felt for his pouch of melted butter, which he kept on a leather string around his neck. He sipped it, washing down the gross peppermint taste of Ash's eyeball.

Hubward hadn't thought about the eyeball until just now. But it seemed to him, it was incredibly lucky he'd gotten that eyeball inside the dragon, just when he needed it most. In fact, it seemed as if he was supposed to have the eyeball juice handy, for just this moment.

The stolen eyeballs of magical creatures often gave you great power.

Power he needed to get through this part of the task. But he was careful not to squeeze out *all* the eyeball juice, just in case he needed it again later.

Hubward snapped his fingers, and the lightning danced down.

Good. Now he was fortified. He felt that rush of

excitement that came with using magic. He snapped again. Another bolt of lightning hit the ground near him, evaporating a few fish-trangles.

Double good. Now the fish-trangles were all swarming toward him and away from Gulchima. Swarming. With their sharp teeth. Swarming. With their blank far-seeing eyes. Hubward realized he hadn't really come up with a plan. He'd just been thinking about the distraction.

The fish-trangles left Gulchima. She stood alone in the center of the mud flat. He waved. She waved back. Then she jumped into the sinkhole.

What was the giant trangle doing exactly? Hubward looked up. It seemed to be preoccupied with the trees. It was systematically ripping out each tree, then stripping the branches.

A tree trunk hurtled at him.

Hubward dove for the ground. The tree trunk whistled above his head, then slammed into a limestone boulder, shattering into splinters of wood.

Hubward waggled his left pinky and lightning hit the giant trangle square on the forehead. It left a smoking crater, but that sealed up within seconds. The giant trangle roared in anger.

Hmmm. Maybe it was time to find a nice safe place to think.

Hubward started to back away. Now that Gulchima was safe, maybe he could go and get his family. They'd know what to do.

As Hubward turned, he noticed a red robed figure who stood in the center of the lake. A protective faded blue aura engulfed the figure like a shield.

Hubward could see the beginning of a massive spell taking

place within the blue aura, the sparks and shudders of high-energy magitrons pinging around.

It was the Sorcerer! Here! And she was casting a powerful spell.

Hubward took a step backwards and crashed into someone. He turned and saw Man-of-Arms standing before him.

Hubward knelt down and picked up two large metal fishhooks. Both had been teeth from the destroyed fish-trangle. They were six inches long, and though pitted with rust, they were both strong.

Man-of-Arms sniffed at him. His nose seemed clogged with boogers, and his dark green skin was almost gray. Only one of Man-of-Arms' arms was working and it held a sword. The other seven looked quite shriveled, and each had a gold shackle around the wrist.

It was the same metal from inside the dragon. The same metal that sat next to the hairbrush where they'd found Ash. Hubward remembered it.

"What happened to you?" Hubward asked. "You were so powerful! You need to remove those golden shackles you wear, help me fight the Sorcerer."

I need them, Man-of-Arms said. *I must not use magic. The war is over. I must remove magic and make sure the world is safe for my children.*

With only one arm, Man-of-Arms (or was he now, Man-of-Arm?) had to use short choppy sentences. He was usually much more eloquent. But Man-of-Arms could no longer flick boogers, and his armpit fart noises were too soft to be heard over the *rawrps* of the fish-trangles.

"Safe?" Hubward asked. "You're being tricked. I know you Man-of-Arms. You are the greatest magical swordsman in Baltica. You fight by sense of smell."

The shackles don't make me strong but they make me safe, Man-of-

Arms mumbled. *I have children now. The world must be safe for them. I must not use magic.*

"If those golden handcuffs help you, then how come I can do this—"

Hubward feinted at an overhand chop with his fishhook. Man-of-Arms moved easily to block him, but could not stop Hubward from kicking a sharp piece of wood at him, and slicing off his lower left arm.

The arm, almost entirely decayed from lack of use, fell off. A new arm grew in its place. This one was strong and well muscled. And it held a sword.

That was the remarkable trait of these creatures. When you chopped off their arms they always grew back. With weapons.

You will pay for your insolence, said Man-of-Arms. His armpit farts and hand waving were much more believable now that he had two working arms.

"Yeah, yeah, all magic has its price," Hubward said with a smirk. "And yours is safety. What are you so afraid of, huh? Are you afraid because you have a family now?" Hubward taunted. "Too afraid to try any real magic?"

Man-of-Arms charged at him. Hubward neatly backflipped, but dragged the sharp metal hooks behind him as he spun through the air. The hooks sunk deep into Man-of-Arms, and Hubward yanked, pulling off two more of the creature's arms. It was like pulling the drumsticks off an over-cooked turkey.

Man-of-Arms screamed. Two fresh arms grew from his arm sockets.

"I should have hit you more during training, Hubward," Man-of-Arms said. With four arms, he could make sounds approximating speech. "Your father was wrong about you. You are no great warrior."

"Yeah, then how come I just defeated the greatest

swordsman in Baltica?" Hubward asked.

"Because I am crippled by these things!" Man-of-Arms bellowed.

Man-of-Arms tore the rest of his dead arms off. All eight arms were now fully grown. All eight were now powerful. All eight held swords.

Was this such a good plan? Hubward wondered.

"Now Hubward, prepare to meet your doom," Man-of-Arms growled.

Hubward started to laugh. He put down his metal hooks. "You're back," Hubward said. "You're you again."

"Of course I'm back," Man-of-Arms said. "I was challenged to a duel."

"But you can talk now," Hubward said. "Well . . . You can make sounds in the air by farting with your armpits."

Man-of-Arms stopped. "I feel wonderful," he said. "I wanted . . . I don't know what I wanted Hubward. I wanted to be safe, to provide for my family. I suppose I put on these golden shackles to do just that. But my hands were made for sword-fights; that's just what they do."

"And you lost your magic. You gave your power away."

"I allowed it to be siphoned off, absorbed by these metal pieces." Man-of-Arms slapped his nose. "It was the Sorcerer. She tricked me. And Jaroo too. They said I could remove magic from the world, if I worked at their factory. They promised me medical benefits and a small pension."

Hubward pointed at the red robed figure, casting the spell in the center of the lake bed.

"It was her. She's the Sorcerer. It's Lady Keyhide!"

"Then she will pay!" Man-of-Arms yelled.

He threw two swords to Hubward, then cut off both of those arms.

That was another remarkable trait of these creatures. They sometimes cut off their own arms.

Except this time, one of the new arms was waving a rolling pin. Man-of-Arms chuckled then lopped that one off. A fist holding a sword grew in its place.

Man-of-Arms charged into the fish-trangles, chopping heads from bodies, destroying the skeletons that kept them alive. He was like a tornado moving through a field of wheat. Man-of-Arms whistled as he worked and the fish-trangles dropped.

Hubward struggled to keep up. He took out as many of the trangles as he dared. But the giant trangle held his attention, and the occasional tree trunk caused him to dive out of the way. Man-of-Arms seemed not to notice the danger.

"Fish-heads, chop-chop-chop," Man-of-Arms sang gleefully, playing the music from his left boogery nostril.

Hubward saw the giant trangle narrow its mean red eyes.

"Look out!" he called.

But Man-of-Arms did not *look out*. Man-of-Arms sniffed the air, as if searching.

A tree trunk smashed into Man-of-Arms, breaking his nose. He spun away, nose bleeding, which was a serious injury for a creature with such a large nose. Blood poured out.

Man-of-Arms coughed. He chopped off his upper right arm until an arm with bandages and medicine grew in its place.

"Okay, I can heal myself," Man-of-Arms said. He sneezed and blood sprayed across Hubward's face. "I think."

The medical arm applied a never-ending bandage to his bloody nose, and eventually stopped the bleeding.

"Got a little excited," Man-of-Arms said, or rather, armpit farted.

"Well there's one really good reason to get excited,"

Hubward said breathlessly. "Sniff behind you."

Man-of-Arms turned.

Piles of white bones were reforming themselves mid-air. The Sorcerer's spell was completed.

The white bones! He'd forgotten to tell Gulchima about the caverns, and the bones he'd seen in the fizz factory. Now, unfortunately, it all made sense.

The dragon hadn't been murdered. Bayadev was a place where dragons came to die. This place was a dragon graveyard!

How did he know this? Because the bones in the lake bottom were from dragons. Hundreds of dragons had died here. And thousands more were underneath the ground. The dragon bones were in the fairy nest, and the older dragon bones were leaking into the fizz-water. The dragon bones were what gave this place such strong magic.

A dragon graveyard! And the Sorcerer was known as a necromancer. She knew magic to bring back the dead!

Hubward realized her plan a few seconds after the Skeleton Dragon flapped into the air. Of course. The Sorcerer had brought it back to life.

That's why she had come here to Bayadev.

The Sorcerer was creating an army of dead dragons.

Things were bad, but Hubward knew they would get worse.

And he was right. Because a few seconds later, the Skeleton Dragon started to breathe fire.

CHAPTER 41: GULCHIMA RESCUES THREE

GULCHIMA LEAPT INTO THE SINKHOLE.

She fell for an eternity, or perhaps three seconds, and then she was whisked away into the dark, rushing through the cold troubled water. The fish-trangle mud melted away and she was clean. She was herself.

We are the leviathan, we laugh at the rattling of the lance

As she was carried into the darkness, Gulchima heard those words. They weren't quite real. Gulchima knew this because she could hear them clearly, even though she had to keep ducking her head under water to avoid the rough stone of the cavern roof.

We are harder than the lower millstone. Arrows are like dandelion fuzz to us.

Whose words were these? Who was speaking? Gulchima did not have to think. She knew it was Ash, the Zeitgeist. The Ash of Empires.

We live in the path that birds move, yet we are more real than mud and iron.

Gulchima knew she'd face Ash here, in the dark. Perhaps she had always known this would happen. After her five years away, after what she had seen . . . it was too important to be forgotten. The Great-Clinch. The Joining of Worlds.

And *something* had warned Gulchima not to tell what she'd seen at the end of her five year journey. Something had warned her that by telling, she would doom the world.

We are kings of all that are proud, we have no tongue for fear.

But why would she trust a *Something*? Why accept that warning?

For all Gulchima knew, the *Something* that had warned her was the thing that had trapped her. Why do what magic wanted?

The cold water brought Gulchima exactly where she needed to go. The river slowed, and Gulchima came to a room, lit by three torches. She pulled herself out of the water. She was half frozen now, her legs numb. She struggled to the shore.

Her sister was there. And so were two others.

Lady Keyhide and Jaroo glared at her.

"Gulchima, it's about time!" Lady Keyhide said. Her false smile dropped. "What took you so long?"

* * *

Her sister was there, blindfolded. Isolde was tied to an abandoned machine from the fizz factory. There were dozens of dusty machines in this room, some tipped over, some dismantled. Parts lay strewn haphazardly around the floor.

Jaroo and Lady Keyhide were tied up too. Their blindfolds hung loosely around their necks.

Gulchima crept over to her sister, and her heart swelled when she saw Isolde was still breathing.

"It's me," Gulchima said in a whisper. She took out her knife and cut Isolde free.

Isolde removed her blindfold. She looked dazed. "You saved me?" She stretched her arms above her head. "Don't go getting a big head about it. All you did was jump into a hole."

Gulchima smiled. "Yeah the water did most of the work."

"Exactly. Is Hubward . . . did he survive?"

"He's alive," Gulchima said. "He's taking care of some small things for me on the surface."

"Helloo? Children?" Jaroo said. "Don't forget the two *other* hostages here."

Should she cut them loose? Lady Keyhide was maybe the Sorcerer and Jaroo was just a jerk. But if so, then why was Lady Keyhide tied up? And why did she have a black eye? Better to play the game, even if she didn't know the rules.

"Where's the Fizz-Meister and Ninestone?" Gulchima asked, stalling for time.

"Washed away," Jaroo said. "Tragic devotion to their duty I'm afraid. Cut us loose Gulchima, before Menja and Frenja come back. They're possessed."

"Maybe they're angry about not getting paid overtime," Lady Keyhide muttered.

"Perhaps," Jaroo said dryly. "But you must cut us loose."

Gulchima thought hard about the situation. Okay, the Fizz-Meister wasn't the Sorcerer then, and Ninestone had been scanned, so it wasn't her. But something odd was going on. Gulchima asked Jaroo the questions, but she watched Lady Keyhide's reaction.

"What were you doing at the dragon with that glowing ball?" Gulchima asked.

"Casting a spell," Jaroo said. "Or trying to. These metal bracelets allow one to borrow magic for a short time. But it didn't work. The dragon remained."

"Stupid idea," Lady Keyhide said. "I told you the fizz-water would stay corrupted by magic. The problem was festering long before the dragon showed up. That's why I hired you as a plumber, remember?"

"A water filtration specialist," Jaroo corrected her. "But the magic in the fizz-water increased once the dragon crashed. Our filters couldn't keep up."

He gestured at the wire mesh and the pile of yellow cakey stuff near an abandoned machine.

"We derive that from the natural waters, the pool deepest in the caverns," Jaroo explained. "It has anti-magical properties. I tested it on your Outfit and none of you died. So I assume it's safe."

"You *tested* it on us? When?" Isolde asked.

"That free fizz-water I delivered was my first batch that had been filtered," Jaroo explained. "None of you were sickened by it. As far as I know."

A pile of yellow cakey stuff . . . hmmm.

Gulchima took out her knife. She walked over, then slid the knife blade into the yellow cake. Hubward had told her it was dangerous, especially to magic.

Gulchima walked over to Lady Keyhide, then pressed the back of the blade against Lady Keyhide's face.

Nothing happened. Okay, then she wasn't the Sorcerer.

"My makeup is already ruined," Lady Keyhide said sourly. "I don't think that's going to help."

Gulchima did the same to Jaroo, pressing the back of her knife blade to his neck. Again, nothing happened.

"Give me your metal bracelets, the one you used for magic," she said.

Isolde walked over to Jaroo, and detached his bracelets. She tossed them at Gulchima's feet.

Gulchima pressed the cake covered knife against the metal links. They flashed brightly, then turned into ash.

So the yellow cake ate magic. That made as much sense as

everything else.

And it meant that neither Jaroo, nor Lady Keyhide was the Sorcerer.

She tossed her knife to Isolde who cut Jaroo and Lady Keyhide free.

The sound of heavy footsteps interrupted her thoughts. Gulchima looked up to see two towering figures standing in the doorway. Their eyes glowed like coals.

Menja and Frenja strode into the room.

"I thought I smell rabbit-poo," Menja said. "That other girl here."

"Good," Frenja said. "Now Brunhild not know about our mistake."

Lady Keyhide and Jaroo cowered away from the two guards. They moved to the edge of the flowing water.

Isolde and Gulchima stood still. They looked at one another.

"There's only two of them, there's four of us," Gulchima said.

"Hmm, migssht want to countsh again," said another voice. A dozen heavily armed bandits entered the room. They all glittered with magic.

Their leader had an evil smile. He was quite handsome, if you ignored his teeth, which were magical teeth, made of diamond. Magical teeth? What a stupid idea. They were pretty to look at, but he sloshed his words around in his mouth.

"Now I'm gonna guessh, one of yoush is named Gulssshima, am I righsht?"

But Gulchima didn't have time to answer.

Because just then, Lady Keyhide threw something at the man.

And then, the battle started.

CHAPTER 42: BRUNHILD GETS STUCK

IT WAS A STICKY SITUATION.

Often, Brunhild would use that turn of phrase to describe a period of uncertain footing, or a time where caution was warranted. But in this instance, Brunhild knew the phrase was particularly apt. It *was* a sticky situation, because someone was shooting syrup at them.

And they'd made a small swamp. Well, a small syrupy swamp anyway.

The man called Soltanabad had barricaded himself in a long row of two-story shops in central Bayadev. He was head of the loggers, and he and his crew had been systematically clear-cutting the haunted woods over the last few months. Soltanabad and his men were dressed identically, they all had wild hair, wore purple cork boots, and had an unlimited supply of syrup it seemed. Such garish men, such ridiculous fashion sense. Who wore purple in late summer? Who had that much syrup?

Brunhild stood with Kondo and her River-Hag sisters, watching the attack. Besides this pocket of resistance, most of Bayadev was captured. Parts of it were already ablaze. Once this sticky situation was dealt with, Brunhild could relax.

Above them, a purple-booted man kicked open a window on the second floor, dumped his syrup from a pot, then disappeared before the bandits could get a shot off. Another window opened a few shops down, and a similarly dressed man, dumped a similar pot of syrup on a bandit. It was maddening.

The syrup was extra sticky, she could see why it had slowed her attack. And magic had no effect on syrup. Everyone knew that.

In the center of the homemade syrup swamp, a few of the bandits lay unconscious. Though exactly how that had happened, Brunhild could not imagine.

It seemed as if the bandits were focusing their attack on a very small boy, who stood on a box in the syrup swamp and punched the air. Nothing dangerous or magical about that, Brunhild thought. And though the bandits were slowed, they weren't stopped. They could struggle through the knee deep syrup. The boy couldn't be more than four-years-old. What was the problem?

But Brunhild wasn't particularly worried. Not all of her army walked on two legs.

"Fairies, attack!" Brunhild yelled. She pointed at the shops.

The pack of fairies sped up into the air, darting toward the first open window. The man carrying the syrup pot was surprised, even more so when the fairies yanked him into the street by his nose hair. A bandit grabbed him and tried to push him down, but the bandit was stuck to the man, and they rolled, coating themselves in syrup.

"Delicious," Kondo chuckled.

The fairies darted toward the shop windows again, giggling cruelly. Once the shops were taken care of, Brunhild would have the fairies deal with the young boy.

Suddenly, a figure appeared on the roof.

"Clearwise, with eyes!" the figure called.

He waved his broad brimmed hat in the air, and his golden teeth flashed in the firelight. That was Soltanabad. She knew it.

"Grab him!" Brunhild called.

Several figures popped up on the shop roofs (or was it rooves?). They had those ridiculous backpack sprayers they used in the woods.

"Glacier water won't work on fairies," Brunhild said, an evil smile growing on her face. "This will also be *delicious,* Kondo."

But then she saw the first fairy fall.

Brunhild sniffed the air. The backpacks contained, not water, but watered down syrup. The fairies fell to the ground, struggling against the syrup.

The River-Hags groaned.

"Not to worry sisters," Brunhild said. "Fairies are strong."

And they were, but not strong enough. The basement doors flew open, and two more of Soltanabad's crew emerged, each carrying bellows, the fan shaped tool used by blacksmiths to blast air.

Except these bellows were hooked up to hoses. Brunhild could smell the hot air wafting from the basement.

"Save the fairies," she yelled.

But it was too late.

The two men stomped on the bellows. Gusts of extremely hot air roasted the fairies, crystallizing them into their syrupy prison. The two men scooped up the candied fairies, jabbed them with a wooden stick, then disappeared back into basement.

"FurnaceFairy for sale! Delicious candy treats," Soltanabad called. "We make small profit only, but guaranteed fairy inside. Great for enemies and tricking bad children. Memento of battle against magic. Good price, good price."

The doors and shop windows slammed shut. Soltanabad

disappeared.

Brunhild screamed in frustration.

One of the River-Hags rushed over and pulled on the basement door, but found it was stuck shut with syrup.

"Burn it down!" Brunhild called to the bandits. But they seemed to be occupied.

The four-year-old boy had knocked all of them unconscious.

Did Brunhild have to do everything herself?

"Kondo, take care of that boy!" Brunhild commanded.

Kondo, second in command of the band of bad bandits, strode forward. He held up his magical sword. It crackled with energy.

The boy jumped into the air, kicked twice, spun, awkwardly backflipped, punched twice more, then slapped the air and smiled.

Kondo tensed, but after a few seconds, nothing happened. Kondo grinned. "Looks like your luck has run out."

Kondo threw his sword at the boy.

It stopped an inch from the young boy, and hung in mid-air, still crackling with magical energy.

The boy stared into the distance, as if listening to someone speaking, then he nodded. "Emm, yes. But don't forget the slap at the end."

He turned to face Kondo, and his eyes widened. "Oh and also, the sword should explode, like ka—"

Without warning, Kondo was lifted up into the air, kicked twice in the head and the stomach, then spun and flipped, until he smashed into the shuttered window on the second floor of the shop. Kondo slid down the side of the building, groaning.

The magical sword sparked. It accelerated hilt-first into his stomach, where it shattered in an explosion of sparks and green fire. All that was left of Kondo was an ashy outline.

"Ka—Boom!" the young boy said. He clapped. "Now let's get those other mean ones." He pointed at Brunhild.

"Get the boy!" Brunhild called to the River-Hags.

But her sisters were gone. She saw the last of them, ducking down an alley.

They couldn't be afraid. Could they? Perhaps they had decided to attack a different part of Bayadev, suddenly, without warning.

Brunhild ran and caught up with them, and she realized what was happening.

Uncle Roog, their white-haired tormentor from the houseboat, stood in front of the River-Hags. He was naked, except for his towel, and he was eating a potato. He did not have his cannon.

"Get out of my burgh," Roog sneered. "It's men's sauna time. River-Hag sauna time is in ten million years." He threw his potato at the closest River-Hag, and it bounced off harmlessly.

Roog's eyes grew wide. He turned and ran.

The River-Hags pursued him, their claws extended.

Brunhild called for them to come back. With the fairies turned into candy and the powerful bandits defeated by a lone four-year-old-boy, the River-Hags were Brunhild's last chance to capture Bayadev. The lunkers hadn't even entered the burgh.

Brunhild ran after her sisters, and away from the sticky situation.

They entered a small courtyard.

It was damp and smoky. It smelled like a sauna. In fact, she could just see the outline of Roog's sauna built into the wall. The door was wide open.

Brunhild realized they hadn't escaped. They'd been herded.

A net was pulled across the entranceway to the courtyard. They were trapped!

She tried to pull down the net, but her hand sizzled when she touched it. The net dripped with a red and orange pulpy slime.

It couldn't be potatoes because she had temporary protection against potatoes. But then . . . what was it?

The River-Hags huddled together.

In the steamy sauna air, they heard Roog's sing-song voice. "Potaaaato. Potaaaaato."

Something hard and vegetal slammed into the River-Hag next to Brunhild.

Her sister fell, unconscious.

"Potatoes don't work, we're immune!" Brunhild cried. *But how?*

Then she heard the children calling down to them. "Potato! Potato!" they chanted.

The children were standing on wooden walk-walks above the courtyard. They had many cannons pointed down at Brunhild and her sisters. And many more pots of bubbling stew.

"Potato, potato, potato, shoot!"

The vegetables rained down. The River-Hags fell.

It was impossible! Brunhild was going to lose.

But the proof was in the pudding, her voices told her.

And her pudding was made of potatoes.

CHAPTER 43: HUBWARD CAPTURES THE SORCERER

THE SKELETON DRAGON SPEWED FIRE, and the pale blue flames flashed across the fish-trangles, incinerating them where they stood.

The dragon turned and glared at Hubward.

Its eyes were neither red, nor glowing orange as he had expected, but a surprising shade of faded blue. The dragon's left eye had a diamond shaped freckle that gave off sparks of purple and white. It winked.

How can a skeleton wink?

Hubward stood dumbly, as if his feet were stuck in the mud. He didn't even remember to backflip. He and the bleeding Man-of-Arms should have been toasted already. Except . . . .

Except the dragon fire wasn't aimed at him. The skeleton dragon was attacking the giant trangle!

Monster fight!

The trangle roared in fury, then tossed two spears made of tree trunks at the dragon. This was, of course, entirely useless, and the trees were soon turned to ash.

Didn't trangles know about fire?

The pale blue dragon fire cracked the skin of the giant trangle, turning it gray and ashy. But though it seemed annoyed, the trangle wasn't seriously hurt. The flame just angered the trangle.

"What should I do?" Hubward asked Man-of-Arms, who was still bleeding profusely from his nose. Man-of-Arms waved his sword weakly.

Fight it? But who should I fight first?

The skeleton dragon struggled to stay in the air. This was not surprising given that it didn't have any skin or feathers with which to flap. Bare bones made terrible wings. Didn't skeleton dragons know about air resistance?

The dragon trundled forward awkwardly, then bit off a piece of the trangle's forehead. But the mud just fell through its rib cage, and then rolled back into the body of the giant trangle. *Useless!*

The giant trangle picked up a boulder, digging it out of the mud near the island. The boulder slammed into the dragon, scattering its boney tail. It screeched in anger, then redoubled its stream of fire. The Sorcerer waved her arm hurriedly, and the bones on the dragon's tail reformed.

The magical monsters are too evenly matched! This battle would go on forever.

It was time for Hubward to attack. It was time for him to choose. But who should he attack first?

What would Gulchima do?

Skip the dragon. Defeat the giant trangle, then go right for the Sorcerer.

Hubward pointed both pinkies at the giant trangle, closed his eyes and—

Ka-Bloooosh! An immense lightning bolt hit the giant trangle, piercing its chest. The trangle staggered backwards, holding its hands over the hole in its chest. The clay that poured out was wet and soft. It was as close to trangle guts as you could get, but the wound was already starting to heal.

The dragon roared in approval. It focused its fire at the hole in the trangle's chest, drying it from the inside. The trangle flailed its arms and legs, as if it was dying.

Then, something weird happened. Well, something weirder than a skeleton dragon fighting a giant clay gingerbread man.

The dragon started to suck its fire back in.

The Sorcerer was waving her arms wildly, and the blue flame seemed to flow backwards, sucking the energy from the trangle. It grew hollow, its red eyes widened in fear.

The trangle's eyes faded to pink, and then to black.

As the trangle thinned, the dragon grew more substantial, each of its bones thickened and took on a brownish hue. It was as if the trangle was being fossilized *into* the dragon bones.

With a crack that sounded like the start of a landslide, the trangle crumbled to the ground. The smaller fish-trangles stopped their endless marching, and they too fell apart, puppets of a stronger magic.

The dragon flapped its boney wings thrice more, then dropped, its brown bones piling up in a jumble around the Sorcerer.

The battle was over.

Hubward hadn't won it, but he'd helped turn the tide. Now it was time to capture the Sorcerer.

Hubward leapt over the trangle pieces and dragon bones, swords at the ready.

The Sorcerer lay on her hands and knees, gasping.

At last. He had her. Now he could speak the lines he'd practiced. Hubward held his swords above her and said:

"Hello, my name is Hubward Trumblebutt, and today I'll be avenging evil, thank you very much." Hubward grinned. It didn't sound as good as he planned it. "Now stand up Lady

Keyhide, so I can see your pretty face."

With a trembling hand the Sorcerer pulled back her hood.

It wasn't Lady Keyhide.

It was Ninestone.

* * *

"Very, believable," Ninestone wheezed. "Your backflips have—" she started to cough, "—really improved."

Ninestone looked drained. Her face was bone white, her eyes a dark smudge sunken into her skull. Her hair had turned white as well, it was streaked with gray and brown. A scarlet line of blood ran from one of her nostrils, the only part of her that wasn't coated with mud or dust. A few pieces of burnt metal lay at her feet.

Hubward surprised himself. His sword did not waver. He did not blink, or freeze, despite the surprise. *Ninestone was the Sorcerer?*

"Stand up," he said.

Nothing made sense. The Sorcerer was Ninestone the herbalist, the woman who had cooked him breakfast, lunch, second breakfast, dinner, and midnight snack, for half the summer. Ninestone, the evil Sorcerer who killed his family, had made him brush his teeth and eat vegetables. How could anyone be so cruel?

"I know your full name Hubward, I was at your parents' wedding," Ninestone said.

Hubward narrowed his eyes. He kept waiting for some glimmer to show him this was an illusion. But no, Ninestone had used all of her magic. She was the Sorcerer. No go-backs. Somehow, it was true.

"I am your aunt, your mother's sister," Ninestone said.

"My mother doesn't have a sister name Ninestone,"

Hubward said quietly.

"It's a secret identity, Hubward. I'm a war criminal," Ninestone said. "My name is Desi, I'm your mother's older sister."

Hubward stared at her. He hadn't seen his aunt in years, but yes, he could see the resemblance. The mannerisms, the faded blue eyes. They were his mother's eyes.

No wonder he'd liked Ninestone so much. Hubward had thought he'd just been missing his mother, but that wasn't it. Ninestone looked a lot like her. No wonder he'd been so easy to fool.

"Is that why you helped me fight the trangle?" Hubward asked.

Ninestone shook her head. "No. I helped you just now, to save Bayadev. I gave Novvy the seeds to help Bayadev too. I tried to defeat the Zeitgeist to save Bayadev. How that evil thing got past my defenses I'll never know."

Hubward jabbed at her with the sword. "No matter if you're my aunt. I'll still take you in, take you to the King. You killed my family."

"I have no magic," Ninestone said. "I am helpless." She sat up in the mud, breathing heavily. Her lower lip trembled.

Was she afraid? Or was this all an act?

She would regain her magic ability soon. Hubward had to decide.

"Saving one town doesn't make up for all the evil deeds," Hubward said. "I'm bad at math, but I'm not that bad."

"I didn't do all those things. I haven't been the Sorcerer that long," Ninestone said. "And I tried to change things once I took over."

"What?"

"Sorcerer is a job title, not a person!" Ninestone said. "I

took over when Kidal, the old Sorcerer, got ill. I was his herbalist, and we grew close. But I wore that horrible armor, I fought the Scythians, and when the Gutlanders turned on us, I fought them too. We were invaded Hubward! People forget we were invaded, and the Scythians would have killed us all. I did what was necessary, but I didn't . . . I didn't want to."

"The Sorcerer got sick?" Hubward asked. "I thought he was invincible."

"The armor eats you from the inside, like a cancer," Ninestone said. Some of the color had returned to her face. "Like a fire burning a house from the inside. All the Sorcerers have died slowly. But someone has to do the job, otherwise Baltica will fall. We didn't start the war Hubward, and yes some of our cures were harsh. But I did what I needed to do, to save Baltica."

"Like sending the dragon to kill my family?" Hubward asked. His sword arm trembled.

Ninestone shook her head. "Why would I? Yes, the dragon did kill your family. Because *they* were trying to *kill it.* Shouldn't a dragon protect itself? Or should it die because a human wishes it to be dead?"

"Intended or not, evil is evil," Hubward said.

Ninestone sighed heavily. "I suppose I'm asking for your judgment, aren't I? You are best to give it. You Hubward: Magic user, last of my family, veteran of the war. Maybe that's why I'm asking you to decide. It is cruel to ask. But I need someone to judge. So it's going to be you."

"Then you'll go to the King. He can decide," Hubward said.

"The King is my executioner," Ninestone said. "I need you to hear all of it, to confess . . . ."

"Go ahead," Hubward said.

"I was once a mother, I was once married," Ninestone said.

"I was once a herbalist in Rakvere, near the eastern border. I was once worried about my two sons, and the annual festival, and my husband's pain in his left leg. I once thought about our chickens, and their thin eggshells, and whether or not we should purchase another home to rent out, to expand our business. Once, that was my concern—" she laughed bitterly. "And then—"

Ninestone shook her head.

"—And then the Scythians came galloping in on their horses. They seemed to enjoy killing. They killed my family. They killed my *village*. Every chicken. Every child. Do you see? Intended or not. Evil is evil. They brought about their own destruction when they attacked. I had twin boys. They were your age when they . . . ."

"And your husband?" Hubward asked. He felt numb, frozen in place.

"My family was killed, and I was so angry at the Scythians. I was so angry! I was right to be angry. Maybe that's why the Sorcerer's armor chose me. That's why it wanted me next, because I was blinded by rage. Because I was right."

"And then?" Hubward asked.

"Small things at first," Ninestone confessed. "The armor must grow on you, adapt to your strengths. My anger would slip out, and the most horrible things would happen to the Scythians. Things I didn't even want. I started to lose control, to grow paranoid. I knew the war had to end, I had to get rid of that armor. It was cursed. So I found a horrible spell. It was the worst thing imaginable."

"Is that where Ash came from?"

Ninestone shook her head. "Ash has plagued us since the beginning. No, I cast the spell that made the mud ring, it protects Baltica for hundreds of miles. No horse, no creature, can pass through that mud. But that wasn't enough! I had to hurt them, I had to hurt the Scythians too."

Hubward licked his lips. They tasted like salty mud. "What did you do?"

"When was the last time you've seen a horse?" Ninestone asked.

"What?"

She smiled bitterly again. "My spell killed every horse. Every single horse. Haven't you wondered why there are no horses in Baltica? Why we use oxen?"

That was it?

"It's the mud," Hubward said. "Horses can't deal with the mud."

"True, they can't," Ninestone said. "But the Scythians practically live on their horses. I wanted the war to end, and so many people had died already. I thought when I took over for the Sorcerer, that I was smarter than he was. So I cast the most horrible spell, to save humanity. I killed every horse in the world. My family was dead, and I was angry and I killed every stupid wonderful horse. And the war was over."

Hubward nodded. "Better horses than humans."

"Is it?" Ninestone asked. "Is it really? But remember the Scythians lived on those horses, and their families depended on hunting from horseback. They live in the eastern plains. Without a horse, they had no ability to get food. They starved to death. The grandmothers. The children. The weak. That's who died, Hubward. And I caused it. Millions of people died. Slowly."

"But you didn't mean to."

"So what if I meant to? Intended or not! You just said that. 'Intended or not, evil is evil.' After that, I swore off magic for a long time. Once we had won the war against the Scythians, I let the other sides unite against me. I was evil, but not for the reasons they thought. The Scythians were defeated. And when the Gutlanders and Balticans attacked me, I let them win. They trapped me, and I abandoned that horrible suit of armor, and it was destroyed and spread across the kingdom. Except . . . ."

She pointed at the metal rings scattered near her feet.

"Except someone is bringing it back together. Someone is rebuilding the Sorcerer's armor. And even now, I use the power. As evil as it is, I used the magical power from the armor to save Bayadev."

Hubward touched the metal rings with the back of his hand. This was the same metal Jaroo and the others had worn. The same clasps that Man-of-Arms had been using too.

"I've seen this. Ash, the Zeitgeist was repairing it inside the dragon."

"No surprise," Ninestone said. "That creature is working to destroy all of us. Not just Baltica."

Ninestone took a deep breath. She stood up. "So Hubward, that is my story. Nothing is left out. And now you must judge me. I am sorry to do it to you, but someone must. It falls to you, the last of our family."

And there was the story, laid bare. Hubward felt as if his head was spinning. "But my family, you killed them, made them undead anyway. I can't judge you fairly."

"I've been trying to *save* them," Ninestone said. "Why do you think I took you in? The stews, the vegetables. I've been working day and night to heal them. You must have noticed an improvement."

Hubward had noticed. Was that why his team had started to act more normal? Why they had been able to care for the garden? "And the seeds you gave them?"

"A half-measure," Ninestone said. "If Novvy planted a few,

they'll have an unlimited supply. The pumpkins can make them almost live again, while I work on a permanent cure."

Hubward said nothing. He had to decide. He had to before Ninestone regained her power.

"So send me to the King, Hubward, or let me go. You have the ability. Will I be another death, another soul for the war to claim? Or shall I keep trying to fix the problems I caused? Do I receive the grace of second chances?"

He looked at Ninestone and thought of all the truths and lies and how she had befriended him and fed him and taken him into her home. Nothing in her behavior marked her as an insane murderer, he thought. She'd lied with words, but her actions were true. *Was she evil?* If this was a play, the audience would never believe it.

What would Gulchima do? He didn't think she would have a clue. Perhaps this was a job only for him. Something for a perfectly normal magical boy, who was bad at math, and liked bacon, to decide. Who better to judge the world?

He looked at Ninestone. A part of him roared for vengeance. Vengeance for what? Did he want vengeance, or did he want to restore the world, to set it back on the right path?

Maybe, there was a way to defeat the Sorcerer without killing it. Maybe Ninestone would help. Maybe he *could* give her a second chance.

He looked at her tattoo on her inner forearm, which read "Once . . ."

There had been enough death.

Hubward dropped his sword.

"Go," he said.

Ninestone bowed to him, then disappeared in a puff of smoke.

He'd hoped for some insight from this, some great revelation. But it was not to be. Ninestone's smoke was neither the red of evil, nor the white of good. It was purple. And so Hubward didn't know if that meant she was evil, or good, or something else entirely.

But she was gone. And he'd let her go.

That was important.

CHAPTER 44: GULCHIMA FINDS THE YELLOW CAKE

THE BANDITS HAD WEAPONS, POWERFUL MUSCLES, AND MAGIC.

Gulchima had cake.

It wasn't even fair.

Lady Keyhide's first cakeball whizzed through the air, hitting the bandit leader right in his magical teeth. He didn't just drop. He *flew* across the room, flipped over the top of an old fizz factory machine, and then slumped unconscious.

The battle started.

Arrows and cake whizzed across the room. The bandits hid behind the machines, despite Frenja and Menja yelling at them. They were being picked off. Their magic made them weak.

The nearby wire mesh was easily molded into plates, which made it easier to hit the bandits. Isolde flung a plate of cake, and a bandit stiffened, then toppled to the ground, as if frozen stiff.

Gulchima threw a plate at one, and missed, then had to duck as a blast of magic shot toward her.

Jaroo scooped up a handful of cake, packing it down like a snowball. He had a good arm, surprisingly, and the cake thwacked into the head of a bandit, who was peeking out to see where they were.

One of the bandits decided to throw the cake back. Since that bandit was strongly magical, she had to use a broken lever she'd found on the ground to even touch it.

The cake sprayed across Lady Keyhide's forehead, but had no other effect, except to enrage her. She ran toward the bandit.

"Get out of my burgh!" Lady Keyhide yelled. She head-butted the bandit, and since the cake was still spattered on her head, the bandit rocketed away and then splashed into the river.

"Oh you are such fun orphans!" Lady Keyhide said gleefully. She clapped her hands and returned to the cake pile.

"We're not orphans!" Gulchima and Isolde said simultaneously.

Between Isolde's cake plates, and Jaroo's cakeballs, the battle was over quickly. One-by-one the bandits were taken out.

Only Frenja and Menja remained. They leapt out from behind a machine, and charged at Gulchima, screaming.

She started to back away.

But the others were out of position too. If Frenja and Menja took control of the pile of yellow cake, there was no way Gulchima could defeat them.

Gulchima threw her last cakeball and it hit Frenja's sword. But her sword wasn't magical. The guards kept coming.

Menja and Frenja hurdled the last machine, and then they were in front of her.

They glowered at Gulchima and pushed her away from the pile of yellow cake.

"We were told to bring in girl," Frenja said, stepping toward her. "But you too hard to catch."

"Maybe we cut you into pieces," Menja answered. "That

make you easier to carry."

Frenja held up her sword, ready to slice off Gulchima's head. But a movement in the pile of cake caught their eye.

It looked like a large rodent was burrowing out of the cake!

Isolde popped up, out of the cake pile. She was holding two plates.

"Care for some dessert?" Isolde asked. She mashed both plates of cake into the guards' shocked faces.

Frenja and Menja were thrown back, as if hit by a runaway ox cart carrying bags of potatoes. They slammed against the wall, and the fire coals in their eyes went out.

The room was silent, save for the sound of groaning.

They'd defeated the bandits! At least the ones in the caverns.

Lady Keyhide went around the room, kicking the unconscious bandits.

"Why are you doing that?" Jaroo asked.

"I just like kicking them," Lady Keyhide said. "I like the sound it makes."

"Oomph," said one of the bandits.

Jaroo scowled. Then he kicked one of the bandits. "Say, that is fun. If you hit them just here, they curl up. Watch!"

Jaroo kicked another bandit and laughed. He looked almost happy.

Gulchima wished she was done, and that she could go around kicking bandits. But there was one small task that awaited her. The dragon. Well two tasks, actually: The dragon and the evil creature Ash that lurked inside it. She had an hour. How hard could it be?

"Isolde, take Jaroo and Lady Keyhide and get up to the surface," Gulchima said. "There's fighting at Bayadev. Brunhild has invaded with a magical army, so take as much of this yellow cake stuff as you can carry."

"And you?" Isolde asked.

"I have to take care of that dragon," Gulchima said, "and the monster that lives inside of it." She held up her hand. "And I have to go alone. Otherwise it will use you to manipulate me. You know: take one of us hostage, use our love against us, that old trick."

Isolde paused, as if ready to argue. Then she agreed. "If you don't come back I'm going to burn all your clothes. Especially your bedding. Seriously, have you ever even washed them?"

"Yeah," Gulchima said, annoyed. "Once. Last year. I think."

She hugged her sister, then jogged toward the water, afraid that she might stop, and if she did, she wouldn't be able to go through with it.

Gulchima grabbed the dragon tooth from her boot, and leapt into the flowing river. The water carried her down until, as she suspected, Gulchima was transported.

The river carried her into the dragon.

But this time, she was in the belly of the beast.

CHAPTER 45: BRUNHILD LOSES

TURNIP BURN.

SQUASH SQUISH.

BEET FEET.

The children laughed and taunted and fired down vegetables. Only Brunhild, SwampWeed and Stranguela remained. The rest of her River-Hag sisters had fallen unconscious when they were hit. They couldn't be hurt by potatoes this night, but other root vegetables still worked. Especially if they were shot from a cannon.

"Potato, potato, potato . . . Tiktok!" cried the children.

A handsome boy gestured for the other children to be quiet. He stood on the wooden platform above her, and was eating an onion.

"How about some . . . Onion Fun?" Tiktok asked the crowd. He threw the half-eaten onion at Brunhild's feet. It bounced twice, and she heard an ominous hiss.

The onion exploded in a miasma of eye stinging smoke.

The boy had placed a small package of Roog's fire medicine inside the onion. Brunhild wasn't allergic to it, but Stranguela dropped as if hit by a giant's boulder.

Stranguela had always been allergic to onions. Not every River-Hag was affected by every root vegetable (except potatoes, that was a universal). But the children had so many vegetables to try. And they had a lot of time to experiment.

"Potato, potato, potato . . . Tormo!" yelled the crowd.

A small boy with a glow-in-the-dark beard walked to the edge of the wooden platform. "Radish Smash?" He dumped a bucket of radishes on them.

Brunhild and SwampWeed jumped away. The radishes clattered against the wall behind them, but did not explode. They were a distraction.

"Radish Splash!" Tormo said. The children cheered.

An entire cauldron of radish juice splashed down on top of them, dousing Brunhild and SwampWeed. SwampWeed fell, her allergy to the juice of radishes exposed. She lay face down in the puddle of juice, her arms spasming.

At last, Brunhild was alone. Her scale armor was filthy. She couldn't take the chanting of the children any longer. Eventually they'd find something that worked on her.

Brunhild ducked into the sauna, then slammed the door shut. She took off her scale armor and tried not to weep.

Perhaps she could wait them out. Perhaps without the armor, they wouldn't recognize her. Perhaps . . . .

Roog sat in the sauna, eating honey from a jar with his fingers. He was dressed in white robes, and his white hair sprouted from his head like a geyser. From outside she heard the giggling voices of the children.

"Ah so you must be Rattbone's wife," Roog said. "Bunhead is it?"

"Brunhild," Brunhild said. It was getting hot in the sauna. The stove was glowing red, and on it sat a bubbling stew. She reached for the door behind her, but it was locked from the outside.

A small trapdoor in the wall, probably for firewood, was her only escape. But Roog sat in front of it, grinning and eating honey.

"Right now, sauna is closed. But since you're family," Roog took out a ladle and scooped some of the bubbling stew. He poured the liquid onto the stove, and it hissed. The sauna got much hotter. She felt as if she might explode.

"There, how's that?" Roog asked.

Brunhild started singing, meaning to enchant Roog.

"Deaf in that ear," Roog said. He dipped his finger into the small jar of honey. "Must be all the fire medicine."

Brunhild stiffened.

"I see you noticed the stew bubbling on top of the stove," Roog said, scowling. "I've been cooking that up for you since we got here. I figured you'd be back."

"What is it?" Brunhild asked in a small voice.

"Every root vegetable known to man, and some known only to worms," Roog said. "I call it: Roog stew." He ladled out more stew and poured it on the stove.

Brunhild sniffed the air. It smelled of onions, but something in it immediately caused her face to break out in hives. She staggered away from it.

"It's like the opposite of a love potion," Roog said, "because that's what you deserve. I'm not your brother-in-law, but if I was, I'd tell you what I really think."

"Oh, what's that?" Brunhild gagged.

"I think you're terrible," Roog said with a sneer. "You were terrible as a wife and you're worse as a villain. Chasing us around, bothering my coworkers. I don't like them much either, but I *really* don't like you. Wanna know why?"

Brunhild pressed her lips together. She shook her head.

"Because you don't have to be this way, Bunhead. Things are bad enough, and you're making them worse," Roog said. "You could have given Rattbone a chance to pay you back. But no, you had to get all hurt and grumpy, because your heart was broken. Well boo-hoo for you!" He poured more stew onto the stove, then took out a large bag of explosive powder.

Brunhild started to cry. Such an awful man. Such an awful truth.

Roog ate the last of the honey, then put the empty jar on the seat next to him. He pointed a honey encrusted finger at her. "Just because nobody loves you, that doesn't mean you get to destroy the world Bunhead. It's not the world's fault. It's your fault!"

Roog tossed the fire medicine into the stove, then dove out the steel trapdoor in the side wall.

Brunhild tried to follow him, but the stench of vegetable stew was too strong for her.

At least she was alone, she thought.

No, she was *trapped.*

Brunhild asked her voices for guidance . . . but her voices had abandoned her.

Her sisters were defeated. Her plan had failed. And now, all Brunhild could do was watch the explosive powder as it grew hotter and hotter.

Brunhild closed her eyes. "I'm sorry," she whispered.

She heard an explosion and felt a cornucopia of vegetables slam into her.

Roog stew. It really did feel like the opposite of love in every way.

But perhaps, it was what one needed.

Brunhild went dark.

CHAPTER 46: ENTER THE DRAGON

THE UNDERGROUND RIVER LED HER into the dragon, as Gulchima knew it would. There was simply too much magic for it to work any other way.

This time she emerged dripping wet into the belly of the dragon. Ash was there, coiled, and waiting. She knew it would be.

She stood in a smaller cavern, perhaps the size of the houseboat. The dragon's yellow stomach acid lay in a swirling pool above them. Occasionally a drop landed on her, sizzling holes in her tunic.

Why wouldn't it be up there? Gravity was strange inside a dragon.

Gulchima held the dragon tooth in front of her. A small bag of yellow cake swung at her side.

"Have you come to defeat us?" Ash asked. Its eyes flared, as if daring her to try.

"I've come to talk," Gulchima said, warily stepping closer. "To negotiate your departure."

Ash curled around in the air. "That tooth would have worked, up there," it pointed with its tail. "But here, we cannot be touched by magic."

That meant the yellow cake wouldn't work either! Somehow she knew Ash was telling the truth.

"Then what are your terms?" Gulchima asked. She had learned about negotiations from her father. The first person to speak was at a disadvantage. So she'd let Ash do most of the talking.

"A debt is owed," Ash said. "We demand payment."

"It's not my debt," Gulchima replied. She stepped closer to Ash.

"You will pay, whether you have reason or not," Ash hissed. "Or do you sssuggest . . . another take your place?"

There. She had its terms. Someone had to pay. Gulchima was here. She would do it then. Save the family, save Baltica, get rid of the magic. She would do it. Or die trying.

"It's not my debt, but I am responsible," Gulchima said. "I'll pay. I'll tell you what you want to know. But you must leave and never come back here."

"Agreed—" Ash started to say.

"—And," Gulchima said. "I want eight knives made of this tooth."

Ash's eyes dimmed for a moment. "Yes there is a way," it said. "The splitting is not a problem, but the handles would require Sacred Oak . . . but yes we can do it. We can. We can do it as payment."

"And I want some answers," Gulchima added. "Did you cast the spell, kill the dragon?"

"Ninestone cast the spell. She is currently the Sorcerer," Ash said. "But no one killed the dragon. Dragons come to Bayadev to die. That is why the water is tainted with magic. Thousands of dead dragons lay under the soil."

"She brought you here?"

Ash twirled in the air. "She did everything to keep us away. When she realized we had found a way through her barrier, by tricking the dragon into eating us, she stripped away all magic. But we were protected. Her pet dragon's scales protected us."

"And you control Brunhild, and Frenja and Menja?"

"Control? No. But we have many powerful magical objects, swords in stones, unbeatable dice, powerful armor and so on. That magic comes with a price. We are the voices that whisper, and occasionally, we ask the users for assistance. We don't force, yet, we are persistent."

Gulchima swallowed. Now she would ask the final question. Her heart thudded in her throat. "Did you—did you set the trap that sent me away for five years?"

Ash paused. Its eyes narrowed. "We set it for another. But you showed up and stepped into it. We required an explorer and we . . . had someone else in mind. But you survived, and all would have been well except, we couldn't find you afterwards."

"What?"

"We could not find you," Ash repeated. "You have been stripped of all magic. There is nothing magical about you Gulchima Brixby. Not one freckle, not one hair on your head. This should be impossible, we thought. But there is much we need to learn."

Ash puffed up. "So Gulchima now is the time to pay what is owed. The lies have ended. The threats have ended. You are here by your own decisions. Now tell us what you saw."

* * *

Gulchima told Ash what really happened the five years she was gone. It wasn't the true-truth, it was THE truth. And this is what she said:

To the outside world, Gulchima probably looked like a happy young girl in a pretty dress, collecting berries and singing, free from cares.

In reality, she'd only worn that stupid dress, because all her normal clothes were dirty. Gulchima was wasting a perfectly good morning collecting berries, because her mother had made her gather some for one of the carpenters who had a urinary tract infection. And she was only singing to make sure a bearded bear didn't stumble upon her and attack.

Still, it looked ridiculous. A young girl in a pretty dress, singing and gathering fruit. Perhaps that was why she got trapped.

At first, she remembered nothing. Gulchima had stepped forward, stooped over to pick a berry and—

—then she stood up. Her lower back was sore. The fresh berries were still in her basket, but it was the wrong season. It was winter. She was still wearing the same stupid dress, but the cold wind tore through it like it wasn't there.

Gulchima started to cry, and the tears had started to freeze to her face. Because where did the snow come from?

Because . . . .

She wished there was more to the story, some secret, some magic prince. A map with runes on it. A friendly slug. Some payment in gold coins. But it was just a trap, a five year trap. And trapped animals never got anything. Except eaten.

And if you believed *that*, then you haven't been paying attention. There was always something between the dots with Gulchima. Something that wasn't said when she trailed off. Because she'd left some things out. Because she'd said, dot-dot—

* * *

—dot. She remembers the nothing.

For a long time there is nothing. Occasionally a streak of

light is visible out of the corner of her eye. When she turns her eyes, she finds they won't focus on anything. Gulchima stops counting at three-hundred-forty-seven streaks of light. She never thinks of pacing around. She never gets hungry. She just waits. It is magic and she is afraid.

There is water, and she drinks it by scooping it with her hand and slurping it out. The water tastes like medicine, like a tincture. She never eats anything. She never blinks. She never goes to the toilet, and she thinks that will make a good story, when she is done. No potty breaks? Magic is ridiculous.

It isn't five years for her. It feels like a month. Sometimes she opens her eyes, so that means she must have closed them. Perhaps she is sleeping. It is weird that Gulchima isn't bored. She drinks water. She waits.

At last there is something.

She opens her eyes and sees a small mountain, not much larger than a hill. It isn't remarkable in any aspect, other than the fact that she's seen absolutely nothing for so long. Nothing except for the zips of light.

It is dusk. At the top of the mountain are flashing lanterns, red and white, on a scaffold of some sort. The scaffold surrounds a tower that is half-built. She sees metal carriages, a caravan of them, moving on a black road that winds to the top. She sees words spelled out in white rocks on the mountain, in a language she doesn't understand. It looks like her mother's native tongue. She memorizes the rocks.

Later she will draw those letters, then look up what they mean.

S-U-N-

D-A-

N-C-E.

Sundance. There is a pulling in of the sky; an unnatural

darkness like the light is all bunched up in a bed sheet. Sundance. The mountain is called Sundance. Or is it a description? Perhaps that is what you were supposed to do there.

In the distance, she sees a flat topped mountain, like a volcano that had been sliced off. It has deep gouges up the side as if a giant bear has scratched it. That mountain seems more impressive and powerful, but it isn't. The power is here at Sundance.

She sees the darkness, and through that, another world. Perhaps it is her own world. Perhaps it is another. Either way Gulchima knows what it is really.

It is a portal. The true-truth: She sees a portal at Sundance mountain.

A portal! To another world.

How boring.

* * *

Ash had the look of a snake who has just eaten a hearty meal of mice, and was now sitting by a warm fire. Satisfied.

"Sundance Mountain," Ash said, contemplatively. "We were aware of it, but had no idea that would be the location. There is no warning you see. It just happens and then it is over. The magic flows out of the world for a time, so we must be in place before it happens. No zipping about in puffs of smoke. There is no magic available."

"No warning for what?" Gulchima asked.

Ash smiled faintly.

"Are you the Sorcerer?" Gulchima asked.

Ash said, "Let us speak plainly. We are not the Sorcerer. We are not the dragon. We are not destroyers of worlds. But we seek the portal. And you've found it."

"Plenty of portals around. What's so great about that one?" Gulchima asked. "Every fairy tale I know has a portal. Every battle against magic has a magical gateway. Otherwise most of the story would be about trying to find a place to sleep for the night, or buying comfortable footwear."

"Plenty of *magical* portals, yes," Ash said. Its orange coal eyes flared. "But what we seek is a *non-magical* portal. What we want is the Information that travels through."

"Information . . . ."

"From when we were *skimmed*," Ash said. "There is a prophecy—"

"STOP!" Gulchima yelled. "If you tell me a prophecy, I will head-butt you."

"What if I call it a fable? Will you listen?" Ash asked.

"What if I put a pig in a wedding dress? Will you marry it?"

Ash paused. "You really ought to hear the prophecy. But you've already fulfilled your part. Are you sure you don't want to hear it?"

Gulchima took a deep breath. She was curious. But the thing about a prophecy was that once you knew about it, you'd see it everywhere. Like if you suddenly thought about the color blue, and then noticed all the blue things in your room.

Prophecies destroyed your filters. Nope. No prophecy this time. If she was destined (or even pre-destined) to do something, she'd find out after it happened. Gulchima would be *post-destined.*

"I won't," Gulchima said. But she had an idea it wouldn't be so easy.

"But you musssst," Ash whined. "It is *foretold* that we will tell you the prophecy."

"Let me get this straight: It is foretold that you will foretell?"

Ash chuckled. "We hadn't thought of that. It is humorous. Still, we must."

"Okay I'll listen to what you have to say," Gulchima said. She crumbled up a bit of the yellow cake from her bag, and stuffed it in her ears. All she could hear was the roaring of the sea.

When she was sure Ash was done speaking, she nodded for a few seconds, then cleared the cake out of her ear.

"Will you take me to the tail now?" Gulchima asked.

"I've been taking you this entire time," Ash said. "Look up."

Gulchima did.

She was on her stomach, laying in rotted dragon flesh. The smell made her gag. She choked and then her vomit splashed hot onto her arms.

Gulchima reached for her bag of knives. There were eight dragon tooth knives, as promised, each attached to a handle made of oak.

She selected one of the knives, then started to cut.

The flesh cut easily under the dragon tooth knife. After all, that's what dragon teeth were designed for.

To cut other dragons.

As she sawed through the dragon, the flesh started to firm up. The creature smelled of the Western Sea. It was not rotted entirely, but it was not so tough that she couldn't get through it.

As she poked a hole through the scales, Gulchima heard someone speaking

"The lemonade mystery is solved?" said a muffled voice.

It was Hubward. He was putting on his play. The one about

the lemons.

The crowd laughed. That was good. She could tell when Hubward was playing it for laughs.

Gulchima heard an answering voice. That was Isolde. She was there, helping Hubward. And Lady Keyhide too. She heard the crowd gasp. They were drawing out the laughter. No, they were stalling. They must have seen her knife cut through the dragon.

Hubward was making sure that everyone would see Gulchima's grand entrance.

"And yet," Hubward said from above her, "there is still the mystery of the dragon."

"The dragon?" asked Isolde.

"The dragon," gruffed Lady Keyhide.

The dragon, Gulchima thought. She sawed madly, pushing away the last string of sinew that attached to the dragon scales.

The crowd gasped and then cheered. It seemed as if Gulchima had appeared out of thin air, had crawled out of a trapdoor in the dragon.

Gulchima emerged from the dragon, holding her gleaming dragon tooth knife above her head.

"Who wants dragon for dinner?" she asked, blinking in the early morning sunlight. "I mean—brunch?"

The crowd erupted. Isolde, Hubward, and Novvy, ran over to hug her, slipping on the dragon goo. Jaroo and Lady Keyhide hugged each other, then looked away awkwardly. Uncle Roog, and the children, and the inhabitants of both houseboats and everyone in the burgh, all cheered for her.

They were all there, they were all witnesses to Gulchima's birth back into the world.

And they cheered her return.

CHAPTER 47: THE PLAY IS OVER

THE CROWD CHEERED WILDLY now that Hubward's play was over.

They were gathered around the dragon, and had stood patiently and watched his play, even after a long night of fighting off magical monsters. True, there had been free ale from the Alewife, but the play had been the real reason they gathered here.

Well, that and the dragon.

Isolde, Lady Keyhide and Jaroo had all agreed to help with the production, with Hubward filling in by playing the other twenty-seven roles.

It took many sets of eyebrows, and three long hours, for the audience to find out what had happened. After a twisty-turny showdown scene on the roof of the apple-cider building, the play resolved the central lemonade mystery.

The villain was not the evil sheep-shearer.

The butler did it.

Then Gulchima had cut through the dragon, and Hubward had introduced her too, as if he had been planning it all along.

What an ending!

"Thank you for being hostage to my art," Hubward said. He gestured at Gulchima. "As you know, the Romaic people had a *deus-ex-machina*, the god in the machine, in all of their plays. So today, I give you a *herois-intra-draco!*"

"A what?" Isolde asked

"A hero inside the dragon," Hubward said. The crowd laughed in that polite way, which meant they appreciated the effort, but the joke wasn't really all that funny.

His play was over, the monsters were defeated, and his family was still undead. They seemed better, less confused, but still undead. Their faces were striped with orange, like a tiger. And they sat clustered together, watching Hubward with rapt attention. They were undead, but they had hope. Maybe Ninestone could cure them. Maybe not.

Hubward was at peace with his decision.

Gulchima gave a short speech. When she was done, the noise was tremendous. There were no words for the thunderous joy of the crowd, at least not in Aestii, the language of Baltica. It was loud.

Gulchima smiled awkwardly with her too small mouth. Then she handed out the dragon tooth knives (or was it knifes?), and everyone started cutting.

There was quite a feast after that, and more speeches, and even Jaroo smiled. Slightly. Lady Keyhide promised more work for Gulchima's Outfit, given that the fizz factory would need to be completely rebuilt. She claimed the contract was completed, and Gulchima would be paid in full. Minus *certain* expenses.

Novvy and Tormo sat together, equals again since one-eaten-finger equaled one-glow-in-the-dark-beard, as everyone knew. And Hubward overheard Isolde say to Tiktok, "Well it's quite a lot of spit, if you're really asking for feedback on your *technique*."

The local burghers were roasting bits of dragon flesh over a fire, while others were salting it, preparing for dragon bacon.

But it was Soltanabad who had the greatest idea. He

whispered something to Gulchima, and they shook hands.

"A third of profits," Gulchima said, before releasing his hand.

Soltanabad agreed.

His crew set up large bags inside the dragon, stolen from the fizz factory flood. Soltanabad used his hot air hoses and bellows to inflate the bags with air.

Gulchima took out her dragon tooth knife, then sawed near the end of the dragon tail, leaving the last five feet of tail on the ground.

As she sliced through the very last scale, the tail sunk into the ground, absorbing the many years of deferred gravity. It left only a hole.

The rest of the dragon shifted forward, now free from its gravity debt. With poles to nudge it into the water, Soltanabad sailed on top of the dragon. The bags of air floated it down the river, and away from Bayadev.

The dragon was removed. It would be destroyed, or maybe cut into smaller pieces and resold for a small profit, which was really the same thing if you stopped to think about it.

Gulchima and Hubward watched it go.

"I did it," Hubward said.

"Yep," Gulchima said. She punched him on the arm. "What do you mean *you* did it. I'm the one that defeated evil."

"I mean the play," Hubward said. He peeled off one of his eyebrows, then reapplied it. "Everyone laughed when they were supposed to. That's a success."

"Yeah, but did you defeat the Sorcerer?"

Hubward shook his head. "I let her go, it wasn't who we thought."

"Ninestone was the Sorcerer," Hubward and Gulchima said at the same time. They both laughed.

"I saw her do magic," Gulchima confessed.

"She's my aunt," Hubward added.

They looked at one another, then laughed again. Hubward took a bite of dragon, which tasted like a cross between ox-tail and horned oryx.

"You look better without that smelly fish monster on your head," Hubward said.

"You look better with those new eyebrows glued on straight," Gulchima said. "I'm glad we're friends."

"Best friends," Hubward added. "Will you tell me what happened in the dragon?"

Gulchima shook her head. "You wouldn't be interested. It's all about the end of the world."

"Oh! Was there a prophecy? I love prophecies," Hubward gushed. "My next play is all about prophecies. It's called *Remembro*, and it's about a magical boy who can't remember his prophecy because he got kicked in the head by a camel. Anyway, when will the world end? Do I have time to write it?"

"Ask me tomorrow," Gulchima said. She took a bite of dragon steak, and chewed thoughtfully.

"Today is for celebrating."

CHAPTER 48: RATTBONE RETURNS

"ORPHANS! DON'T YOU JEST LOVE 'EM?"

Days turned into weeks, and Ash did not return. Neither did the Sorcerer. Gulchima went back to work.

There was still magic, especially inside the fizz factory caverns, but it wasn't nearly as strong as it used to be.

Gulchima stood at the Bayadev docks, watching the lone wonder worm. It hadn't moved since the night Brunhild had attacked. Was it planning something inside that cocoon of silk?

Jaroo and Lady Keyhide had insisted she take care of it. They were tough negotiators in private, but in public they gushed over the Outfit. Gulchima, Roog and Isolde had eventually worn them down, and were now part owners of the fizz factory. It would be a steady stream of income, and the houseboats were perfect for selling fizz-water.

Gulchima had also bought partial ownership of "Uncle Roog's Dragon-Hot Sauna Service". The saunas, fueled by Roog's fire medicine, were popular in all the towns along the river. Roog was quite rich now, which transformed his natural meanness into *good business sense*, while his offensive smell was now considered *rugged* to certain older ladies in the burgh.

"I said, do you love them orphans or what Gulch! Hello?"

Gulchima whirled. Uncle Rattbone was there, his beard fresh and combed out. He smiled at her.

She ran over to hug him, to make sure he wasn't a ghost. But he was as solid as ever. He dropped his war-axe.

"I heard you've been cleaning things up around here," Uncle Rattbone said. "But I had no idea. I'm proud of you Gulch. And I see you finally took my advice and had Hubward help you."

"Hubward wouldn't leave, no matter how many mean things I said to him," Gulchima said. She looked at the burgh, at the progress she'd made. It looked good.

Uncle Rattbone laughed. "The war against the Gutlanders is over too," he said. "Had to kill the Soldier-King of course. That old magic-abuser had to go."

"You killed our king? I thought he was against magic."

Uncle Rattbone rubbed his nose. "Ah well. Turns out he was a shape shifter. Only one way to kill a thing like that."

"How?" Gulchima asked.

"Scissors, unfortunately," Uncle Rattbone said, wrinkling his nose. "Takes a long time to cut up all them shapes. Anyway, we have a queen now, and she's a friend of mine." He held up his hands. "Now she's half Scythian, but she's one of the good ones. Good Queen Eneli, they call her."

"How do you know she's good?"

"Oh no, that's just her name," Uncle Rattbone said. "She was worried about being called an evil queen because she was Scythian, so I told her, 'just add good to your name'. And so far it's working."

"So does she use magic?" Gulchima asked.

"Well good magic only, she says." Uncle Rattbone raised his eyebrows. "Light magic, she calls it."

"Light magic? You mean there's a color of magic?" Gulchima asked.

"Dunno. I read a good book on that once. Great book

actually. Said it was kinda purpley."

Gulchima grimaced. "How do you know if it's good magic? This is my business we're talking about here."

"Oh that's easy," Uncle Rattbone said. "Whatever magic the Queen don't like is evil. Whatever magic she does like, is good."

"So nothing's really changed," Gulchima said. "Magic is bad, unless you need to use it."

"Depends on your perspective," Uncle Rattbone said. "If you're looking down on Baltica, measuring good against evil on your abacus, then no, nothing's changed."

"But?"

Uncle Rattbone put his hand on her shoulder. "But if you're measuring the fortunes of our family, then a lot has changed. And all for the good. We're nearly debt free, we got a name for ourselves as dragon removers, and magic tamers. And then there's your parents Gulch . . . You can go to that big island of Saaremaa, and maybe you'll get them outta there."

"Out of prison?"

"Well, they're not exactly in *prison*," Uncle Rattbone said. "That's just an easy way to explain why they're locked up."

He handed a letter to Gulchima. It was gilded around the edges and signed by Good Queen Eneli.

Gulchima read it. It appointed her as *Marduk* of Baltica, and requested that she travel to the island of Saaremaa, to "clean up certain problems" that had arisen.

"What 's a *Marduk*?" Gulchima asked.

"It means, 'she-who-makes-ingenious-things-out-of-the-dragon-of-chaos'," Uncle Rattbone said. "It's a prophecy the Scythians have—"

Gulchima held up her hand. "No prophecies, thanks. This is a prophecy-free zone." She bit her lip. "Will you help me travel to Saaremaa, it's far."

"I'll take you as far as they'll let me," Uncle Rattbone said. "But promise me, you'll come back."

"Back for what?"

"For the wedding. I'm getting married," Uncle Rattbone said.

"To the Good Queen?"

Uncle Rattbone winced. "No, to Brunhild."

He waved to someone standing behind him, and Brunhild appeared. She was not wearing her scale armor, and had cut her hair very short. She seemed smaller, less sure of herself. But she seemed happy.

"Hello," Brunhild said. "I am sorry . . . for trying . . . to ruin your life . . . enslave your family . . . and burn your home."

"And?" Uncle Rattbone said.

"And I have destroyed my magical armor, and the voices that commanded me to do evil things have left."

"And," Uncle Rattbone urged her.

"And, I am pregnant," Brunhild said. She smiled.

Gulchima looked at Brunhild and Uncle Rattbone. There was too much emotion for her tastes. "Sounds good," she said. "But I thought you were already married."

"Yes but, well, it's a bit confused you see," Uncle Rattbone said. "Technically, when she kidnapped your sister—under the evil spell of the Zeitgeist of course—well technically we weren't never married. As we see it. Plus we never got any presents or had a big to-do about anything. So we thought—"

Brunhild cut him off. "We must stand in front of our beloved families, and make the most solemn of promises." She smiled briefly. "And we must eat cake."

"I won't leave you," Uncle Rattbone said, staring into Brunhild's eyes.

"And I won't let you," Brunhild growled. They embraced, and Gulchima looked away as they kissed.

After several moments, Gulchima could not stand to watch them kiss any longer, so she walked away. She kicked the wonder worm cocoon into the river, and it floated away, a small burp of gas showing its displeasure. But that was all.

Above her, a rock from Suur Töll floated across the sky, cutting a line through the clouds. Gulchima wondered about Saaremaa. Would she meet the giant there? Would she save her parents?

She wondered about the future, about Hubward, about Novvy's finger. She wondered about Isolde, and Tormo's glow-in-the-dark beard, and the stupid, useless, left-over magic that was still ruining Baltica. Gulchima hadn't really defeated evil, or figured much out. But she'd cleaned up Bayadev, and fulfilled the contract, and now her family was safe and had enough to eat.

And Gulchima felt glad of it, glad to have a stable place in the world from which she could work against magic. Give her enough time, and enough friends, and enough rope and pulleys, and Gulchima would straighten out this world. Eventually.

After all, Gulchima Brixby was head of the Outfit.

She could fix anything.

THE END

A SECOND NOTE FROM THE AUTHOR

WELL. WELL. WELL. Wellington wellburson. I hope you enjoyed this story.

It was difficult to write, difficult to balance, difficult to stop writing. Mostly, it was difficult. It was my first foray into the dream place, where all novels are born. There are other Gulchima stories to be told, I suspect. I know enough about Saaremaa Island to start writing. I think there's a school there, or maybe it's a prison, or maybe it's both.

And there's a giant who guards it.

Eric "E.C." Stever
Runesday, January 3, 2019
eric@ecstever.com

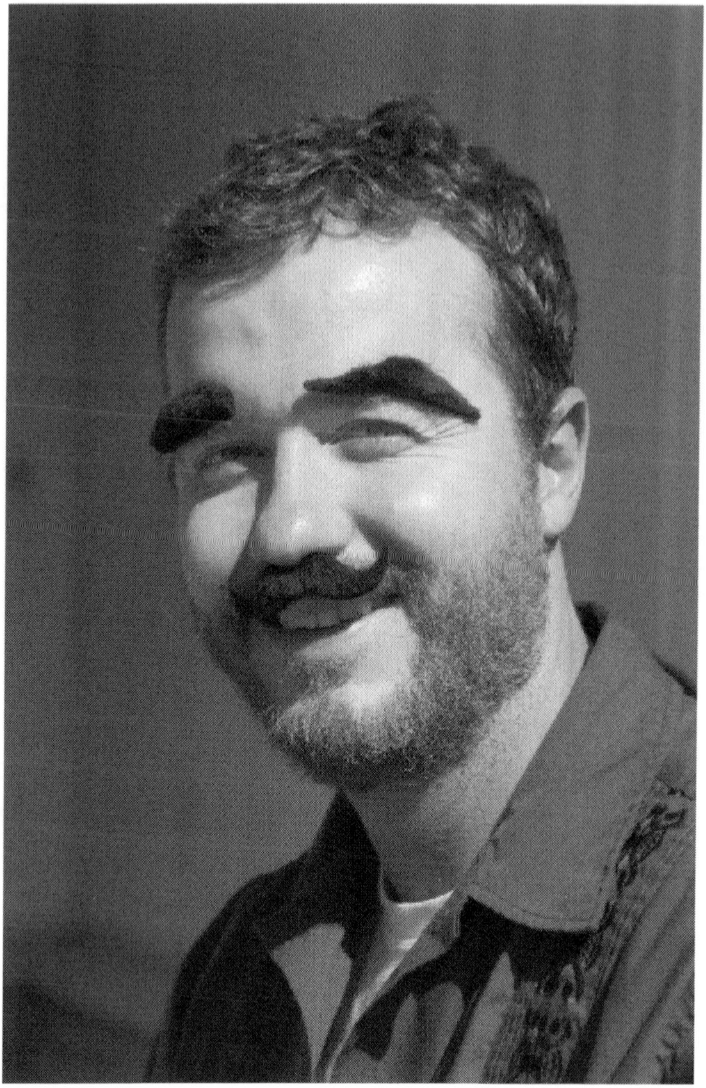

ONE OF THESE EYEBROWS IS FAKE!
To find out which, contact eric@ecstever.com

ABOUT THE AUTHOR

Eric "E.C." Stever is the author of humorous fantasy, and science fiction adventures. He has been publishing for over a decade.

Eric is a professional archaeologist in Idaho, a former Forest Service employee, and has also worked as a computer programmer. (Dear NASA: If you're recruiting for an expedition to those alien ruins on Omicron-Persei 8, he's the ideal programmer-archaeologist you've been looking for.)

He lives on the River of No Return with a geologist, two unrepentant marshmallow fanatics, and several hundred eyebrow mites (don't judge, you have them too). Alas, the coyotes have eaten his cats.

More information can be found on his website
www.ecstever.com/dragons

OTHER BOOKS BY E.C. STEVER

The Moctezuman: A SciFi Horror Comedy
Sisters Under The Skin: A SciFi Caving Novella
Non Metallic: A Near Future Science Fiction Collection
A Magical School, for Magical Fools: Book 2 in the *Dragon Removal Service Series* (Coming December 2019)

Printed in Great
Britain
by Amazon

32108333R00194